# Here In No Place

# Here In No Place

## A.W. Timmons

NEW ISLAND

HERE IN NO PLACE
First published 2013
by New Island
2 Brookside
Dundrum Road
Dublin 14

www.newisland.ie

PRINT ISBN: 978-1-84840-275-1
EPUB ISBN: 978-1-84840-276-8
MOBI ISBN: 978-1-84840-277-5

Typeset by JVR Creative India
Cover design by Andrew Brown
Printed by Bell & Bain Ltd, Glasgow

New Island received financial assistance from
The Arts Council (An Comhairle Ealaíon), Dublin, Ireland

10 9 8 7 6 5 4 3 2 1

*for my parents*

*...This gone-already feeling*
*here in no place with our heads on upside down.*

—Les Murray, *Pigs*

# I

# Stomach & Heart

# 1

In this light, the sky was a sea, and the land had no place between them.

Murt waited, his boots sinking in the slurried sand, but he knew she was not coming. For something to do, he counted again the buttons on his jacket, coins in his pocket, the steps he was taking. No need to count the years.

Out there, the sea was a leady expanse that gave nothing away. It charged forward like a desperate animal, then crawled back, beaten, before rushing in again. Land began along the fringes of beach and froth. A strip of slick sand. Waves cracked and broke near the shore and farther out. Somebody once told him that people here love the sea. It protects us from something, they said.

Eighteen years. That was how long it had been since he had known his daughter. When he wrote the letter asking her to meet him the beach had seemed like a good idea. He was a fool. Why would she come here? They were strangers.

A sneaky wind streamed in from the sea. Constant and trained on him, it was a menacing gaze that he could not avoid. No place to hide. He tugged the coarse woollen collar of his donkey jacket, pulled it up to his ears and kept moving.

Damp, snowy sand stuck to his boots as he made circles up and down the shore. The beach curved for miles in both directions, buffered along its length by iron-grey dunes. What if he started walking and the beach never ended? He'd like that. How long would it take to go around the country by beach and cliff, to see every headland and lighthouse, the nooks and inlets of local lore? To descend into fishing villages from coastal brows and see long-slimed rubble piers, hear tales of trawlers rusting in scrapyard harbours. He would know the whole country for sure then. The stories he could tell her.

Ashen clouds skulked low across the sky, ready to smother the land. Way ahead along the beach, he could make out three figures like black day-stars against the grey. From this distance, he could not tell if they were approaching or going away. One of those dots could be her. Of course she might not come alone. One shape—a dog maybe—broke from the others, shot towards the dunes, then returned.

Once, when he was a boy, Murt's mother had brought him to a beach. He nearly drowned that day. The sting of salt as water gushed through his nostrils and his throat closing in. Above, sun and cloud trembled in a golden blur. The air in his flailing hands was an emptiness that could not save him. And then something real, as if he had been caught by a wave. An arm dragged him back, his chest and throat gasping together like a starved engine. On the beach, older children covered their mouths to laugh or sigh. He looked for his mother in the crowd. Why was she not there beside him? Maybe she was drowning too. Her voice then, reassuring as she held him. It was she who had pulled him out.

The dots up ahead were moving towards him and he was hopeful now. A red jacket huddled beside a long duffle, two woolly hats for heads. And yes, definitely a dog. The three figures ambled along the fringe of sea, hopping sideways to avoid the onrushing tide.

They were getting closer now. What would he say if it was her? He wished he could disappear, turn into sand and be washed away. They might as well have been meeting on the moon, or be the last survivors on a forgotten island. Nobody else in sight on that endless stretch of ocean, sand and sky greys. Out on the horizon, a cargo ship was making its way up the coast. He remembered from somewhere that it was sailors who understood, before anyone else, that the earth was round: the farther away a ship is, the less you can see of it. The horizon is an illusion.

Something about the approaching figures dampened his hope again. They were so close to each other, gripped together arm in arm, a tangle of scarves. Her boyfriend maybe? She could have brought a boyfriend along. And a dog; for a stroll on the beach and a chat with her long-lost father. The straws he could clutch at.

As their faces became clearer, Murt's jaw tightened. A lump pulsed in his throat. It was not her. He cursed his own stupidity and backed slowly up the shore. Could they see his shame as they passed? The young woman smiled and waved.

'Beautiful morning,' she said.

Slowly he nodded as if reminded of something long forgotten.

'Like we have the country to ourselves,' the man shouted, a gust of wind catching him square on, freezing him for a moment like a statue about to take its next step.

Murt felt something wet then against his hand: the dog, its coat spiked with damp sand. He gave its head a rub, felt the soft tongue lapping between his fingers. The woman came towards them and called out.

'Sorry,' she said. 'Mad for strangers, this one.'

She was too old to be Murt's daughter. Closer to the age his dead wife would have been. It was so long ago now that sometimes, when he really wanted to picture Cathy, the glass was broken in his mind's frame and cracks ran across her face, tearing it into shards.

When the woman kneeled in the sand and slapped her thighs, the dog ran to her. On they strolled, not a glance over their shoulders at the strange man walking in circles behind them. The figures became specks again, then disappeared from view.

He had waited for nearly two hours. No sign of Gráinne. Even though she had not replied to his letter, he had taken a chance, hoped she might show up. It was all he could do.

The waves were louder now. He listened to the water wash-whoosh and creep up the shore. It reminded him of something more familiar: wind through a canopy of trees, a living forest.

As he made his way along the sandy track towards the dunes, he wondered what Gráinne might be doing at that moment instead of meeting him. It was a thought in which he often imprisoned himself. How happy she probably was with those two she called her parents. Maybe they had a hand in the situation. If they had seen the letter, if they knew he was trying to contact her, they would not allow it. He wondered what lies they had told her about her own father: that he had abandoned her; that he was to blame for what had happened to Cathy; that he was dead now. He knew how they could twist things. Nothing was beneath them.

Over the crest of a reedy dune, he could see the road ahead of him and the cab of his little blue truck parked in the lay-by. Farther on, near the boarded-up shop, something caught his eye. His legs stiffened and he stopped as he made out the shape of a man standing beneath a tree. Was he being watched? His boots anchored in the sand. The wind caught him now from all directions like he was a timber post planted atop the exposed dune. The roar of the sea in his ears was replaced by a rush of panic. The figure was too far away for Murt to make him out. A quick tilt of his head then and he twisted his body behind the tree and out of view as if he had wanted to be seen for a moment only, like your own shadow when you turn around.

Murt walked on, his boots heavy. He was not safe from his past, he knew that, but he had tried to keep out of its reach. Maybe one of his shadows had finally got ahead of him. He kicked the front tyre of his truck to knock the sand from his boots. The road was deserted. When he climbed in and closed the door, he felt safer.

He stayed on the coast road. He passed the barren forecourt of a petrol station, its shutters half-open. Next, the hotel and pub, the golf course, the holiday village with its neat rows of caravans. But no people, not at that time of year. The beach was one of the famous ones. People used to flock to it every summer. He imagined the narrow roads jammed with convoys of cars and jeeps towing trailers and caravans loaded with blankets, towels, tents, all the inflatable rings and beds on which children float away. That was back when a holiday here was good enough for people.

The beach was a bad idea. There had been an image in his head of the two of them walking along the shore together. The years of talking they would have, even if he had never been one for conversation. But late October and the place was like a sick aunt, sharp-tongued and pale with spite. And the sea no better than that two-faced wind. Why would she meet him there, this girl whom he had neglected? How scared she would be on that blustery coast, having to face the father she did not know.

She might say that he had forgotten about her, wiped her from his mind. How could he argue? That was not true though. He thought about her every day. Gradually, the whispering guilt got louder. As time passed, it began to buzz and then ring in his ears until the idea of ever meeting her became a deafening crash. Give it up, he told himself. Have a drink. Gráinne had slowly merged with Cathy to become part of her memory.

The road swung gently inland. He could no longer see the coast out to his right. Instead, he passed through villages and boreens. As each lonely Guinness sign faded in the rear-view mirror, he dreaded the pull of the next, like red lights ordering him to stop. Two things he knew—guilt and the drink—bound together in a black knot inside his gut.

He had heard people say how they did not know when their lives were going wrong, that by the time they realised the shit they were in, it was too late. Murt was not one of those people. He knew the exact day.

Another Guinness sign enticed him, hanging from the flaking plaster of an isolated house. At the gable, a rusted lean-to shed engulfed by weeds. He thought of how their old cottage must look now, and that day when the rot started. Road and ditches reeled past him as the memory replayed.

That last conversation he had had with Cathy. She had wanted a lift to her mother's house—a simple thing.

'Why do you have to go over there today?' he had asked her.

'You know what she's like. Has my heart broke about this cardigan she's knitted for Gráinne.'

'She won't come here of course.'

'The car apparently—something's wrong with it.'

'When was the last time she left that house? And your sister too—how long has she been learning to drive?'

Cathy did not like when Murt said anything critical about her mother and sister, but they had no time for him and his jaw clenched at the mention of them.

'Murt, can you give us a lift or not?'

'All right. I'll try and get back around three. But if they start at you with the guilt trip—'

'I know, I know.'

'You don't live there any more,' he said. 'They need to understand that.'

The motorway was below him now as he drove across a bridge. He slowed to see if the car behind would close in and pass. Its headlights flickered in the dull day, catching his eye in his rear-view mirror.

She had wanted a lift to her mother's house, only a few miles away.

'You won't forget,' she said. 'You'll have to leave early.'

'I'll leave early.'

He was taking the car to work, had to drive to the next county to survey a forest. She called out to him from the doorway as he left, told him that it didn't matter. 'I'll call,' she said, 'tell her I'll go over another day. Tomorrow maybe.'

'It's grand. I'll get back.'

'Three o'clock then. Be careful.'

You can't help the future, that's what Murt's uncle would say. Just do what you do, live your life and hope there is no kick in the arse at the end of it. By which time it's already in the past. And you certainly can't help the past.

Be careful, she had said.

He came upon the scene on his way back that evening. It was well after three o'clock. He had been delayed at the forest but had forgotten as well. Ditches flashed blue and grey in the dusk. Guards beckoned him on. There was barely enough room to squeeze the car through. Men in white suits with cameras and clipboards hovered behind the Garda tape. Debris lay scattered along the road. Where were the vehicles involved, the ambulances to take away the injured? Then he saw it: the wheels and undercarriage of a car upturned in the dyke. He must have stopped, because he remembered shouts telling him to proceed. He wondered if she might have set out walking with Gráinne in the pram; if they had been the accident.

When he got home, the cottage was cold and empty.

He took the turn for Balroe now and watched to see if the car behind would follow. That man disappearing behind the tree had stirred him. The car did a full lap of the roundabout and came along the Balroe road. Murt did not trust coincidence. Tightening his grip on the steering wheel, he drove on. Boot to the floor was pointless in his old rattletrap.

Soon, Dwyer's pub was ahead of him. The final pub before home, standing on the corner, its blistering walls of green and orange daring people to enter. Whenever he passed the place, he could feel its draw. The lazy haze of the locals smoking—ban or no ban—at one corner of the counter; stale drink mixing with dust and smoke and damp curtains. Mumbling, coughing, the drag of a stool across worn floorboards. The steady stream of racing commentary from the television, watched by lolling heads or glued faces; men arguing and throwing money around as if they had it.

He looked in the mirror again. Could wait here, he thought, go into Dwyer's and see if the car passes. In the car park, he stopped the engine and wound down the window. A stillness in the Balroe air that had always made him wary.

Balroe itself was nothing to crow about. A few streets, more than enough pubs and full of its own importance. The people liked to say that it had this and it had that—only an hour from Dublin, and such a writer owns a cottage out the road. For years, the town had been on the up. Murt got sick of hearing it. Other than floating away with people's ideas, it was going nowhere. Just another town, no different to any other sleepy hole. They could dress up the shop fronts like packets of crayons, build as many shopping centres as they liked, but it wouldn't make anyone throw a second glance at the exit sign on the motorway.

No car passed.

He stepped out onto the gravel of Dwyer's car park. From the upstairs window of a house across the road, an old man raised a hand in slow motion. Some days everything was like that, as if it were not really happening or had happened before.

The door to Dwyer's offered little resistance to Murt's push. A waft of smoke burst past him, as if it were drunk itself, gasping for fresh air or rushing out to get sick. A hum of voices followed. Murt went through the timber-panelled porch and stood inside like an outlawed cowboy. Faces turned, heads nodded, idle eyes returned to the television, the newspaper, or some point behind the bar that did not exist.

Too late to walk back out now. From the depths, he heard a familiar roar.

'Be the Jesus, if it isn't Doran.'

A blunt hand burst through the smoke and beckoned Murt down to the far end. His boots dragged along the floor as he made his way over. Leaning against the counter, the sleeves of his shirt rolled up, buttons open halfway down his chest, was Donoghue. A curl of hair, broken from the slicked-back mop, dangled in an arc across his forehead. He threw an arm around Murt and pulled him close.

'My good friend the nomad,' he said. 'Are you back to us?'

A whiff of turnips stabbed Murt's sinuses. He struggled to free himself. Donoghue's bottom lip bounced around like live fish bait as he called to the barman, telling him to throw up a whiskey.

'I'm not staying,' Murt said. 'Just looking for someone.' He watched the road through the window. Still no sign of the car passing.

'Who?' Donoghue asked, tilting his head back and frowning. 'Now who might you be looking for?' He shouted down the bar for support, but nobody was interested. This was the problem with Donoghue: he was a nosey fucker and not likely to let the matter rest. If there was the sniff of a story, he would want to find out.

Donoghue and Murt knew each other well. They both lived in a guest house on the outskirts of the town. When Murt first arrived in Balroe a few years before, the council had given him a flat in the terrace. It had suited him fine until part of the building collapsed. The place was condemned for demolition and everyone had to find somewhere else to live. The residents were promised other flats, but since that day Murt had been staying at a guest house—the council's solution, supposed to be temporary. To Murt, it had sounded like a halfway house or a shelter, and he said as much to the woman from the council. She had a spiel then about how they solved the problem of social housing for *this group* by putting them up in guest houses. This group being him and his type—losers and misfits, single men with no dependants, no job, no prospects. It had been a long time since he had shared his space with other people, and could not see how this would work for him.

Oscar Donoghue was already staying at the guest house when Murt arrived. Older than Murt by maybe ten years, he gave the impression of being in charge, that everything in the house needed to go through him. Murt soon realised he was all talk. Donoghue had an answer for everything, and he defended it into the ground. Little could be gained from arguing with such a man. Around the guest house, Murt tried to avoid him, but this was no easy task. He was a man who could never get enough of himself, and expected everyone else to feel the same way about him.

Murt kept his eyes fixed on the road outside as Donoghue talked. The car should have gone past by now. How long had he been inside? If he stayed much longer, he might get sucked into the banter and fall under the spell.

'I'm away,' he said, cutting Donoghue off.

'And what about your friend?'

'He's not here.'

'I'll tell him you were looking for him,' Donoghue laughed, as Murt walked out. The door closed itself behind him, a clap of timber sealing the place shut, the draw and stir of voices contained. Maybe it was the morning's events, but standing outside Dwyer's he felt like he was on top of the dunes again. He looked around. Was he being watched right now? The car had not gone past, he knew that. Maybe his mind was playing tricks on him—his mind, Donoghue, this place.

One thing about the people in Balroe: everybody loved stories. About someone they knew, neighbours, cousins, friends. Even a good story about a stranger went down well. They loved stories because they could tell them to someone else, even if they weren't true. It made people feel important, that they mattered because someone was listening to them. Stories, half-truths and lies were passed around like notes between schoolchildren. Whether true or not, it was best to play your part and pass the rumours on. If you held back something, for whatever reason, suspicions were turned on you.

Annoyed with himself for going into Dwyer's, he quickened his steps across the car park. He'd breathe easier once he was behind the wheel.

Most people who were born in the town would die there. Some travelled to the city for work, but hurried back before night. Murt had heard plenty of people threatening to get out of the kip, to never come back. Those who did actually leave had returned, broke and convinced they were different. Nothing to do then but settle down and fatten up for the long haul.

Murt would always be an outsider around Balroe. Trust was hard-gained, and questions were only ever a whisper away. There was little you could do if someone had an idea about you. He was civil to everybody, but kept to himself as much as possible. When their initial talk went stale and Murt had settled in, the locals knew him as someone who was not afraid of work; they knew where to find him if they needed something built or fixed.

He let the truck crawl through the car park and stopped at the entrance. He looked down the road. At the far end, by the gateway to a lock-up yard, a car was parked. Above the thick front bumper, squinting headlights glowed patiently. Was it the same car? As he pulled out of the car park and drove up the road, he reckoned that it probably was.

# a touchy subject

I've never been good with people. Can't understand them. Not the accents, but what makes them say the things they say, how their heads work. I struggle enough with my own head not to bother with other people's. The things I remember from my past are twisted out of shape. There's a scrap pile of rusty memories inside in my skull. It's hard to tell a seized slab-saw from a crumpled car bonnet. I try to lug things out of the way till something real shows itself. Like the pup snapping at my hand. I can't even be sure things happened this way: It's spring, I think—a school morning. She snaps then sits back on her rear legs and growls up at me. The butty tail is going ninety across the lino. I swipe my hand in front of her nose and she snaps again, just playful like. This is the latest thing I've found out about my pup—that she's hands mad. Never takes her eyes off my hands. When I try to pet her she watches the hand and twists her whole body around so that she's lying belly-up on the floor ready to play. Then the paws start, kicking with the back and grabbing with the front. A snarl and the teeth appear—fangs and a tiny serrated row between. She's all tongue then, mad for licking. Ma tells me I'll have her wicked. Watch this, Ma, I say. I lift my hand from the pup's snout, clicking my fingers. Ma spins around to face me. Did you not hear me? Wicked. I sit back to the table and take a chunk out of my toast.

In school, all I can think about is summer—fresh cut grass and making a camp by the river. And the pup running along beside me the whole time. The teacher has set us an exercise in our copybooks. She pretends to be reading as we work, but she's watching and listening for sounds—paper rustling, chairs shifting, sniffles, a cough. A right hawk-eye that one.

I keep my head down until I hear a lawnmower—the first cut. I look out the window. How can I do work now with summer here? Hawk-eye is staring right at me tight-lipped. She doesn't say anything then so as not to disturb the others. After class she starts into me. Rabbiting on about how disruptive I am and can't I concentrate on anything for longer than a minute? The real world is only around the corner, she says, and I'll have to buck myself up for it, especially if I won't be going to secondary school—wherever she got that from. Her blabber is smothered by the lawnmower and the crop of ideas sprouting in my head.

Still a few weeks left until the holidays at that stage, but summer was within reach. Mornings would be easy from then on, especially with my new snappy friend. One morning after Easter I walked into the kitchen and there she was, scrambling to get out of a cardboard box. My mother wouldn't say where she'd got her from. Didn't matter to me. I took her in my arms, and she pissed down my jumper. She pissed all over the house. I was too busy playing and acting the eejit with her to bother training her.

Don't have her at that snapping, Ma says to me. Eat some more toast. The pup watches as I chew, hoping for a crust. Where did you get her from, Ma? Ma puts a mug of tea on the table and sits opposite me. You're not even dressed for school yet, she says. Easy on that butter. I work the knife back and forward along the toast. There's no hurry on me—sure isn't it nearly summer?

Ma was always in a panic. That was one thing about her. Up running around from seven every morning. Chop chop, Murtagh, she'd be shouting. By the time I'd get up, she would be dressed and ready for work with ages to spare.

She worked for the local councillor, de Paor. His secretary apparently. Dogsbody as far as I could see. Forever running around after him she was. Sometimes he called to the house at weekends and she'd be gone out the door soon after. Mr de Paor needs a favour, she'd say, or Mr de Paor has an important meeting on Monday. She never called him by his first name in front of me, and always put on a law-dee-daw accent when she said *Mr de Paor*, as if he were a man too important for me to understand.

Still sickens me to think about that fella and him swanning around all smiles and loud talk with everyone. He knew my name too, which I didn't like, and he always tried to put his arm around me or mess my hair. And then the same nonsense talk. How are the Reds doing? Think they have her in the bag this year. He might slip a few shillings into my hand. I told Ma I didn't like him and that she should look for a different job. Mr de Paor is very good to us, she'd say—you be nice to him. I reckoned he was involved in getting the pup, but that didn't make me like him any more.

When I finish my toast I ask Ma was it the animal pound or the side of the road? What does it matter? she says. The pound yes. Now eat up. I knew it wasn't the pound. She was always at that craic to keep me quiet. If she said the pound, then how could I argue? But I don't let up easily. What about me? Did you find me at the pound too? She makes a buck-lep out of her seat and over to the counter like a bee has stung the neck off her. At the sink with her back to me she rinses her cup then looks around for the tea cloth. She dries the cup so much that it lets out a squeal.

This was a touchy subject with Ma. Whenever I brought it up, she told me not to be at my silly talk. Of course you have a father, she says to me then. A fine man. Unfortunately he's no longer with us. She always said she would explain things to me when I was older. What was there to explain if my father was dead?

And pictures, I say, there must be pictures. She doesn't have much of an answer to that. And what age was I when he died anyway? Enough, she shouts. When you're older I'll tell you all about him. Not now.

She was a great woman for the long finger all the same. When she was unsure, or just didn't want to do something, the long finger would come out. I pushed and pushed, but it was no good.

Was he a brave man? She stands gazing out the window as if the answer might walk past. Did he fight in the war? I ask, knowing that this will really annoy her. Don't be ridiculous, she says. What war? There's a scowl on her face when she turns. She did that a lot too—put on faces to warn me, to pretend she was angry. The war that they all fought in, I say. She takes a fit of coughing and is gone out the door to the bathroom.

I wasn't even sure when the war was, but I imagined a man dressed in army uniform standing in the doorway. I must have seen it on the telly. The timing was all wrong. The war was years before, but she didn't give me anything to go on so I had to make up things. I never knew what it was like to have a father, so in some ways it didn't matter. There were times when I saw other boys with their fathers and I wondered what it would be like to have a big man around all the time. Someone who could shake the house with a laugh or a roar and who could hold me and Ma tight, fit the both of us into his arms, throw us way up into the air and catch us before we hit the ground.

# 2

Murt drove up the driveway to the guesthouse and parked beside the stone outhouses. His truck was a small flatbed Dyna, deep royal blue and covered with dents and scratches from years of hardship. For loading, the sides and tailboard could be opened and let hang down over the wheels like a tablecloth.

A local merchant had given him some old pallets that he could cut up and sell for firewood. As he unloaded the pallets, he wondered how long he would be stuck living at the guest house. He missed the silence and freedom of his own space. Rooted to the bottom of the housing list, as he no doubt was, there was little chance of his getting a new flat. Families and single mothers had priority. That was only fair; they needed a home more than him. Being thrown into a guest house to live with strangers was a sorry reality. And he past forty years of age. Still, there were worse places he could be than the guest house—those years he had spent in a caravan would never leave him.

Mrs Kelleher, the owner, was as nice a woman as you could meet. The guest house was a mile outside the town, within walking distance, although the bends and pencil-narrow footpath were chancy. Elevated above the road, the house itself looked out across the town beyond. A white board dangled at the entrance from chains that were flaky and coarse with rust. Close up, the ghosted impression of old letters could be made out on the surface: B&B.

A line of hardy weeds divided the driveway into two gravel tracks that made it seem more like the access road to a quarry than a house. After hitting every pothole the first day he arrived, Murt had parked by the gable wall and walked around. Standing in front of the house, he wondered what he was letting himself in for. Would he even last a week in this place? A man's face appeared at a window. This, he would soon learn, was Donoghue.

At the door he was met by Mrs Kelleher. A butty, short-armed woman with a crop of curls that were fit to harvest. She looked around uneasily, and Murt wondered if he had come to the wrong house. After satisfying herself that this was the man she was expecting, she ushered him inside and told him to have a seat in the front room. As she poured tea, she apologised and proceeded to tell him about how the Jehovah's Witnesses had her plagued of late.

At the porch now, he took off his work boots. He never knew what to expect when he opened the door of the guest house—the atmosphere could be different depending on who was home. Inside, the house was quiet. He liked it that way, and could sometimes imagine it as his own home.

In the kitchen, he unpacked the few bits he had bought in the shop and put them on the table: crumbed ham, a sliced pan, lettuce, tomatoes, cheese. He took a plate from the press and butter from the fridge. When he heard the gush of a tap, he turned around. Mrs Kelleher was filling the kettle at the sink.

'Sandwiches?' she said. 'And there was dinner here for you.'

'Sorry. I thought I'd be back.'

'I don't know what you do be at. And that other lad is no better.'

They both had a good idea where Donoghue was, but Mrs Kelleher had a soft spot for him; she wouldn't hear of any bad talk about Oscar.

Murt buttered two slices of bread side by side on the plate.

'You'll have tea?' Mrs Kelleher asked.

'Please.'

He layered the sandwich bottom to top: ham, lettuce, cheese, tomato, laid the top slice over and cut the whole lot straight across. When the kettle boiled, Mrs Kelleher made tea and sat at the table. Murt wanted to ask her about the new lodger, but was unsure of how to broach the subject. He never felt right asking questions about people, and was himself suspicious of others asking about him.

Mrs Kelleher looked to be deep in thought. She sat sideways on her chair, facing the window above the sink as if watching for rain against the glass.

'Big auction down at the sales yard,' she said. 'Is it Wednesday or Thursday?'

'Friday.'

'Himself used to love things like that.'

On the rare occasions when she talked about her husband, Murt had never heard Mrs Kelleher refer to him by name, but always with a loyal smile. He decided to keep his snooping questions to himself.

Ursula had arrived at the guest house the previous week amid spills of rain. She was drenched. Eely hair stuck to her skin as if she had lifted her head out of a barrel of water, a startled smile splashed across her face, all teeth and tongue. The carpet in the living room had darkened in a circle around where she was standing. When Mrs Kelleher ushered her off to the kitchen, Donoghue looked at Murt.

'See the ring,' he said. 'Husband must have kicked her out.'

Ursula was drunk that night. And had been every night since, as far as Murt could tell. He wondered about a woman like that being given a place at the guest house. There was something strange about the arrangement.

'Nothing but junk at those auctions anyway,' Mrs Kelleher said. 'That's all.'

'But you'll go down anyway?'

'I suppose, if I'm idle.'

He washed down the last of his sandwich with a gulp of tea.

Mrs Kelleher had been keeping a close eye on Ursula, shielding her from the two men as if they were shady characters. Donoghue wanted the story: who this woman was, why she was at the guest house, and whether he had any chance with her. He reckoned she

was forty odd. Ursula was one of those people who wore life's hardships on her face. There was youth in her smile, Murt thought; she was attractive, but the effects of the drink were starting to show. When he talked about women, Donoghue growled in a low voice, his eyes squeezed tight with lust. Murt had never seen him as much as chatting with a woman. Dwyer's was not known as a hotspot for the ladies. It was a rare occasion when a high heel graced the floorboards. Around Ursula, Donoghue had his own brand of sleaze, which he considered charm. He fawned over her, made a big deal of her presence as if she were a child, all the while angling for a grope.

Murt and Donoghue were in the front room when Ursula came back from the pub that night. Donoghue fixed himself, straightened up in the chair.

'There you are now,' he said. 'Will you have a nightcap?'

She flashed the drink-vague smile and shook her head.

'We must have a few together sometime, you and I. You know nothing about me, nor I you.'

Remembering that Murt was in the room, he corrected himself.

'We all must have a drink sometime, get to know each other. You'll be staying around a while anyway?'

As she went through to the kitchen, he turned to Murt, jerked his head to one side and winked—the wink of a man who thought he was in.

Later, as Murt lay on his bed, he was irritated by Donoghue's wink and the alliance between them that it suggested. Donoghue had not cared if Ursula saw his gesture; probably thought she would appreciate him more because of it.

How little Murt and Donoghue knew about each other. When they talked, the conversation went around in circles about articles in the newspaper, stories they had heard in the town, idle gossip. When it came to themselves, there were limits to the information they shared. Murt did not like it when Donoghue asked him questions, and if he did answer, it was with a question of his own.

Donoghue, too, avoided straight answers. For a man who liked to talk, his defences went up when the spotlight got too hot, turning instead to bravado and tales in which he was a hero or victor.

Donoghue thrived on information about other people, on knowing things that they did not. Most of all, he wanted to be the first to hear. People came to him with side-of-the-mouth talk, rumours that they wanted confirmed or started.

Nobody, including Donoghue, knew that Murt had a daughter. He never spoke about his past, about Cathy or about what had happened to the driver of the car that hit her. Murt's past was his own. If Donoghue did find out, the whole town would know that very day.

Murt opened his eyes. The glow from an outside light took the edge off the darkness. It was a rare night when he slept right through. In the corner of the room he could make out a dark shape, like a man watching him sleep. He sat up in the bed, squinted, moved his head cautiously. Hanging like a scarecrow from the corner of the half-open wardrobe door was his coat. There was no man. He took a breath and lay back, wondering again if someone had been following him. Lately, it felt as if the past was watching him through cracked and filthy panes.

Maybe it was time to leave the town. Where would he go? As much as he could settle anywhere, he had settled in Balroe. Some other place would mean different people, but the same questions, the same whispers and mistrust that take a long time to shake off.

He thought again about the beach and the possible reasons why Gráinne had not shown up. The country was small, it would not have taken her that long to get to the beach—if she really wanted to meet him. Maybe she never got his letter. This was the reason that he wanted to believe, but he could not keep deluding himself. Surely she was interested in the kind of person Cathy had been, even if she did hate him. She would have heard biased stories from her family. There was little he could do about those.

nted. Anyway, he says, they'll hardly be thinking about us
n they're up there spending money.

rp ringing sound echoes around the shed when the wrench
skids across the concrete floor. Quinn starts cursing like
n then. He drags himself out from under the tractor,
his hand around as if it's been bitten by a beast. Always
rn cods you, he says through gritted teeth. He holds the
nd against his stomach and his face is twisted so tight
ain that it looks like he has no eyes. I winced at the sight
d asked him if he was all right. Anything but the hand, he
zing it under his armpit.
the stinging had eased, he looked at the wound, shook
few times, opened and closed his fist and shook it a
Clumps of skin were piled up behind the middle two
if it had been peeled back. There wasn't much blood,
ulled the lumps of skin off and let water from the yard
his hand till it was nearly blue-numb with the cold.
d wrenches from a height, said they're a cunt on the
dy up those tools now and we'll give you a spin. I'd sat
n sometimes, reaching for the pedals, humming the
tretching my neck to see out, but I'd never had the
nning engine in my hands.
et, and Quinn stands on the tractor step beside me.
the gears—first to sixth, high and low. Clutch there
ose two pedals on the far side are the brakes, one for
ck wheels. Now start her up. She won't start in gear,
eutral first. Here, like this. My hand grips the key. I
and when the engine coughs I let go from the fright.
to hold it till she bites. The tractor shakes under me
a start. Quinn points to the throttle, and I pull the
engine.
jolts, I was driving slowly out of the shed. Not even
ut I was happy enough. The steering was stiff and
ds, as if it had a life of its own. That's only because

Awake now, his mind spinning, he got up and turned on the
light. From the locker, he took the small notebook he had bought
in the shop a few weeks earlier. It was an idea he had had about
memories. When he could not sleep, he tried to scribble things
down, bits of his past, stories, fragments of his life. Maybe one day
Gráinne would have questions that only he could answer; and if
they never met, at least she might read what he had written.

His Uncle Quinn had hundreds of books on the country's
history that Murt used to read: stories, accounts of events with
dates and facts, something real that he could understand. He had
heard many stories told too, handed down and recounted.

Opening the notebook, he read the last page.

There were some things that he did not think he could write
down: what he felt shame and guilt about, the shadows he had been
running away from for years. Some day he might make sense of
how his life had panned out, the decisions he had made and their
consequences.

# learning to drive

Every young lad wants to drive. The bigger the machine and the blacker the smoke, the better. I can still remember the thrill of that first time. But the day is important for reasons other than taking my uncle's tractor across his yard. Everything changed that day.

I was eleven, and the school was closed down for a week because of rats. That was the story on the school bus anyway. One week off, and it not long after Easter. You'll be under my feet now I suppose, Ma says to me. I tell her I could go to Uncle Quinn's and help him out. She throws me a look, suspicious-like, but I can see she's thinking about it. Any excuse to get rid of me for a while.

Quinn and Maureen were always happy to have me over. They'd no children themselves. There was a little girl once, but she died being born. Whether they just didn't bother trying after that, I don't know.

Ma drove me down there the next day in the Datsun. Herself and Maureen had arranged to go to Dublin for the day—shopping and maybe the pictures. It was Maureen's birthday and they never got many chances. Go easy, Quinn says to them when they were leaving, with the driving and all. No reply, just their hands waving out the windows as the Datsun drove away. You wouldn't know when we'll see those two again, he says, nudging me with his elbow. Come on so, we've plenty to be getting on with. The back field first. Will you be able for a bag of meal?

I wasn't, but that didn't stop me trying. The bag started on my shoulder, same as Quinn's, but it was slipping the whole time.

Before I even got across the yard, I ha
back in a half-stagger. At the gate, I ha
Quinn was laughing, and told me to go
I wasn't able for it. No, I said, I've go
not to think about how far I still had
the feeding trough, I was dragging th
arse was covered in muck that lodge
tried to haul it up. I'll get it now, Q
same. He lifted the sack with one h
the trough.

After lunch we went out to the
asked me if I was any good at mech
All I had to do was hand wrenches,
was lying down under the back wh
you think they'll bring us anything
me then. Like what, a Viking or s
he says, if they find one of them
the only history they do be tea
I said, and asked him what he'd
stuff straight from the brewery.
jam jar. I never tasted much of
anyway, I asked him, in Dublin
the tractor. That's where the m
Or what they call a governme
in the box there? I rooted
wrench. Quinn was laughing
other things that wouldn't c
he said. This had me intere
said, and fancy buildings th
Liffey. Surely you've heard
Men and women. Take e
you. Is that where the telly
right. And hospitals and u
yourself some day. I said

just gru
two whe

A sh
slips and
a madm
throwing
the last t
injured h
with the p
of him an
says, sque

When
the hand
bit more.
knuckles as
and Quinn
tap run ove

He curs
knuckles. T
in the Datsu
noises and s
wheel of a r

So in I g
He shows m
on the left, th
each of the b
so put her in
turn it real eas
Quinn tells m
and splutters t
lever to rev the

After a few
walking pace, b
jumpy in my ha

Awake now, his mind spinning, he got up and turned on the light. From the locker, he took the small notebook he had bought in the shop a few weeks earlier. It was an idea he had had about memories. When he could not sleep, he tried to scribble things down, bits of his past, stories, fragments of his life. Maybe one day Gráinne would have questions that only he could answer; and if they never met, at least she might read what he had written.

His Uncle Quinn had hundreds of books on the country's history that Murt used to read: stories, accounts of events with dates and facts, something real that he could understand. He had heard many stories told too, handed down and recounted.

Opening the notebook, he read the last page.

There were some things that he did not think he could write down: what he felt shame and guilt about, the shadows he had been running away from for years. Some day he might make sense of how his life had panned out, the decisions he had made and their consequences.

# learning to drive

Every young lad wants to drive. The bigger the machine and the blacker the smoke, the better. I can still remember the thrill of that first time. But the day is important for reasons other than taking my uncle's tractor across his yard. Everything changed that day.

I was eleven, and the school was closed down for a week because of rats. That was the story on the school bus anyway. One week off, and it not long after Easter. You'll be under my feet now I suppose, Ma says to me. I tell her I could go to Uncle Quinn's and help him out. She throws me a look, suspicious-like, but I can see she's thinking about it. Any excuse to get rid of me for a while.

Quinn and Maureen were always happy to have me over. They'd no children themselves. There was a little girl once, but she died being born. Whether they just didn't bother trying after that, I don't know.

Ma drove me down there the next day in the Datsun. Herself and Maureen had arranged to go to Dublin for the day—shopping and maybe the pictures. It was Maureen's birthday and they never got many chances. Go easy, Quinn says to them when they were leaving, with the driving and all. No reply, just their hands waving out the windows as the Datsun drove away. You wouldn't know when we'll see those two again, he says, nudging me with his elbow. Come on so, we've plenty to be getting on with. The back field first. Will you be able for a bag of meal?

I wasn't, but that didn't stop me trying. The bag started on my shoulder, same as Quinn's, but it was slipping the whole time.

Before I even got across the yard, I had it in a bear hug, leaning back in a half-stagger. At the gate, I had to drop it and take a rest. Quinn was laughing, and told me to go back and get the barrow if I wasn't able for it. No, I said, I've got her. I struggled on, trying not to think about how far I still had to go. By the time I reached the feeding trough, I was dragging the sack along the ground. The arse was covered in muck that lodged around my fingers when I tried to haul it up. I'll get it now, Quinn said. You made it all the same. He lifted the sack with one hand and tipped the meal into the trough.

After lunch we went out to the shed to fix the tractor. Quinn asked me if I was any good at mechanics. I told him I'd give it a go. All I had to do was hand wrenches, bars or hammers to Quinn, who was lying down under the back wheels, talking between curses. Do you think they'll bring us anything nice back from Dublin? he asks me then. Like what, a Viking or something? A Viking! Be the Jesus, he says, if they find one of them up there, we'll be rich men. Is that the only history they do be teaching you in school? Pretty much, I said, and asked him what he'd like back. A big pint of the black stuff straight from the brewery. Or a bit of that city air caught in a jam jar. I never tasted much of it in me time. What goes on up there anyway, I asked him, in Dublin? He stuck his head out from under the tractor. That's where the money is, he says. And the government. Or what they call a government. Is there a nine-sixteenth spanner in the box there? I rooted through the toolbox and found the wrench. Quinn was laughing as he took it from me. And all sorts of other things that wouldn't concern country boys like you and me, he said. This had me interested. What things? Big, long streets, he said, and fancy buildings that the English built. There's the River Liffey. Surely you've heard of that. Plenty of troublemakers too. Men and women. Take every penny off you as quick as look at you. Is that where the telly is? I asked. Radio Telefís Éireann, that's right. And hospitals and universities. You might go to one of them yourself some day. I said that I'd never been in a hospital, and he just grunted. Anyway, he says, they'll hardly be thinking about us two when they're up there spending money.

A sharp ringing sound echoes around the shed when the wrench slips and skids across the concrete floor. Quinn starts cursing like a madman then. He drags himself out from under the tractor, throwing his hand around as if it's been bitten by a beast. Always the last turn cods you, he says through gritted teeth. He holds the injured hand against his stomach and his face is twisted so tight with the pain that it looks like he has no eyes. I winced at the sight of him and asked him if he was all right. Anything but the hand, he says, squeezing it under his armpit.

When the stinging had eased, he looked at the wound, shook the hand a few times, opened and closed his fist and shook it a bit more. Clumps of skin were piled up behind the middle two knuckles as if it had been peeled back. There wasn't much blood, and Quinn pulled the lumps of skin off and let water from the yard tap run over his hand till it was nearly blue-numb with the cold.

He cursed wrenches from a height, said they're a cunt on the knuckles. Tidy up those tools now and we'll give you a spin. I'd sat in the Datsun sometimes, reaching for the pedals, humming the noises and stretching my neck to see out, but I'd never had the wheel of a running engine in my hands.

So in I get, and Quinn stands on the tractor step beside me. He shows me the gears—first to sixth, high and low. Clutch there on the left, those two pedals on the far side are the brakes, one for each of the back wheels. Now start her up. She won't start in gear, so put her in neutral first. Here, like this. My hand grips the key. I turn it real easy and when the engine coughs I let go from the fright. Quinn tells me to hold it till she bites. The tractor shakes under me and splutters to a start. Quinn points to the throttle, and I pull the lever to rev the engine.

After a few jolts, I was driving slowly out of the shed. Not even walking pace, but I was happy enough. The steering was stiff and jumpy in my hands, as if it had a life of its own. That's only because you're going so slow, Quinn says. If you were flat out, she'd be all yours. All yours. I liked that.

The afternoon closed in quickly for the time of year. The air was stuffy and hung around like a lazy dog, making us tired. When we got back to the house, we sat down for a rest. Quinn said it was a whore of a heavy evening. I'm a May man myself, he said, but you couldn't do much in that. What do you think? I told him I liked autumn—October. Halloween and bonfires. We may fix up our own tonight, Quinn said, about the supper. What will you have? I told him that I'd eat anything. Anything, he said. That's what I like to hear.

He shuffled around the kitchen, opening and closing presses. He took out a pot, put it back and found a bigger one. After going to the pantry twice and coming back empty-handed, he pulls out a packet of mince from the fridge and leaves it on the counter. He was muttering to himself the whole time—plates, cutlery, salt, butter. Out to the pantry again and back with a sack of potatoes. I set the table.

Beans may do for a veg, he says, as he wrestles with the can opener. Grand. Will I throw on the radio? Do, he says, must be nearly news time. The electric kettle is making a fierce racket, sending steam all around the kitchen and fogging up the window. Quinn waves a hand to clear the mist. Won't be too long now at all, he says. Just peel these spuds and fry up the bit of mince. I flick on the radio switch but nothing happened. Plug it in at the back there, Quinn shouts. Maureen's petrified the place will burn down some day.

I reach in and feel for the plug at the back of the dresser. Something heavy falls on the floor but doesn't break. A pile of bills and magazines spills like a waterfall over the edge. Up on one leg, I manage to get hold of the lead and fish the plug into my hand. I plug it into the socket. Static and voices crackle as I turn the knob backwards and forwards. Finally, I find a man talking in a serious voice, and I sit down at the table to think about the day I've just had. The tractor's steering wheel is still alive in my hands, pulling with the stones and ruts of the yard. Maybe tomorrow I'll take it out to the field, and it will be all mine then. I can open out the throttle and feel the roar of the engine as it takes off. Quinn is standing beside the table then, drying his hands with a towel. He stops. His face turns the colour of an old photograph as he looks at me. Mother of Jesus, he says, rushing forward to turn up the volume.

In Dublin, bombs were going off.

# 3

He dipped the clutch and dropped to second gear. A burst of higher revs and the engine held steady, having been losing power since the foot of the incline. Seamus Cowman's farm was near the top of a sour-grassed highland called Blackgate Hill. Roads up and around Blackgate were wicked as tinker's curses. Even with no load in the back, Murt's truck struggled to handle them.

Today, the Dyna was loaded. Engine and body rattled under the pressure of the climb. The clutch had been replaced only the previous spring. Not that he blamed Blackgate, but a hill like that would do a machine no good. Potential danger, lurked around every corner: milk lorries, delivery trucks, tractors, stray beasts.

More of a small mountain than a hill, but Blackgate was not big enough for the locals to classify it as a mountain. The hill formed one side of a valley that stretched for miles out west to where the mountains proper spined around the back of the county. Seen from Blackgate, the land below, the fields and forests, the roads, ditches and rivers were stitched together like a vast landscaped quilt.

The engine dipped again at a steeper part of the incline. Murt bounced in the seat, urging his truck on. Not far now. The western sky was painted yellow with evening sun. He shaded his eyes from the watery glare. Murt struggled to see what was ahead of him. Finally, around the next corner, the road levelled out. He indicated right and turned onto Cowman's dog-rough lane. Seamus appeared from a shed and stood watching as the truck crawled towards his yard.

'Not a bother on her,' Seamus said, tapping the windscreen.

Murt got out. A sulphury waft of burning clutch caught the back of his throat.

'Wouldn't have taken much more,' Murt said, pointing to the load of concrete blocks on the flatbed. 'Where do you want them?'

'Hold there now till I get something.'

Seamus came back with the tractor, and Murt lifted the concrete blocks from the truck into the front loader bucket. When it was full, he followed the tractor into one of the sheds and they both stacked the new blocks beside a collapsed wall.

'I might be able to reuse some of these old blocks,' Seamus said.

Murt grunted to himself. 'It'll break your heart knocking that hard mortar off them.'

'You got the cement?'

'Two bags.'

'Only two?'

'You told me two bags.'

Murt was well used to Seamus Cowman. He had told Murt exactly how many blocks and bags of cement to pick up at the merchants, had even rung ahead to agree a price with the manager—excluding delivery. It worked out cheaper if Murt collected and delivered for him.

Murt had got to know Cowman through Donoghue, who had worked for him around the farm. 'He used to miss the odd day,' Seamus told Murt once, 'but he went to be fucked then, and I couldn't rely on him.' After that, Seamus started getting Murt more and more. Odd jobs, farm work, whatever needed doing.

Having the Dyna meant that Murt was rarely idle. When people asked him to do a job, they got the truck too. There was always something to be shifted, someone wanting a hand. Across the far side of the valley, he brought hay and feed for horses. Before Christmas every year, he would load up with trees for the markets. He had a few regular jobs around the town too. It had started with one person and then they told their friends and neighbours. Sometimes people called him to move furniture, soil, plants for their garden. When he was not doing casual work for people, he spent his time cutting timber, bagging it and selling it for firewood. He knew just about all there was to know about timber.

'How are you fixed for the end of the week?' Seamus asked.

'You definitely have sand?'

'There's some of that heap left over from last summer. Friday would be the handiest.'

'I think I'll stick my head in at the auction some time Friday.'

'That fucking junk sale. We'll leave the wall till the following week so,' he said, throwing his hand in the air as if he was batting away flies at the height of summer.

Murt could still catch a whiff of the clutch, like burnt carpet, as he opened the door and climbed into the truck.

'They're taking down an old shed beyond,' Seamus said.

'Kavanagh's?'

'Probably give you the timber if you ask them.'

'I'll drop over.'

Down at the road, something had caught Seamus' attention. He held a hand to his forehead to shield the light from his eyes. Sitting in the van, Murt half-turned but could see nothing over his shoulder.

'There'd be good dry firing in that timber,' Murt said.

Seamus didn't answer. He took a few steps down the yard. Murt got out and walked over to where he was standing.

'Look at this nosey cunt,' Seamus said.

Down at the entrance gate, Murt could make out the shape of a man leaning on a car roof and looking through binoculars in their direction.

'I'll see who it is on my way out,' Murt said.

'Not the Knackers anyway; they'd drive straight in. Couldn't be the fucking Customs again.'

A few weeks earlier, two Customs men had driven into Seamus' yard and started asking questions about laundered diesel. He had been edgy ever since.

Murt said, 'Maybe it's the Welfare, after me.'

As Seamus turned for the shed to fetch his shotgun, the man got into the car and drove off. Murt watched the slick roof-line coast along the ditch in no hurry at all, before disappearing behind a copse of trees.

Donoghue raised his head from the table when Murt walked into the dining room. Most days, Donoghue was full of talk, questions mostly. On other rare days—good days for Murt—he was quiet, withdrawn even, as if there was something on his mind. Thinking days, Murt called them.

Today was not a thinking day.

Murt closed the door, said hello to Donoghue and sat at the table farthest away. The only flaw in this arrangement was that, although they were at different ends of the room, they were still facing each other.

'I wonder where Ursula eats,' Donoghue said. 'Not in here with us anyway.'

He stared at the ceiling as he chewed, the fork hovering close to his mouth. Murt gave a not-knowing shake of his head. The door from the kitchen opened, and Mrs Kelleher came in with a plate of stew for Murt. She and Donoghue were on a first-name basis.

'I was wondering, Martha—'

'What's that then?'

'Is Ursula ok? I mean, does she not eat?'

This was probably not the question Donoghue had intended, but his concern had been expressed.

'Not that I know of,' she said, smiling over at Murt.

'I'd be a bit worried about her.'

'I'm sure she'll be grateful for your concern, Oscar.'

Murt had still not figured out what was going on in the house. Ursula had one of the downstairs rooms towards the back of the house, and yet the guest rooms were upstairs, Murt and Donoghue at either end of the corridor. Sometimes they came out of their rooms at the same time and faced each other like two lost strays across the dimly lit passage.

If the lodgers wanted to be fed at the guest house, they paid for it themselves; meals were not included in the council's subsidy. And it was not an arrangement whereby they could decide to have dinner one night and not have it the next as they pleased. Mrs Kelleher, as she said herself, was not their mother. They either paid for the full week's evening meals, or ate elsewhere.

A room off the main kitchen served as the dining room. There were six small tables, laid out in three rows of two. Although the tables could probably seat four at a push, there were only two chairs at each. Donoghue sat at the same table every day, making it clear that this was his table. Murt tried to stagger his dinnertime so as to avoid eating with Donoghue, but this was not a fail-safe strategy.

When he had finished eating, Donoghue flicked open his newspaper. Donoghue, the great Irishman with his English tabloid. Rants about the English were standard fare for him, with that red top under his arm or waving it around like a baton. Them and their fucking empire, he'd say. The only thing they ever fought for wasn't theirs to begin with.

Of late, he had taken to the horses in a big way.

'It's a pity you're not a gambling man,' he said to Murt now. 'With all the tips I get.'

'Any winners today?' Murt asked.

'Not so many today. Some days though.'

As he rustled through the newspaper, Murt stood from the table.

'You'll be going to the auction, I suppose?' Donoghue said. 'Wouldn't know what you'd find down there.'

'Might drop in for a gander at some stage,' Murt said, not wanting to be drawn on the subject in case it was suggested that they go along together.

Without looking up, Donoghue nodded.

'Can't resist, same as meself.'

When the front door to the guest house closed with a bang, Donoghue lowered the newspaper. He cocked his head and gave Murt a that-must-be-her-now look. Raising the paper again, he waited to see if Ursula would appear in the dining room.

# telling stories

I'd never been next nor near a coffin and suddenly there were two side by side. The sight of them rattled me something fierce. Still does. All I could think about was how long it would take the wood to rot in the ground. I couldn't stay in that room, so I ran out to the kitchen where the auld ones were making a big fuss about nothing. Here he is, says one, and she throws her elbow out for the others to whisht. Neighbours shuffled in. They brought things along—tokens I suppose you'd call them—and left them down on the table. Plates of sandwiches covered in tinfoil and cling film, currant cake, bottles of Paddy and Jameson. There were prayers first of course—a lot of muttering and hands on Quinn's arms, shoulders and back. I sat in the corner holding the pup by her collar in case she made a bolt for the door. Her little chest was shivering like an alarm clock at the sight of so many hands coming at her. People asked me in whispers how I was getting on. Mostly though, they just mauled the pup. How old is he? She. She? Sorry, how old is she? What's she called? Do you have her long? Where did you get him? Her. Sorry, where did you get her? I don't know, I said, Ma got her somewhere for me, didn't tell me where. At the mention of Ma, they remembered. Oh, sorry.

I must have been cried out because I didn't shed a drop at all that night. Quinn didn't either. I think it was on account of me, in case he started me off like. Sometimes you can't help crying though, it's that strong. He was in the other room with the coffins for a while. Everyone who went in there cried. When Quinn asked me if I wanted to go back in, I said no way. It's ok, he said, the lids are closed. No, I don't want to, no.

Later when the talk started, Quinn pulled me aside. You'll be in charge of the whiskey, he said. Keep us topped up. Red Doherty insisted I have a drop myself and the others agreed. I threw it straight down and the face on me must have been a sight. I thought my throat was melting. It'll burn you a bit at first, Red said, but you'll get a taste for it all right. He wasn't wrong about that.

Doesn't one story always swell into the next? Around the table, everyone played off each other, having small digs when they could. When one of the women mentioned some dead local—a man who always mumbled and liked his Guinness warm, they all had a comment. Didn't he used to tell the barman to throw his pint bottle into the kettle for a bit? And soup too, Red said. I saw him throw a cupful of Oxtail into the glass to warm up the stout. Across the table, a man mocked the long-dead mumbler and they all laughed. I didn't know the man they were talking about, but a furry warmth from the whiskey had me giddy, and I laughed too. Twas no easy life for him, Quinn said about the mumbler. Wasn't he got by the Tans? someone asked. The room rumbled with voices. Sure nobody knew what side he was on, someone shouted. You couldn't give that lad a slingshot, he'd have gone looking for water. The laughing was soon shushed by the women.

I had an auld slingshot myself but didn't know how you could look for water with it. I took the lid off the bottle and went around the table topping up glasses. And my own.

After a short drink and reflection, one man sighed and said, the Tans were some cunts all right. And off they start again. What about yer one with the two husbands? Two husbands? A younger man over in the corner had never heard this one. That's right—Mrs Carmody. One of the husbands—the first one—was supposed to be dead. Wasn't he a wanted man? Would have been executed for sure if he'd been caught. Only way out was to pretend he was dead. So that's what they did. Had to stay in hiding, moving around from safe house to safe house. And if the wife didn't go off and marry someone else in the meantime. Go away. Did she know he wasn't actually dead? Sure wasn't the whole thing her idea?

Even though most of them seemed to know the story, there was uproar. And on they went until some time later when there was a knock at the door. Everyone looked at each other as if they had no notion or else knew exactly who it could have been. Quinn went to the door. Voices dropped to a whisper. Might be himself, Red Doherty said. Must be. Could be the other lad. True. I didn't know who Himself or the Other Lad were, but I listened anyway. The door closed, and Quinn reappeared with another bottle of whiskey. O'Neill, he said. Red Doherty eyed him. Wouldn't come in? No, just stopped to—. Fair enough.

I woke up some time in the morning, my head resting on Red Doherty's shoulder. Here he is now, Red said, and the few heads that were left nodded over at me. A woman put a cup of tea in front of me, and after I drank it, I slipped off to bed, the pup still in my arms.

Most of what I know of the past, I got from Quinn. How the country came to be the way it is, the things that went on before. There were books too, but the books didn't have stories. Not like Quinn's—stories he got from his parents and grandparents, my ancestors. His crowd came from a small farmstead three or four miles from the nearest village. The secrets they had were deadly, what they had to do to protect themselves. Quinn's grandmother would whisper tales to him late at night. To survive, she told him, you had to believe. Everyone was active in some way—family, neighbours, priests. Against the monarch, the Tans, and later, worst of all, against each other. They went about their simple lives, making bread, foddering animals, barely surviving but at the same time harbouring and feeding volunteers, hiding weapons, passing information, under threat of death if they were caught.

Quinn told me tales that could just as well have been made up. How would I know the difference? He was never angry or upset, didn't curse the empire or the soldiers. They were yarns about a way of life and how things were. It seemed important to him that I knew about the past. It's always there behind you, he said. It's who you are.

# 4

When Murt first arrived in Balroe, Monday was mart day. The farmers would flood down from the hills, blocking roads, queuing from all hours of the morning. Tractors, jeeps, trailers and lorries lined every route in and out of town, packed tight with panting sheep and cattle, their breath rolling into the air like hundreds of stews on the boil. Later, when the buying and selling had finished, rubber-booted farmers thronged the pubs, eating sandwiches and drinking until the cows were brought home.

A local auctioneer had owned the mart at that time. Being so close to the centre of town, the yard itself was worth more than its few sheds suggested. A developer offered a lot of money, made a big scene about the town complex he was going to build on the site—something for the community, he said.

The developer, it turned out, was really a speculator and never had any intention of building a town centre. The way prices had been going, he was set to double his money in a year or two. So the gates were closed and the mart yard was forgotten about. Tufts of grass appeared between cracks in the concrete, rust began to eat away at the steel.

Murt didn't know much about economics and that sort of thing. He knew only what he read in the papers, what people were saying— that the money was gone and there was no bottom. Whoever owned the mart yard now was stuck with it.

Today, Balroe was like the mart days of old. The sale and auction had been advertised for a few weeks. There would always be people who, even if they didn't want something, would buy it anyway for the sake of a bargain.

Murt parked near the church and walked down.

Traveller men and boys, clad in leather jackets and slip-on shoes, poured from frantically parked vans. If there was junk being sold, they would be sniffing around, moving in packs so that it looked like they had taken over.

Machines of various size were lined in an arc around the main yard: pumps, motors, power washers, hedge-cutters, tractors, trailers, JCB diggers, track machines. People sauntered, some pointed, others inspected. A man walked past Murt examining the catalogue and scrawling notes in the margins as he went.

The nosey ones and others who couldn't make up their minds darted from one lot to the next. Two children climbed atop a bulldozer and ran along the tracks. The auctioneer's assistant waved his clipboard furiously from across the yard and another man, probably their father, ordered the children to get down.

At each lot, the auctioneer stood on an upturned crate, his megaphone fizzing gibberish through the dank morning air. A group of men were gathered in front of the megaphone now, farmers by the look of them, bidding for a cattle trailer. Heads nodded, fingers were raised coyly from chin-rubbing hands, a rolled-up catalogue was pointed at the back.

'Sold. Next lot.'

A spill of rain that morning had left the yard in a mess of puddles and gravel that squelched and spat underfoot. Murt found a catalogue curled on the ground, wiped the back of it against his leg and turned to the front cover: Machinery Auction, Bankrupt Stock. The back cover invited people to make their way indoors to the main shed for the open market bazaar.

The main shed ran along one perimeter and opened onto the yard. Murt remembered when, a few years before, they had sold sheep in there—hundreds of pens, the auctioneer running along a timber platform, weights and starting prices crackling through the megaphone. There was no chorus of bleating animals today. Tables, stalls, boxes and furniture occupied any available space on either side of roughly defined routes.

People dallied, browsing out of nosiness, seeing what remnants of their lives other people wanted to sell or give away. Puzzled looks followed detailed inspections. They discussed cost and value. What was worthless to one could be someone else's find. Tastes change. Children grow up. Parents get old. Items once beloved become obsolete—hideous, awkward, gaudy, broken. A nod of the head here, a shake of hands there.

Some of the sellers had made signs, handwritten on cardboard. Murt stopped at *Ann King's Rummage*. Four large cardboard boxes lay on the ground in front of a woman whom Murt presumed to be Ann King.

'Have a root,' she said. The boxes were arranged roughly by item size. He picked up a picture frame and three more came with it, bound together with green wool. 'Five euro,' she barked. He put them back in the box and pulled out what he thought was a trouser belt but turned out to be a dog leash. 'Two euro, if you like,' she said, softening her technique. Another box was full of nothing but candle-holders and half-burnt candles.

Beside Ann King, a tall man in red trousers stood next to a fridge. He leaned forward and opened the fridge door to reveal shelves packed with delftware—cups, saucers and plates. 'I like to keep the light off them,' he said, leaning towards Murt with flared nostrils.

Barter was rife. A woman took off her hat and received a painted vase in return. Murt watched to see if she would put the vase on her head, but she wrapped it in newspaper and tucked it under her arm. Some of the furniture was in good condition and decent amounts of money were exchanged. There was a constant stream of people in and out of the shed carrying chairs, sideboards, a glass table, a timber bureau. Two men toppled a wardrobe onto its side and a boy cleared a way for them through the crowd.

And then there was Donoghue, jumping clear of the oncoming wardrobe. He was holding his arms out wide, warning people of the danger. 'Careful, careful,' he shouted. 'Mind out of the way. Coming through.'

Murt turned the other way and busied himself at a stall. He picked up the nearest thing to hand, glancing over his shoulder to make sure Donoghue had not spotted him. He looked then at what he was holding: an old carbide lamp. When he was a boy living with his mother, he had found one of these in a box in the attic. After examining its parts, trying to understand how it worked, he had shown it to Quinn, who took the lamp and held it in his hands like an egg. 'Well now,' he said, inhaling through tight, impressed lips, 'isn't this a find.'

The lamp in Murt's hands now was in no better condition than the one that he had found in the attic. Still, he and Quinn had got that one working eventually. Murt remembered his uncle's face, the nurse-steady run of his fingers over the metal as slowly, over days and weeks, he brought the lamp back to life.

'Big with cavers,' a voice interrupted him.

Murt looked up at the girl standing behind the table. How familiar she was. But from where? Then he saw it—a version of Cathy or maybe his daughter, or whatever image he had of Gráinne in his mind. This girl could be Gráinne, he thought as he stared. The girl rocked on her heels and smiled at him.

'Cavers?' he asked.

'Carbide lamps. Cavers are mad for them. Much safer. And some miners too. They mark the rocks with black soot from the flame, so they know where they are. Like dropping sweets in a maze.'

Her hair was bunched together in thick clumps like animals' tails, and tied up some way with a scarf. As she talked, she played with the loose wool around a hole in her jumper.

'I had one of these before,' Murt said. 'Years ago. It was battered and rusted; didn't work at all.'

'Don't think this one's much good either.'

'Got it going in the end though; brought it back to life.'

The girl leaned her head to one side, and her face turned mock-sad as if she might cry.

'Was there a genie?'

Murt smiled and shook his head.

'No genie, no. Maybe I'll get one out of this.'

'It's not every day you see something you like,' she said.

'Where did you travel here from?'

It was a stupid question, none of his business, too personal. She weaved a tail-thick length of hair through her fingers.

'Sorry,' he said. 'It's not important.'

'Kildare,' she said. 'Athy.'

'I've been there. Nice place.'

She scoffed and threw back her head, as everyone seems to do at compliments about their home town. The ropey tails swung across her face.

'My daughter,' he said. 'She's about your age. You remind me—'

What right had he to talk about her? He was a fraud. What right to call her his daughter? Keeping his head down, he rooted through another box, hoping the girl wouldn't see the shame on his face.

'What's her name?'

Murt looked up and when he said her name, he burned with the imagined stares of every face in the shed.

'Gráinne.'

'Tell Gráinne that her father has a good eye for things.'

He wanted to stay here with the girl, to buy more of her wares, everything she had. As long as he could listen to her talk, take in the lines of her face, etch the details in his mind. She wasn't Gráinne, but that didn't matter. From nothing, at least he would have something.

'I'll tell her,' he said, 'if I see her.'

Another stupid thing to say. The girl smiled again and reached forward into another box.

'My eighties box,' she said.

She held a white plastic contraption in front of him like an offering—a tape machine.

'You can record a message for her,' the girl said.

Murt pressed the buttons: rewind, forward, record, play, stop.

'Tapes still work,' she said, tilting her head, pleading with him to take something else off her hands.

He asked her how much for the two things and she added on her fingers.

'That's a crazy price you're charging,' he said with a grin.

She laughed and lowered her price, but he handed her more than she had asked for. Somebody nudged in beside him then, and the girl's attention was lost to the next customer.

As he walked out of the shed, eager to avoid Donoghue, he felt a tug on his sleeve. The carbide lamp jumped from his arms, but was rescued from falling to the ground by a woman's hand.

'Eliza!'

She pulled him close and asked how things were going. Across the yard, a machine's engine roared to life. Black exhaust smoke rose into the sky.

'If you have a minute,' she said. 'I'd like to show you something.'

Eliza lived across the valley from Blackgate Hill. She owned a crumbling estate house, the Moss Hotel. Sometimes Murt delivered hay and straw for her horses.

Like a child, she led him through the crowd by his sleeve.

'Chickens,' she said, when they stopped at a van, the back doors of which were propped open, revealing cages of Bantam hens.

'Going to buy a few of these Banty's, but I'll need a coop too.'

She pointed to some sturdy timber coops beside the van.

'I thought you might bring it up for me,' she said, 'in the truck.'

Her hand lingered on Murt's arm as part of the plea for this special favour. There were other times when she would barely talk to him.

'Will do,' Murt said, 'But it'll have to be another day.'

The man with the chickens interrupted to say that that was not a problem, he could leave the coop in the sales yard. There would be people coming and going for the next week to collect what they had bought. But as for the chickens, she would have to take them today. And cash up front for the lot.

'I can throw the chickens in the boot of the Fiesta. You'll bring the coop, Murtagh?'

'Tomorrow or the next day.'

She flashed a smile that disappeared as her hand slipped down along his arm.

A commotion erupted behind them, people moving past, some running. A crowd surged towards the back of the yard where a large group of leather coats and flat caps were bunched together, waving arms and shouting. The chicken man was very amused.

'Must be a fight over a battery,' he said.

Donoghue and another man were at the entrance to the shed, watching the ruckus. Murt's line of vision was obscured, but there was something familiar about the man Donoghue was talking to—his height, the set of his shoulders. As Murt watched, the two men shook hands and parted company.

Eliza made a deal and paid the chicken man.

A slap on the back then, and Donoghue was beside them.

'Looking well, Eliza,' he said. 'A few cocks is it?'

'Just the three, Oscar.'

'More than enough.'

He frowned at the items Murt was carrying and tried to take them from his hands.

'Interesting choice of junk,' he said. 'I'll get a spin up the road with you, if you're going that way.'

Murt said, 'I'm not, but come on.'

Sitting in the passenger seat, Donoghue always looked ridiculous, like a child who had been allowed in the front for the first time. Leaning forward, and with his hands planted on the dashboard, he eyeballed and commented on every person they passed. Murt wanted to ask him about the man he had been shaking hands with, but Donoghue would not stop talking about how Eliza was a fine bit, and she wanted a good seeing to, and how he was the man for that.

'I can see it in her eyes,' he said. 'Cocks is right.'

Murt stopped on the road outside the guest house.

'Where are you off to now?' Donoghue asked.

'Up the hills to collect some firing.'

Donoghue got out and held the door open, waiting for an invitation, thinking that maybe Murt would need some help. As Murt drove off, the door swung free of Donoghue's hand and slammed shut.

# prisoners

It had gone more than a year since Ma and Maureen died before Quinn spoke about them. I was starting to think that he'd never say their names again. In he comes from the yard one day, pours himself a glass of whiskey and sits still in his armchair with a look on his face as if he has lost something and is trying to remember where he put it. She was an awful case of a woman, he says. I couldn't get near her at the dances. His mouth twisted to one side as he rubbed his jaw. A pause. I'd have her in my sights all right, but the minute I'd take a step, she'd know my game and be gone. Vanished. Three months that went on for.

I wonder now how long he must have been trying to start that conversation with me. Or maybe it came out of nowhere, and he was just as surprised as me by what he was saying. I hope that's how it came about, for his sake.

After a while, he went on. Then this night I stationed myself by the main door of the dance hall until she was leaving. One dance, I said to her. She told me after that she was more nervous than me. Imagine.

Quinn sought refuge in the parish church after the women were killed. He went to mass as much for the faces and the talk as for anything else. Like most of the men, I suppose. He never insisted, but I often went along anyway. I liked the faces too, the nods and whispers of the older folk.

On the way to mass one Sunday morning there was a slogan painted in fresh white strokes on a shop gable near the church. Trickles of paint still running down like tears from the letters. It was a rough job but I could read it clearly. Free Our Prisoners. The ones in the North, Quinn said. Same ones that killed Mammy and Maureen? I asked. No, the other side—our side. Next thing he picked up the pace as if we were going to miss the readings. Come on, he said, I'll explain it later.

Outside the church after mass, people were talking about the writing on the wall. Somebody said it was shocking. Another said something had to be done. A man in a heavy hunting-type coat came over to Quinn and shook his hand. I'd seen the two of them nod to each other before. They talked out of earshot and it was something serious, not the usual banter. I watched the man rub his face as if the wiry red beard was a disguise that he wasn't used to wearing. Quinn introduced him to me as O'Neill. Young Murt, O'Neill called me. A fine man you'll be. Sorry about your mother. That's what he said—sorry about my mother. And it over a year. His accent was strange. He said words sharp as if he was being jabbed in the arse with a spear. He held my stare as we shook hands, and I couldn't see whether he was smiling or snarling behind the beard. Then he looked around, waved to another man who was standing on the steps and the two of them headed for the gate in a hurry.

The trees around the church swayed in slow motion, huge pines with duffle coats of needles. I remember the priest standing in the doorway, holding his hands in front of him as if he was still praying. He looked towards the sky to see about rain. Others then followed his lead. When they saw the clouds, they said their goodbyes. Down on the road, engines started up and vehicles pulled away.

Quinn was quiet on the way home. When we passed the slogan on the wall, I read it again. Prisoners. They must have done something all the same, I thought. People don't get locked up for no reason. I didn't know much about the fight that was going on, about all the people who had been killed or about all the people who were yet to be killed. I knew fuck all about the causes, the struggles or the people involved. All I knew was that my mother had been killed and nobody had told me why.

# 5

Murt lifted the axe above his head and brought it down on the log. He picked up the two halves, smelled the fesh grains and threw them into a bag. This was the last of the ash and holly he had in the shed. Holly trees were raw and awkward but when dry, they made great firing. Ash timber split like spaded turf, and it spat and crackled when burning.

Expenses in the firewood trade included petrol, oil for the chainsaw, wear and tear on the blade, plastic bags, diesel for the truck. There was money to be made, if you could get the timber for nothing from people who wanted rid of it—fallen trees, pallets, demolished sheds, renovations, off-cuts.

Murt used to sell firewood in old fertilizer bags. Farmers were happy for him to take the bags off their hands. After he struck up a deal with the local garage owner, he was told that he would have to consider the optics—how things look is important to the buyer, the garage owner said. People were less keen on bags that looked second-hand, even though the timber was the same. Murt could see his point. He switched to clear plastic sacks which he had to buy from a local merchant, but they were clean and looked professional.

Beside the guest house were two outhouses. The larger of the two was once Mr Kelleher's workshop. A sturdy workbench lined the rear wall, and his tools were still stored in a cabinet there. The other outhouse was falling down when Murt had first arrived. After he had settled in, he asked Mrs Kelleher if he could fix up the shed and, if it was all right with her, could he use it himself for timber?

She said he would be doing her a favour, and he was welcome to use the workshop too.

After stacking the last bag of logs against the wall, Murt locked the shed and went inside. A perfume of petrol, oil and sawdust followed him around the house. In the bathroom, he washed his hands and face. He put on a clean jumper.

The front room was the lodgers' living room. It was brightest in the mornings when sunlight hit a bay window that faced onto the front garden. A lumpy couch was well established in the middle of the floor. Various items hugged other available spaces: armchairs, a sideboard, display case and television. The mantelpiece was lined with porcelain figurines, and at one end stood a photograph in a small silver frame of two figures in grainy black and white: a man with his arm around a woman, her head resting on his chest, hair tossed in the wind. The photograph reminded Murt of a life he had once had.

Ursula was sitting on the sofa when he walked into the front room. She wiped her eyes and made to leave. Murt apologised, said he was only passing through to the dining room.

'Is everything all right?' he asked.

She nodded, waved her hand and sat back down.

'It will be when I get a drink,' she said.

'Shitty old day all right.'

'Which day is that?'

Her mocking laugh left Murt unsure of what to say. He did not want to be rude and walk out. Maybe she could do with some company? He tried to lighten the mood.

'There was some crowd around for the auction,' he said.

'You went?'

'Scrap hunters everywhere.'

Ursula frowned.

'It's some kind of a vocation,' Murt said.

She thought about this and nodded slowly.

'The obsession is the point,' she said. 'And they're afraid of shiny things.'

'Except for vans and jeeps.'

'Maybe they find new things painful; they don't like being reminded of the fickleness of the world around them.'

Murt searched for a hint of humour in her tone, but could detect only a quiet resignation to whatever she was really thinking about.

'There was a fight down there and all,' he said, sitting into an armchair.

'Well, that's not much in keeping with my theory,' she said with a smile. 'Or maybe it is. What was the fight about?'

'Who knows? Bald tyres, a rusty bucket, flat car battery.'

'Were the Guards called?'

'No, there's not much the Guards can do with that crowd.'

Murt told her about the carbide lamp he had bought from the girl who looked like Gráinne. Except he did not say anything about Gráinne. She was one of his secrets in Balroe, part of a past that had been torn into pieces and scattered all around him. And his daughter was the only piece left that he could salvage from the dirt.

Ursula said, 'Sounds like a right hippy, that girl.'

Her feet were up on the seat, tucked underneath her legs, a cushion on her lap.

'I suppose that's what she'd be,' he said. 'Haven't met too many. If the rest are as nice as her, then I don't know why people are always giving out about them.'

'Jealousy probably.'

'How's that?'

'The whole laid back, couldn't-give-a-damn lifestyle. At one with nature, all that crap.'

She was staring at her own hands on the cushion as if they belonged to someone else and she was trying to imagine all the things they had done that she knew nothing about.

'What about you?' Murt asked.

'You want to know about me?'

'You were upset there when I came in.'

'Bit of a basket case really. Thirty-eight. Alcoholic. Back living with my mother. What else is there to say?'

Mrs Kelleher was Ursula's mother! Murt felt as if he was peeping in through a window and seeing something shocking. How easily she could expose herself. People should not be able to sum themselves up in such few words. Was life so fragile?

'Sorry,' he said. 'Have you children?'

'Two. They're with their father. He said I can't see them until I straighten myself out, sober up.'

'Can he do that?'

'Probably not, but he's right. I'm no mother to them like this.'

Murt Doran talking about parenting. This was not lost on him, and he stopped himself from saying any more.

The front door closed with a bang, and Ursula's hands jumped from the cushion. Donoghue walked into the front room, noted the silence, apologised for disturbing them, and left. Murt knew what this meant. There was a nod and wink language in Donoghue's politeness—himself and Murt would have a talk later about his conversation with Ursula.

In the dining room, the two men were silent as they ate dinner—beef and Guinness pie, one of Donoghue's many favourites. The blow and slurp of hot sauce was accompanied by clinking cutlery and satisfied sighs.

Murt was thinking about the carbide lamp that he and Quinn had restored. Where was it now? At his uncle's house probably, hidden somewhere in the workshop. He had not seen Quinn in months. Maybe he would take a drive over there soon, bring along the lamp he had bought at the sale. Quinn would be impressed, although his hands were not as nimble as they used to be.

Donoghue let out a contented belch and pushed away the empty plate.

'She's still not eating with us,' he said. 'Is it you? Have you been talking her out of it? Warning her away from me perhaps?'

Murt sat back and let him talk. All the information that Ursula had divulged to Murt earlier, Donoghue would want to know: her age, why she was at the guest house, the heavy drinking. This evening Murt would entertain Donoghue's blather. Not because he enjoyed his company or the confusion such information might cause—the niggling and twisting of words. No, not because of that. Murt had his own agenda and tonight, for a change, there would be a trade.

'She was crying,' Donoghue said, half to himself. 'Upset at something—husband, children maybe? The drink? She probably wouldn't tell you though.'

He eyed Murt for a reaction but Murt gave nothing away until he spoke.

'That man you were talking to at the sale yard,' Murt said.

'Or maybe she would,' Donoghue continued.

'I haven't seen him around here before.'

'Yes, she told you something. Which man? Christopher—he's staying at The Moss Hotel.'

The name was a good start for Murt. Everyone, at least, had a name.

'Christopher someone or Mr Christopher?'

'What were yourself and herself talking about?'

'Would you be surprised if I told you that she's Mrs Kelleher's daughter?'

'Martha's daughter? Ah, of course: I can see the resemblance. How come she's never been here to visit her mother before now?'

'They must have fallen out. Where's he from, this Christopher?'

'I suppose the husband kicked her out because she's been hitting the sauce? Has she children?'

'Two.'

Donoghue absorbed this information slowly and savoured it. Murt had said enough about Ursula; any more would be idle gossip. What she had said about being a basket case—that was personal to Ursula.

'You don't know Christopher?' Donoghue asked. 'He seems to know you.'

'He doesn't know me.'

'Didn't I just tell you that he does? Knows your name, what you drive and that you live here. Says he knows you from wherever you were before here. Where did he say it was?'

Murt felt a tightening in his stomach, rising up to his throat as if he was being slowly squeezed by a closing fist.

'Kill— something or other.'

Donoghue sat forward in his chair now and leaned on the table, as if to get closer to Murt across the room, to look into his eyes. Murt broke the stare. Donoghue was no longer interested in Ursula. A new theory was forming in his mind, one that promised many more questions.

'Kiltuam,' Murt said, as Mrs Kelleher entered, interrupting the interrogation.


Outside, in Mr Kelleher's workshop, the bulb above the workbench gave off a wavering yellow glow. Murt held the carbide lamp close to the light. There were dents around the brass body, but no visible cracks.

He tried to move the water regulator to the left and the right. It was seized. If he could get the thing to open, he should be able to remedy this. Being careful not to cause any more damage, he unscrewed the top and bottom chambers. The grainy tear of tarnished metal made his teeth grind. Inside, the mechanism was caked with hard lime. He scraped at it with his finger. The regulator tube would have to be spotless for the water drip to be controlled. The lower chamber, too, was layered with hardened lime. He looked at the tarnished metal and imagined the thing as he would eventually have it: clean and ready for use, pebbles of solid carbide fuel fizzing in the chamber and reacting with the water, acetylene gas passing through the filter to the burner tip where he would spark it to flame for the first time.

The reflector dish around the burner was nicked at the edge and split by a hairline crack. A pity, but this should not affect the beam too much. He turned the lamp around under the light, naming the intricate parts to himself, recalling their functions. As long as none were missing, he was sure he could get it going.

From the guest house kitchen, he brought out a bowl of water and a bottle of vinegar. He washed the lamp and used the vinegar to dissolve the hardened lime. The main drawback with carbide lamps was the waste lime that was left over after the carbide had been used up—like ash after a fire. Holding the top and bottom chambers of the lamp in each hand, he twisted them together, and eased them apart again. Stomach and heart.

The gasket seal between the chambers was perished. It flaked away in his fingers. The filter plate itself seemed to be all right. There was no filter but that would not be a problem. He scratched at the hardened lime, using the flat head of a steel nail, so as not to damage the brass. He tapped and blew the flaked lime from the chamber, held it under the light and scraped again.

Later, the door of the shed opened, and then Donoghue stood behind Murt, peering over his shoulder, pretending to be interested.

'All you need now is a bicycle,' he said. 'I could picture you sitting up on a High Nelly.'

'Maybe I'm going to the mines.'

'Mines?'

'Mind out of my light there.'

Donoghue retreated a few steps. Murt blew at the dusty lime, held the chamber up to the bulb and blew again. He couldn't sense where in the shed Donoghue was standing now, but he knew that he had not left. He wanted to ask more about Christopher, but he had to be careful not to stoke Donoghue's curiosity any more. Donoghue rarely came out to the workshop—something was on his mind.

'Ursula,' he said, 'was asking if you are going for a drink.'

Murt squinted hard at the object in his hand, felt his own breath reflect from its surface.

'No,' he said. 'Sure, you go with her.'

'I wasn't asked.'

Murt put down the lamp and looked over his shoulder. He could see Donoghue's legs in the bulb's light, but his upper body was in darkness. He was in two halves, like the lamp on the work bench, except Donoghue was not seized in a crust of lime. He was racked by a lust for scandal.

Murt laughed and told Donoghue to grow up.

'At least I'd have a drink with her,' Donoghue said, skulking out the door.

Murt could do no more with the lamp until the lime had been loosened and removed. He made up a vinegar solution in an old paint bucket, placed both chambers into the solution and left them to soak overnight.

As for the tape machine, he liked the girl's idea about recording a message, but he knew he would not do that. Cathy had brought a similar machine home one day from the school where she taught. It was broken and she had asked him to take a look. Murt knew nothing about electronics, but he spent the evening tinkering and eventually fixed the recorder. He had never heard his own voice before. He sounded like a different person, no one he knew. And that soup-thick accent of his, the way some words curled as he spoke them. Cathy liked to tease him, and she played the tape over and over. When he told her to stop, she said she would know his voice anywhere—that it was all rust and leaves.

# reilly

A strap of a lad called Reilly joined the secondary school for the last year. No one knew why he had left his old school or if he'd been kicked out. He was a hyper sort, a sharp talker. Mad as a brush and forever coming up with new ideas to cause mischief. When he thought of something to do, he went straight ahead and did it. No time for consequences with a chap like Reilly.

Here he is sitting on my desk one day, peeling an orange with one hand trying not to break the peel. He throws a wedge of orange into his mouth, and you'd swear he's a dog lapping water, he makes so much noise. The full peel springs loose from his fingers. When the orange is gone, he wraps the peel around his head and face like a bandage. Then he remakes the orange by folding the peel back on itself and matching the tears. You see, he says to me, you can't have one thing in this world without destroying another. Is this your desk?

He was clever—cleverer than me anyway—and he had things to say, not just about fruit. The crust, he said, had to be destroyed to get to the juice. If I could take it out through a tiny hole, I'd have an empty orange. What would you think of that, Doran?

He was a whore of a messy eater. When he attacked an apple, he bared his teeth like a horse—helped swirl the flavour, he reckoned. That was him, always looking to get the most out of everything, even food.

It was him introduced me to gambling, but I was never much good. If there was a fight in the school yard, we'd bet for cigarettes.

I can still see him stepping around, flicking a coin in the air and slapping it on the back of his hand. Call it, he says to me. The yard is a shouting match as usual. By a gable wall, the lads playing hand-ball are shouting, and others lads cheer them on. The boys kicking football roar at each other between hocks and spits. The slap of their leather soles on the hard ground is enough to shake the teeth in your head. One lad falls under a wild tackle. The ball is picked up and the game halted. The lad's team-mates offer him a hand. They aren't happy. The tackler is pushed. He pushes back. He has a name for being a bit wild. The injured lad stands up and examines his hands and clothes. A strip of material hangs ripped from his trousers. He looks around for the culprit. The yard prepares for a fight. They meet in a no man's land between the swelling crowd. We are watching all this from the steps. Reilly nudges me—who are you taking? We knew Donal, the lad who had been tackled. He was bigger than the tackler but never looked for fights. The other lad was a toerag. He smirked in Donal's face as the taunts grew louder. I'll have two on Donal, Reilly says. Someone pushes Toerag in the back, and he lurches forward. Donal catches him by the shirt neck and holds him upright. They're face to face. The yard goes quiet as everyone tries to hear what they are saying. When Toerag tries to swing a punch, Donal flings him backwards onto the ground. A few cheers and the crowd disperses.

Reilly says to me, I wouldn't mind a fight sometime. A proper punch in the face like—that must be something. A nose exploding. He flicked the coin in the air and when it landed in his palm, he clenched his fist around it and looked at his knuckles. A powerful thing, he said, the fist.

I told him he should go down and play football if he was feeling rowdy. He laughed, clasped one hand over the other and asked me to call. Heads. I won. Best of three. Call. Heads.

We were sixteen or seventeen. I had a rough band of stubble across my upper lip and sideburns as thick as the history teacher's. Reilly was shaving but didn't seem to be getting too far at it. Apart from the odd patch of pale fluff, his jaw was varnish-smooth. Some lads slagged him, called him *babyarseface*. Reilly didn't give a damn. He joked about it, put himself down before they got a chance. There was no fun in it for them if he laughed at himself. He was smart. He thought about how to deal with people, how to make them look like louts instead of him.

He was some boy for taking lads off too. You've seen them at it, he says to me one day, a cigarette tight between his lips. Like this. His mouth and jaw were twisted tight so it looked as if lighting a cigarette was the bitterest thing any man could do. He struck a match, cupped the flare and met it halfway with the fag. Air hissed through his lips as he dragged hard on the filter. Always a big one, that first drag. Sometimes he'd flick the match, other times he'd let it burn to a charred hair then crush it and sprinkle the charcoal. I don't know how I lit-up, but Reilly never laughed when I did it.

Reilly had a walk too that was all boots and forearms. He talked about films and actors, said he fancied himself on a film set. That'd really piss the auld lad off, he said. Next thing he was taking off his auld lad, the eyes bulging out of his head in pretend anger. You'll do no such thing. There's no son of mine going to be a layabout queer. I hadn't met his auld man yet, but the impression was enough to crack me up.

Some days Reilly would be flat out asking questions. What are you going to do with yourself, Doran? After school like. I told him I didn't know, but that wouldn't do. Come on, there must be something. The farm—you'll work that surely. Maybe. I'd like to see places, I said. Go around the country working at different things for a while. He let out a roar and punched me in the arm. An auld tramp you mean—an itinerant, is that it? Maybe he knew things about the future that I didn't. Ma would have liked me to go to college, I think. If she was still here, I said. Sure we're only young lads yet, Doran. Think of all the whoring around we have in us.

I was getting to that age all right, but what I knew about girls wasn't much. I had talked to a few from the convent, and they hadn't

57

run off, so I supposed that wasn't a bad sign. Half the craic was in the banter, hearing stories from other lads. About how drunk they'd been at the dance, how far they'd got with yer one in the back of the auld lad's car.

When Reilly talked in a low voice, it was serious. What about the real fight? he said a few days after. Would you be up for it? I knew he was mad to join, if he hadn't already. You see what's going on, he says. Tell me it doesn't make you mad. It does alright, I said. Have you thought about it then—your mother and that? I told him I'd considered it, but really I hadn't. There's lads around, he says, you'd be surprised who's involved.

The Cause was only talked about in whispers, but people worried about what was going on. There was no end in sight. Most just wanted to live their lives and not get involved. Some didn't feel they had a duty, but others wanted to do their bit. For young lads like us there was something attractive in the struggle. I've heard it called romance, but I'm not sure if that's the right word. In our daydreams we saw ourselves as heroes in some battle or another. There wasn't much room for reality in heads full of notions like that.

Reilly's house was a fair drive away. I took the Datsun most places now. I felt safe, like Ma was sitting there beside me, her hands on the dashboard and she telling me to slow down. Whenever I needed to think, I'd go and sit in the Datsun. The smell inside reminded me of Ma. The driver's seat still held her shape.

I hadn't even thought of buying a present for Reilly's birthday. You didn't need to bring beer, Reilly says when he opens the door. There's heaps here. I looked around. The hallway was huge, with a high ceiling like a church. Reilly rolled his eyes when I told him I liked the place. Come on, he says, and meet the others. Down some steps he opened a set of double doors to a room with glass on three sides and timber trusses across the ceiling. I remember people scattered everywhere in groups, drinking and dancing. Reilly introduced me to some of them. His father didn't say much. He barely looked at me when we shook hands. He seemed edgy, maybe afraid something was going to happen to his house. I'm hopeless with names and gave up trying to remember. Other than one or two of the lads from school, I didn't know anyone. There were cousins, friends of friends, an aunt, work colleagues of Reilly's father, neighbours, a priest. Mrs Reilly was apparently sick in bed. There was a younger brother running around somewhere, and then there was Reilly's sister.

This is my good friend Murtagh, Reilly said when she came over. She gave me a quick wave, then turned to Reilly and asked him about some record of hers that she wanted to put on. He told her he'd hid it because it was shite, and she called him a pig and stormed off. I'd missed her name.

People floated between groups. Some talked to me as they passed, then turned away when they saw somebody else. I wondered was it the rough clothes or my accent. I drank fast and talk came easier.

I met her again in the kitchen. She was giddy with drink. So, she said, is it Murtagh or Murt? I told her Murt was fine. Where are you from, Murt? The back of beyond, I said. James hasn't mentioned you before. How do you know him? She squinted up at me and twisted her mouth as she wondered. Not his old school anyway, she said. I know all of them. New school? Chess club maybe? No, you don't look like a chess player. Show me your hands. She makes a grab for my free hand, pulls it close to her face and gasps. They're like bark, she says. Her eyes and mouth pretend to be shocked. She holds my hand and tilts her head to look at me from a different angle. Who are you? she asks, as if I'm not real. She lets my hand fall and covers her mouth. You're not in the Ra are you? When she started laughing, I realised she wasn't looking for answers. Someone called her name then—Sarah. Grabbing my hand again, she led me from the kitchen back to the party, and I repeated her name to myself so as not to look like a thick the next time.

Sarah was a college girl, away in Dublin learning to be a nurse. She told me all about a holiday out foreign with her friends. Sounded a bit hectic to me. Daddy had funded the trip. Mr Reilly was a businessman, and he owned a hotel in the next town.

Outside later, Reilly starts talking again about the Cause. Says that he asked this lad he knows and that we can get in. Next Saturday. We'll get pick-up details the day before, he says. It was all a bit sudden for me. I told him I'd have to make sure that Quinn didn't need me, but then Reilly started losing the head. Fuck that, he says. You're either in or you're not. I told him I was. He blew a cloud of smoke into the night. I wanted to ask who these people were and what was going to happen on the day. I would soon learn that questions were frowned upon.

The journeys were torture. I sat on wheel arches in the back of vans, potholes kicking the arse off me. I shifted the cramps between muscles and tried not to make eye contact with the other five lads. Me and Reilly were boys still, but they were men in their twenties, thirties and forties. Men with leathery faces who kept their hands closed into fists just in case. Maybe they were nervous too though—I never thought about that then. Talk was scarce, even between myself and Reilly. The quiet was sometimes broken when briars and branches smacked and squealed against the sides. When the van stopped, there was no delay. The door was flung open to a farmyard of rust-eaten sheds somewhere in the mountains.

One day I jumped out and saw an old man standing in a doorway. The clothes were hanging off him as if he was a washing line. His socks were stuffed with the bunched up cuffs of his trouser legs. The trousers were held up by braces, the shirt buttoned to the neck in case it fell off. He watched us clamber out of the van and walk across his yard. Without even a nod, he turned and went back into the house. I almost dived onto the ground when I heard the front door squeal across the concrete step as he forced it closed.

We walked in file across haggards and through crumbling barns. Meetings took place in newer sheds that were hidden among the crumbling ones. The men all looked like they had come from a fallen comrade's funeral and cared about nothing only avenging his death. Jaws were set and lips tight. Reilly seemed more at ease than me, and he talked with some of the others.

Dempsey was the man in charge. He never stopped pacing around as he spoke. He watched everything, even the floor, for treachery. Rules were repeated, secrecy demanded. Everyone grew very serious at the mention of our country.

Reilly got stuck into training and discussions. Whatever was asked, he volunteered. He tried to drag me into it too, but I stayed on the fringes. I never put my hand up and only did something if I was asked. I took it all in, tried to understand what was happening. Eventually I would come to realise that I didn't belong with these people. Until then, I listened.

After a couple of meetings, we were sent for field training. I had a good eye with the weapons and was being pushed in that direction—wherever it would lead to, I never found out. Reilly tried to encourage me. He could see that I wasn't fully committed. You may make more of an effort, he said. They're always watching.

At school, the boys from the town didn't pay much heed to us country lads. They played football, went to dances and drank. I sometimes had a drink with Quinn, but I'd never been to a proper dance, and it was only a matter of time before Quinn brought up the subject. Must be a few cailíns knocking around in that town, he said one evening. We were driving back home from Ratheen village and had just passed two girls walking along the road. Quinn waved and blew the horn. Suppose there is, I said. He reached across and tapped my arm. They'll be after you yet.

The conversation stuck in my mind. Soon after, when he started to ask questions about where I was disappearing to, I lied without thinking about it. I needed an excuse and only one would be plausible. There's a girl, I told him. A friend's sister. He was surprised, but nodded in approval. Good man. Good man yourself.

The realisation of what I had done came at me in the dark. The shame had me tossing at night instead of sleeping. I was a liar. You can't take something like that back. And what would I do when the truth came out, as I knew it would? After all that Quinn had done for me, I had let him down.

It was announced at one of the meetings that our unit was to become more active—conduct an operation, was how Dempsey put it. This brought nervous smiles to the faces around me. A man I knew only as Bambi, who always wore a green jacket with a tiny German flag on the sleeve, spat onto his hands and clasped them together in a slap. Jack, a burly man with tight white hair—he was the oldest—gritted his teeth with delight. About fucking time, he roared, and the others cheered and clapped. I reckon some of the men hoped they were going to kill someone. Wasn't that why they were there?

The plan was discussed at the next couple of meetings. We were going to hit a local fertilizer merchant and take as much fertilizer as we could. It would then be sent somewhere to make explosives. Details were sketchy and seemed to change from meeting to meeting. I hoped that I wouldn't be asked to go. But everyone was given a task. Mine was to keep watch.

Myself and Reilly were having a pint one night when he started on about flaws in the plan. There's so many things that could go wrong, he said. I was earwigging a conversation beside me, not paying him enough attention. You don't give a fuck, Murt. I do, I said. I hardly want us to get caught do I? The two men to my right were talking about their wives, and I thought Quinn would love to hear their carry-on. One man was convinced his wife was having an affair. She was off into town most days, and this was strange because it had always been such a chore for her before. But Reilly was lost in himself. I'm going to have to say something, he said. Tell them what I think. He wanted me to back him up. They'll only laugh at us, I said. Not when they hear what I have to say.

Beside me, a crude trap was being planned. They both agreed that the man should follow his wife. There was a problem though—she would be taking the car, and he'd be left only with the tractor.

I'm going to try, Reilly said. You'll be at my shoulder if I need you. Fair enough. We drank our pints and to calm Reilly down, I filled him in on the goings-on beside us.

At the meetings, the floor wasn't usually opened for people to speak, especially with the operation being planned. Reilly waited. He sat on his hands, his jaw fidgeting. When his moment came, he stood. Reilly talked quickly and with an authority that he did not yet have. There was no waffle. His points were clear and direct. A murmur of approval followed the pause as he sat down. Thinking about it now, this was the beginning of Reilly's career. Just as in any organisation, I suppose, the powers that be noted his potential. His points were valid, and the plan was changed to incorporate them.

On the night itself, things were running smoothly until a security van stopped for a random inspection. I whistled and hid as I had been told to do, but the security man saw the broken lock and went inside the shed to investigate. When the shouting started, I ran to the shed door to see what was happening. A torch lay on the concrete floor, and I could see a huddle of men swinging fists, boots and bars. Bambi roared at me to get the fuck back to my post. I saw Reilly sitting in the driver's seat of the truck. He waved me to get in.

I had thought I wanted to be involved, that maybe I could learn something about the real reasons for what was going on in the country, but a man left half-dead for doing his job?—that was wrong. I guess part of me had hoped I would find out why my mother had been killed. It was still unreal to me, ridiculous what had happened to her. She went off for a day and never came back.

Quinn found out what I was up to. Is it a liar you're turning into? he asked. I told him I was sorry. You think I'm a fool, is that it? He was too mad to look at me and busied himself with sweeping the floor as if to calm himself. No, I said. Didn't I tell you to stay away, that no good would come of it? I never got any answers, I said, about Ma and Maureen. He flung the brush down and sat opposite me. The Cause, he said, is not about answers. It's not a place for confused souls. Nobody knows where it's all going. Half of these lads down here have fuck all clue about it. Criminals, the most of them, hiding behind a cause. If that's what you want to be, you better get going away from here. He rubbed his forehead with the palms of his hands. That security man, he said. It's all over the papers. If it was you, if you were involved. I told him the truth, that I was a look-out. He stared at me and the whites of his eyes were cracked with red veins. You'd better be off, he said.

I was nearly eighteen, and although I'd thought about it, I wasn't ready to leave Quinn's. I waited to see if he would boil the kettle or turn on the radio, but he left without another word. The outside door closed with a long sigh, and he headed across the yard to the sheds.

Reilly understood. He said that it would be frowned upon, and that they could find me if they wanted. I knew that too. The country was an even smaller place back then. Reilly told me he would have a word, do what he could, but our friendship from that point on would have to end.

# 6

He climbed the stairs of the guest house and stopped on the landing. A loose board squeaked underfoot. This happened every time, and Murt could never pinpoint why it bothered him. He shifted his weight on the loose board; it whined and creaked again.

In his bedroom at the end of the landing, he opened the drawer of his dresser. Beside the notebook in which he had begun writing the stories of his past, his letters—apologies—lay scattered, as if spilled from a postman's sack. When he had tried to write the first letter years ago, he could not even mark the page with ink; it felt as if he was on top of a mountain: bare, treeless peaks and slopes as far as he could see, and no way down.

He had sat in the caravan, half-slumped over the table, and the pen would not move. He repeated her name to himself. Eventually he managed to write it. What could he possibly say? Her name echoed from the mountain top inside his mind, but nothing came back—no answer, no thought. A swig from the bottle, and whiskey dribbled on the page. His mind fuzzed over with static and white noise, as if two hands had clapped hard against his head, cupping his ears. After weeks of this, he had managed to write one or two lines. The words he put down were ridiculous. He was a fraud. So he wrote that down: I am a fraud. Pages and pages of those words. It was all he wrote for days. Then he wrote other things: I neglected you, Gráinne; I deserve nothing in life after that.

And beside the ruins of his house, he sat for months in the rotting caravan and wrote it all out of himself. Then he balled up every scrap of pity, made a bonfire in the grass and watched as smoldering flecks of regret floated through the evening sky.

The words came out of him—lines, sentences, paragraphs and eventually a full letter. He was drinking less—not at all in the mornings. He would post this letter, and she'd write back—that is what he told himself. They might arrange to meet, and he would spend the rest of his time trying to make amends for what he had done. The mountain was receding beneath his feet; there were trees now, fields and some houses. The sea was a long way off, but he knew in which direction it lay. This, he had imagined, was his awakening.

What age was Gráinne then? Ten maybe. A child still, she would not have understood. It didn't matter; he had needed to do it for himself.

And maybe it would have worked out if he had posted the letter that day. But he left it for a few days, and by then he was losing his nerve. The village was deserted, as if everybody was in hiding, expecting him and his great letter. The unease took him to the pub for some sign of life. One drink, two drinks, three drinks. By the time he left, he had forgotten about the letter.

The following day, or maybe it was months later, a visitor had arrived at the cottage. Murt recognised the man and knew what he was going to tell him—that the day had come. The driver of the car that killed Cathy had been released.

Thoughts of letters receded and the nightmares returned. He had stopped trying to sleep. When he closed his eyes, everything was bright. Objects, faces, words, figures flashed in front of him. It was as if he was blinking continuously, ten times faster than it was possible to blink.

In the years since, he had written many grovelling letters, but had never come as close to sending them as he had that day. After finishing one, he would seal the envelope and place it with the rest—in a bag or a box, or as now, loose in a drawer in the room of a guest house on the outskirts of some town. Sealed, with her name scribbled on the front. He could not tell one letter from another.

Finally, a few weeks before now, he had sent his daughter a letter. As it slipped from his fingers into the dark slot, he panicked and tried to grab it back. But his fingers, too rough for writing in the first place, were not able to grab it, and the envelope disappeared, resting with a rustled sigh in the post box. He knew the address, had even driven down there a few times to watch his daughter from afar.

What was in the letter? An apology, a photograph, an offer to meet at the beach. That was all. He was a fool to think she would be there. Red-faced, he slammed the dresser drawer closed.

Across the landing, the floor creaked under Donoghue's footsteps. And it came to Murt like a slap in the face: Curran's pub. That same lazy creak of board against board, nail holes worn loose. He used to rent a room above the pub from Joss McNabb. There was a sense of relief in resolving this simple thing, but also a lingering worry that there could be more, that something greater remained to be unearthed beneath this sound. It crossed his mind how most things do not change much: the sag of loose boards under foot, the past snagging against the present.

It was many years since he had rented the room above Curran's pub—before he had gotten married—many years since he'd left Kiltuam and all that happened there. That did not mean it would ever fade from his memory.

Murt didn't believe in—didn't trust—coincidence. Rarely did things just happen. Opening the dormer window, he leaned on the ledge and looked out past the front garden to the roofs of the town beyond. The orange glow of another night closing in.

Something was happening that he had set in motion—the car, the man following him. It was Murt's own fault. If he had not sent the letter asking his daughter to meet him, the past might have stayed in the shadows. But, then, so would Gráinne. He had always kept his past in a far corner of his mind where it did not seem fully real—a place where he could go to be sentimental. But the sentimental could never be separated from the guilt. One could not be recalled without being confronted by the other.

As a boy, life seemed straightforward to Murt: adults made decisions, they did the right thing. He soon learned the reality. When they get older, people try to give the impression that they know what they are doing, that they are honest, balanced people. They go through life tripping from one mistake to the next, hoping that they won't be found out, exposed for the unreasonable, selfish people that they are.

One letter was not enough. The things he had done would have to be faced if he was going to meet Gráinne. Everything was bound together. Soon he would have to stop running and living his life in vain. This Christopher was no stranger. Murt knew who he was. He had guessed it all along.

# II

# Kiltuam

# joss

Joss McNabb owned Curran's pub in Kiltuam. It had been called Curran's from years before. I wasn't in the place a wet day and Joss had told me all about Mick Curran, so as he wouldn't have to talk about himself. Never bothered changing the sign, he said. This was an old story. There's many a cute whore would be reluctant to see their own name in big letters. If anything, they wouldn't want it known that they owned any place. Publicans are the most secretive people in any village. A well practiced *whowantstoknow* look was the answer to every question put to Joss McNabb. He spent his days pretending he was only a step away from big trouble with anyone from the taxman to the Guards, the Ra, the ex-wife, other pubs. It was nobody's business who drank in his pub, or what the turnover was. When it came to the rest of the village, Joss knew everything. A loaf of bread couldn't be taken from the local shop without him hearing. He wasn't a man to judge though. If the thief was sitting at the end of the bar supping a pint, nothing would be said to him. It was enough for the crime to be known.

Joss was the first person I talked to when I arrived in Kiltuam. This was a good few years after I'd left Quinn and the farm at Ratheen. I walked in and asked about getting work around the village. Joss told me to try the mill and said that he had rooms upstairs, if I intended to stay a while. And would I be staying a while? Where is it you're coming from? And where are you from originally? I see, I see. What has you round these parts? Very good, very good. The stairs is down the back there, stay as long as you like. Settle up the few pound at the weekend. I'd go straight out to the mill if I were you. Mr Shaw will get you sorted, if you're not afraid of work. You say you were out in Tullamore? On the bogs, I said, harvesting peat and turf for Bord na Móna. There's a desert of the shite out there.

I had cut turf with Quinn before and spaded it into small piles. Bord na Móna's operation was serious though. Big whales of machines laid the wet peat out in rows along the bog. Always reminded me of that ribbed material they make trousers and curtains from. I wasn't long getting the hang of the machines. Other bogs were drained first to get the milled peat from April to September when the weather was driest. The crumbed peat was stockpiled and taken to factories or power stations by train. It was good work. A dusty carry-on, but good work. After a day at the milling, I used to be caked in peat. At least it didn't itch like crop dust—it was more like a brown snow, spicy and sweet as the midland air.

Joss threw a pint in front of me that first day and refused to take money for it. He knew a thing or two about the bogs himself. Boring auld work though, he said. He had me at ease in the place already, which made me talk on. The fish, I said, now that's bad work. What's this then? he asked, cocking his lip. Dingle, says I—gutting fish. Worst job I ever had. That so? Be the holy. He wiped patches of the counter and swept over others as the information sank in. You're a bit of a wanderer then? The main door groaned open from the wind, and we both looked around on the off chance that someone might be coming in. I told him I'd been picking up work wherever I'd stopped. Never been too far from this godforsaken kip of a village myself, he said. If I was a young man still—.

A while later, the door whinged again, and an auld stump of a man reversed inside. Joss went straight for the whiskey and put one up on the counter as the man struggled with a barstool. Both men agreed that the day was a dirty one. As they talked out of earshot, I noticed the old man glance in my direction. With my pint getting shallow, Joss raised an eyebrow and I nodded. The mill must nearly be closed for the day, I said. Be still there tomorrow, Joss said. The old man tossed another look along the counter and piped up. The mill's going nowhere, he said. Get another pint, young fella that you are. A laugh rolled out of him then like a ragged and dusty carpet.

Joss was only mad to tell him about me. This fella was on the bogs in Tullamore, Bill, and at the fish in Dingle. When the coughing had eased, Bill eyed me again. Saw you getting off the bus earlier, he said. I knew you was strange.

Sometime later, I looked out the window, and it was dark outside. There was no end to the pints or the questions. I told them about other places I'd been to and the people I'd met. What about Dublin? Joss asked. Wasn't there too long, I said. Did a few deliveries around Guinness'—St James' Gate. I remember the smell of hops following me up and down that river. Can't say I didn't like it.

The pub was getting busy, and other lads were listening in, adding their two-pence worth. The drink was doing most of the talking for me by then. Someone mentioned the other river, the Shannon, and I told them I'd stood on the dam at Ardnacrusha and listened to the roaring waters of Ireland's industrial age. Such a statement to make. Bill, who had been listening but saying little, was very interested in this. The skin below his eyes that was gathered on his cheek in ripples began to twitch. The Shannon Scheme, he says. Three years I worked on that. Biggest in the world at the time. Imagine that, in little old Ireland. I caught a few smirks around the bar like they'd heard this one a few times. Hard days, Bill said. We only stopped to eat and sleep. And the best of men, lost.

When I got to the mill the next day, the bossman, Mr Shaw asked me where I'd worked before and what I could do. I was in luck, he said. One of his forestry workers had been badly injured and would be out of work for a few weeks at least. He said he needed someone who could drive a tractor in the forests and use a chainsaw. We talked money and shook hands. Take it easy out there till you get the hang of it, Mr Shaw said. You'll mostly be dragging logs with the Horse, but you might need to give a hand on the chainsaw some days. Just limbing though. The other men will do the felling.

Having worked farms and forests before, I was well able to handle a chainsaw—everything from cutting trees, logs and stakes to clearing ditches. On a big estate in Laois, I felled twelve acres of wild hardwoods. Cutting branches off pines and spruces wouldn't be a problem.

Forestry days were long and damp. Chainsaws roared as they spat white smoke and sawdust. Forests had their own climate— somewhere between autumn and winter all year round. A peaceful damp. But cold too, especially on the toes. Not a scratch of comfort in Hobnailed boots. Chainsaws offered no heat. Oily petrol fumes hung in the muddy, still air all day, mingling with sap and pine—the perfume of timber harvest. Once felling started, everywhere was muck, dead pine needles and sawdust. I loved the roar of work, the whole forest humming, engines revving like hundreds of motor-bikes scrambling the hill trails and paths all around.

Nothing falls like a tree. That crack, snap and rip as the last piece of trunk gives way. Branches beating through the air like giant wings and the ground quaking beneath your feet as the whole lot crashes down. A man by the name of Marah was in charge. His saw never stopped. Trees fell in steady rhythm. Every tree called for a pause. We watched and listened to the firework of each tree fall.

I worked at de-limbing the trunks. Once all the branches were removed, I drove the Horse—a Ford County tractor with front wheels as big as the back wheels—dragging logs out to better ground where they could be loaded onto lorries. When we sat down on fresh-cut stumps to open our lunch boxes and flasks, all around was still, as if the forest was taking a break too. And the air misty with sweet, white smoke. I worked the harvest for a few months, getting to know the process, and soon enough I was felling myself.

Before the saws arrived on site, we went out to inspect and prepare the forest. Roadways had to be in good enough condition for the trucks and lorries, and ground underfoot had to be sturdy.

That meant no bogs. The area to be felled would be marked out. When all that was done, the saws moved in. Usually it took a few weeks to clear a site. After felling, the forest floor was like a waste-land—branches strewn everywhere, sticking up out of muck and yellow grass as if they were arms and legs on a battlefield. Stumps left abandoned like dead soldiers. It was a no man's land that would then be left for a year or two until replanting, and safe from harvest for twenty or thirty more. Clearfelling was done in sections, never a full forest all at once. Seen from afar, clearfell looked like scorched patches in vast quilts of green.

On the back of the Horse was a steel winch. I wrapped chains and slings around the logs and dragged them out to the forestry road. When the pile was large enough, a lorry would come and load. From a seat up behind the cab, the driver sat and operated the jib—a lifting arm like the back of a digger, but with a grab at the end. He could manoeuvre that thing around like it was his own arm. I can still hear the hiss and whine of hydraulic rams as the grab closed around logs and raised them into the air. After the lorry was loaded, black diesel smoke coughed from its exhaust as it struggled away, heading for the mill yard.

Felling stopped when the weather got rough. Downpours of rain turned forest sites to swamps. Neither man nor tractor could go near them. I started working in the mill yard after that, but I would work many more harvests in the future.

Things in the mill yard were different. Gone was the peace of the forest, the freedom, the scent. At first, I was put to work keep-ing the mill tidy—moving piles of sawdust and off-cuts. The yard was on the edge of a forest. My days were spent surrounded by living trees and stacks of logs. It was a factory—logs in, planks out. Saws ran all day and were fed non-stop, as long as there was day-light. Soon enough, I was feeding logs to one of the big saws that threw dust and chippings into piles around the shed. When the piles became drifts, a loading shovel would carry them outside to heaps like sand dunes at the rear of the site.

The yard itself was a patchwork of galvanised sheds in various stages of decay. Some roofs had already caved in. Along one side of the yard ran two narrow sheds for drying and storing the cut timber. There was always a calmness about the drying sheds that couldn't be found elsewhere around the mill. Away from the cry and ring of steel blades, away from roaring engines and shouting men, timber waited patiently to dry.

An old steel crane from bygone days hogged the centre of the yard. A brute of a thing like a huge tripod, it was manually operated by turning handles and gears. There wasn't much use for the crane, but sometimes a contractor's trailer would arrive which had no jib and we had to work the old thing to unload the logs.

No part of the mill yard was left unused. Heaped in every available place were remnants of the process—off-cuts from trunks, bark slabs, chippings, mountains of sawdust. From sheds to tools and machines, everything was the colour of rust. Even the timber looked as if it was rusting. The surrounding trees kept out the sun most of the day so it was never warm. The yard itself was stuck in that forest climate. In the mornings, dew and rain dripped from pines, bark and steel, and in the depths of winter everything froze solid.

# the mill

First Friday in December, and there I am stuffing the wages envelope into my coat pocket when Sticks Foley slaps me on the back.
I've a whore of a thirst on me, he says. This is his routine. I'd been
in Kiltuam a few months by now and winter had the countryside
by the scruff. Not sure about this evening, I tell him. Every week
it's the same story with you, Doran. And what happens? We fall
out of the place about two o'clock. Exactly. So come on to fuck—
none of your shite. I nudge Foley when I see Mr Shaw's daughter
at the main gate. I had her for a bit of a snobby young one, seeing
as she'd never come into the yard and always waited for Daddy
outside. We all go quiet as we walk past her, nodding and muttering hellos, but when we get into Foley's car, he starts. I reckon
she's gamey, lads. Heard that all right, Smithy says. Not being a
local meant that I'd heard nothing about Cathy Shaw. The few
times I'd seen her waiting for her auld lad, I paid no mind. It was
because of the mud in the yard that she never drove in through
the gates. Instead, she would stand by the open car door until one
of the workers saw her. She'd be up on her toes waving an arm in
the air. Is he around? she'd shout.

Foley drove like he couldn't care less about the road, lighting
cigarettes and turning around to talk. Fridays meant straight to
Curran's after work, and there was never any shortage of takers—
me, Smithy and Foley in his car, and more lads would follow. It
wasn't easy to say no. Besides the pints and banter, I was renting the
room above so I had no excuse.

Inside the door of Curran's, I made for the back stairs. Where do you think you're going? Foley roared. Up to get changed, I said. Well don't be fucking long. Even with the pub below, my room was grand and quiet. It did me fine—double bed, dresser, wardrobe, armchair, a small television, although I never watched it much. The bed was laden with blankets—carpet-heavy and woolly, the old type. A tattered rug covered the floor, and I used to walk around barefoot. It was a dormer-type room with two small windows, and I could touch the ceiling without standing on my toes. In a nook beside the wardrobe, a mirror was fixed to the wall above an old Belfast sink. Off the landing was a bath and toilet with a cistern that never let up hissing no matter how many times I fixed it.

After a wash in the sink, I sat down in the armchair to throw an eye over the local newspaper. The pints could wait, sure hadn't I all night to drink? On the front page was a photograph of Cathy Shaw with a bunch of people from the football club. One of the lads had an arm around her. I flicked through the rest of the paper and turned back to the front cover. A girl like her, I reckoned, would surely have a boyfriend. When I woke later, Foley was banging the door and roaring at me to get downstairs.

There were four pubs in the village, but everyone went to Curran's of a Friday evening. If you got settled near the fire, you could be there for the night. Foley started early on the vodkas. Once the round went that way, there was no going back.

Later, two lads joined us at the table. They were in their twenties, same as us, but they had the snarl of fellas who hadn't much craic about them. Foley and the others knew who they were. I recognised one of their faces all right but couldn't figure out from where. His name was Duffy, and I didn't like the cut of him. He watched everyone from under a brow that was thick as a sod of turf. Now and then his top lip creased into a half-smile. There was something—a sort of patience—about him that made me uneasy. Foley talked to Duffy for a long time and seemed to be licking his arse. When I saw the republican newspapers being passed around, I understood what was going on. You'll buy one, Duffy says, handing me a copy. Around me, some of the lads have a paper rolled up in their hands, others have left theirs lying on the beer-soaked table, but everyone has bought a copy. I shake my head and tell him no, I'm grand. Foley frowns and says, Help the cause, Doran. You a Prod or what? Duffy's top lip creases even more, and he stares at me as if I have betrayed them, betrayed their cause, their country even. But it was my country too, and theirs wasn't the only way to live in it. What the fuck? Foley said after the two lads had collected their money and left. Are you looking for a hiding? Fuck them, I said. I had enough of that shite before. Someone slapped Foley on the back of the head with a rolled up paper and we went back to drinking.

Scattered around the mill yard were warped lengths and off-cuts of timber. One of the men must have fancied himself as a bit of an artist. Timber figures like scarecrows, bits of furniture and other random shapes could appear anywhere. Left where they'd be destroyed by machines, driven over by lorries or crushed under logs. I had a fair idea who was doing it—we all did—but it brought a bit of banter to the place. On the roof one morning was a twisted effort of a star. Whoever it was had come in early, or else stayed late, climbed up onto the roof and fixed it to the ridge of the main shed.

Later that day, I was filling a couple of gallon cans from the main diesel tank to bring over to the forklift when I saw Cathy Shaw making her way across the yard. She had the jeans held up by the knees, and was trying to pick her steps, as if the yard was a shallow river with flat stones. I wondered what had gotten into her. She'd always been too good for the place before. When she saw me, she tried to say something but staggered backwards, first one foot, then two, into a pile of mud. He's not here, I said. She cursed the place blind for ruining her shoes, and her father for not being there. I held her arm and helped her back across the yard. At the car, I took her shoes and wiped them as best I could in the grass, trying not to stain them with my oily hands. Would he not get you a pair of wellies? I asked her. He'd have me down here shoving logs then, she said. I told her there was worse things, and she looked at me as if I was half mad. Thanks anyway, she said. Are you the artist? She pointed to the roof. I told her what was going on, and that nobody knew who was at it. Strange game, she said, getting into the car. She shut the door and rolled down the window. I wondered how old she was, reckoned around nineteen or twenty. Turned out that I wasn't too far off. She was twenty-one—three years between us.

Saw you got caught on the front of the paper, I said. She covered her red cheeks and shook her head. Jesus, she said, don't talk to me. The car's engine turned over and started. Will you tell him I was here? she said. I tried for something else to say to keep her there a bit longer. You were looking well, was all I could come up with, and she drove off slapping at the air for me to shut up.

Back at the forklift, Foley was waiting to quiz me. He had seen us at the gate and wanted to know what was going on. Something in his voice and the forced smile told me that he wasn't happy. Nothing going on, I said. She was looking for her auld lad. With the shoes? Foley said, a bit louder.

Diesel is fierce messy tack. And stinking when it gets on your hands and clothes. It gushed from the mouth of the can as I poured it into the forklift's tank. It sloshed and spilled around the cap. It ran down the metal frame of the machine and onto the ground, and I held steady until the flow eased.

Dirty shoes, I said. I helped her clean them. His smile was now a scowl. I was talking to her last week, he said. He tried to laugh but sounded as if he had just broken one of the machines and was afraid to tell the boss. When the diesel can was empty, I screwed on the lid and lifted up the second can. Why don't you ask her out? I said to him. She's not available, he snapped. I told him to stop annoying me if so. Just making sure you weren't stepping on my toes, he said. I angled the can so as to minimise the spillage. Is that a rule? I asked him. Fucking sure it is. Ask anyone. The can leapt and I nearly lost hold of the thing as I laughed. Diesel arced through the air and slopped onto the ground. Foley jumped back from the splash, but too late. He looked at the dark patch running down his leg. Fuck sake, he said. Then he rubbed it and smelled his hand as if to be sure. If she's not available, I said, what does it matter? It matters to me. He waved a warning finger in the air as he turned to walk towards the shed.

Thinking back on it, there had always been something about Foley that I couldn't figure out. When he got an idea in his head, when there was something he wanted, he'd go to any lengths to get it.

The mill yard was a mile and a half outside Kiltuam village, and I always walked. I stopped at the narrow bridge on my way home that evening and watched the river below. The bridge had still not been properly repaired since a hurricane a few months earlier. It was a temporary job by the council, leaving one single lane for traffic. I couldn't see the river but heard water rushing through the darkness below. I remembered Quinn telling me that during World War II the Irish Army had drilled holes in stone bridges like the one I was standing on. That was how close we had come to being invaded. The holes were for dynamite—the army were going to blow up our own bridges. Quinn thought it was funny, said it wouldn't have made a blind bit of difference because the Germans would already be here. Still, he said, those Germans would have had their hands full with us all the same.

Kiltuam consisted of one street, which curved gently up towards the church and school at the far end. A two-storey terrace of shops and houses, some painted, some not, snaked along the footpaths on both sides. Curran's pub was halfway up the shallow hill, on the corner where Station Road joined the main street. Farther on, close to the church, the street widened for cars to stop outside the school. Derelict buildings and old ruins were dotted around the village. On the outskirts was a Protestant church with its gate lodge, the Old Rectory.

Kiltuam was the same as any other place around the country where I'd stayed. Sometimes I wonder if every village was built to the same blueprint, and then shaped by petty bickering and nastiness.

Later that evening, I picked up the local newspaper again. The caption on the front said that the man standing beside Cathy was Oisín Duffy, the same lad I had met in Curran's. Was she mixed up with that crowd too? I wondered. I pictured her again, red-cheeked as I teased her. And her words still purring in my ears—Jesus-don't-talk-to-me.

# accident

Some mornings when I arrived at the mill before anyone else, it felt like the world had forgotten about the place and moved on. Just me and this abandoned hulk of timber and steel. It had the same peace as the forest itself, until the workmen arrived and machines roared to life.

I put on the kettle in the portacabin and walked across the yard. A spill of drizzle during the night had left every surface with an oil-like smear. On damp days, cut timber smelled stronger. The scent of sap and shavings was gorse-thick in the main shed. I kicked a pile of sawdust into the air and ran my hand along the ledge of a machine as I went past. The dust was like cotton wool in my hand. I flung a handful out ahead of me and watched it fall like snow. A sheet of steel clattered on the roof.

I had done a circuit of the shed when I looked up and saw something hanging from the truss. It spun idly as if there was a breeze in the shed. I stared at the shape until I realised what it was—a workman's boilersuit hanging from the neck and stuffed to make it look like a man. Relieved that it wasn't a real person, I shouted, You'd better take that fucker down before the bossman gets in.

Steam was rushing from the spout of the kettle when I got back to the portacabin. I filled my cup and went to the fridge—no milk. There's nare a bit of craic in you, Doran, Foley said from the doorway. I'd never seem him as happy with himself. Not a drop of milk in this kip, I said. Some in my lunch box, he said. Throw me on a cup there will you. He flung the morning's newspaper at me and I batted it onto the table. There was a rattle and squeal from the yard as somebody opened the gates. Foley looked to see who it was. Shite, he said, and went sprinting across to the main shed to dismantle his handiwork before Mr Shaw saw it.

I was reading the paper when Foley came back, out of breath. Jesus, he said. I'm after getting some earful. He's like a bear today. As the rest of the men dragged in through the gates, machines started up one by one and the day's work began.

Around midday, the first of two lorries arrived to be unloaded. The lorries were supposed to be going to another mill, but a water main had burst in that yard and flooded the place. The owner rang Mr Shaw and asked if he would take the two loads, as a favour like. One trailer per day was as much as we usually unloaded—we were busy enough as it was. Two trailers would be pushing it, but we'd manage. We'll have to, Mr Shaw said. He was wound up that morning about the whole thing. Foley was first on the receiving end. The lorries had no jib either, so that meant we would have to unload them manually with the yard crane. Mr Shaw was running around giving orders. Foley and Smithy worked the handles and gears of the crane as I tied and untied straps around the logs. Everyone was barking different commands.

Next thing I look around, and here's the second lorry at the gate, and the first's not even half unloaded. Course, the crane's handle jams as usual, and with the other lorry waiting, Mr Shaw is losing the head. Rain is starting to fall again at this stage. Smithy swings a sledgehammer at the cogs. There's a loud crack and the handle runs free. Back to work.

Horns blow as the drivers pass each other. When the second lorry pulls to a stop, the driver jumps down into a pulp of gravel, mud and timber shavings that splashes up around him. He holds his wrist up to Mr Shaw, points at his watch and shakes his head. Mr Shaw shouts back that he can't go any fucking quicker. The rain is really starting to fall now.

We work on, as fast as we can, and we're making good headway when the crane's handle jams again. Smithy gets the sledgehammer. I climb down from the trailer, soaked through. If we could just free the handle, we wouldn't be long finishing up. Dark falls with the rain.

Smithy swings the sledge like a track layer might. The lorry driver is shouting from the shed, telling us to hurry up, that he has to get home for his dinner. The men curse him from a height. Smithy lets out a roar as he swings again. Drops of water spray everywhere in the release. The winch slips and the gears turn. Back to work.

There's no talk with the driver when we're finished. Go on to be fucked, Mr Shaw tells him, as the last of the logs are being hoisted off. There's towels in the portacabin, Foley yells to us. He and Smithy are already halfway across the yard. I gather up the chains and slings with Mr Shaw. Logs are piled around the yard in mounds higher than I've seen before. Don't think these are safe, I shout to Mr Shaw, who's making for the portacabin now. A grumbling noise fills the air. I shout again, roar this time. Whether he hears me or the danger, I'm not sure, but he turns around. The logs are on the move. I run towards him but haven't a hope of making it. The first log catches him on the legs just above his knees, more follow as he falls—two, three, four more. That thud of galloping trunks will never leave me.

When the mayhem stopped, there were a few seconds of calm, like a huge engine quitting or the power being cut for an entire town. Rain slapped off steel and puddles. A mist rose from the centre of the yard. Workmen appeared from sheds, running through the slop.

The mill was closed. Nobody knew for how long, and nobody asked. Time needed to pass first—a week for sympathy and mourning. Not a week for questions about the mill or about the workers' concerns. I'd seen it before, a village pulling together at the death of one of their own. Mr Shaw was no tyrant boss. He was a popular figure, and the grief was real. No need to worry—wages would be paid while the mill was closed. The family would see to that.

How many nights did I wake thinking of how that second log had caught him square in the face? If he was still alive, he'd have said it himself—That second bastard of a log. I was looking right at it as it hurtled towards him, bouncing from end to end, trundling—would that be the word?—along like a rickety old cart. Except it wasn't a rickety old cart, it was thirty or forty feet of tree trunk. He hadn't a chance. The rest of the logs buried him.

Never seen the likes of it, they said—they being the crowd that go to every funeral. Couldn't get into the church, they said. Popular man, popular man. Every available cap was in hand. The family invited people back to the local hotel where they put on food. There was a gang who stayed there all day and night, drinking till they could get no more. I suppose I didn't really belong, but I stayed and floated around and got drunk. At some point I met Cathy Shaw at the bar. She said it was strange how things worked out. Only the week before, they had been planning as a family. Her father was always too busy to sit down and talk, but he had been different the past few months, she said—quieter, better. That was the word she used, better, as if he had recovered from a sickness. Not that he was bad or anything, she said, just the usual family hassle. They guessed that he'd had enough and was maybe thinking of retiring and selling the mill. Then this happens, she said. Taken from us by a stray log. A gentleman, I said, into my drink. Thanks, you're kind. When she talked, the words drifted from her mouth. She stared at something outside—a wall, a branch or nothing. I said that he was as decent a man as I had worked for. No one had a bad word to say. Although she had probably been hearing it from people all day, she smiled and then returned her gaze outside. You were there when it happened, she said. You tried to help him. I told her we all tried to help and that I wished I could have done more. I watched her finger circle the base of her glass as if she was feeling for a lump or a chip to make the smoothness more real.

Will you be staying on in Kiltuam after Christmas? she asked me. You won't leave because of what happened? From the far side of the room, I saw Oisín Duffy staring at the two of us. Dad laughed when I told him about you cleaning my shoes. A solid chap, he said. What has you in Kiltuam anyway, working at the mill? It's the smell, I said. The smell? Freshly cut logs and sawdust. Keeps me straight. Strange, she said. But I kind of like it myself. For years he used to come home covered in sawdust. I don't think our house will ever lose that smell. Hope not anyway.

Duffy was making his way across the room. I thought about moving but decided to stand my ground. Wallace, I said, is he going to keep the place running? Wallace was Mr Shaw's right hand man. She let out a huff. I think so, she said. He likes to do his own thing, but he'll look after the place, for a while anyway. He's not so bad. Then she leaned forward and kissed me on the cheek. It was soft, the way a leaf might land on grass. I didn't know how it happened, but she was holding my hand too, squeezing it tight around the fingers as if she was afraid to let go. Those arms, skinny little things, peppered with freckles, like her face. I tried to whisper something as she pulled away after the kiss, but no sound came out. I wondered if her lipstick had left a mark on my face that I might see later.

A smash then. The glass had slipped through her spidery fingers. Her other hand too, slipped from mine. Duffy was there beside her then, holding her by the shoulders, glaring at me with black eyes. Sorry, I said, although I'd done nothing wrong. She freed herself from Duffy's grip and wanted to help clean up the glass, but people insisted it was under control. Holding one arm tight with the other as if it was injured, she hurried past me. You're up at the mill, Duffy said. I am. Nodding as if he knew something I didn't, he took a few steps back, turned and walked across the room.

# snow

Nothing is straightforward, especially a favour. I hadn't long set foot back inside Kiltuam after Christmas when Joss said to me about the loose slates and asked if I'd have a look. There's a few tools out the back, he said, someone may as well use them. The barn looked like an old cow parlour with thick stone walls. Reminded me of Quinn's barn, where he kept everything from tools to things he might use sometimes and other things that he'd never use. There was a small window with a rotten frame and planks across two tar barrels for a bench. Many's a day I spent in there hammering and cutting anything I could lay my hands on.

I rooted through a stack of rusting tins in Joss' barn and found all sorts of nails. Using a plank and timber laths, I banged together a ladder. The pub's roof was a mess of pitches, valleys and gables. I hooked the nose of the slating ladder behind the ridge tile and made my way onto the damaged roof. Already, a few slates had slid down into the valley on the far side. As I shifted my weight, the hammer slipped from my hand and rattled down the slates as if it was on tracks. It stopped with a thump in the valley gutter. I cursed my awkward hands. If the lead was damaged from the hammer, it'd be a bastard to fix. I climbed down the ladder, stretched across to get the hammer and inspect the damage. There was a small dent in the lead but no puncture.

It was one of those brittle January days when the east wind could cut the snot off you. The snow had not arrived yet but it soon would. Way out east the clouds were gathering like a mass of white that was inhaling and puffing up. They'd stay out there for a few days before moving inland. First though, a biting wind to dry the ground. Then the snow would stick.

The roof looked to have been damaged for a while. Loose and broken slates had left a football-sized hole into the attic. The supporting laths were half-rotten and nearly gave way under a bit of weight. Major work was needed. I was sure Joss knew this too, but he had told me to patch it up as best I could. I laughed to myself because Quinn used to say the same thing—Just patch it up for today, we'll come back to it in the summer. Always the summer with men like them.

As I was finishing up, Joss appeared in the backyard and shouted at me to have a look in the front chimney while I was up there. I should have known there'd be something else to do. The jackdaws were squawking like fuck last year, he said. Might be a nest in there. Pull it out if you can. Then block it up to stop the bastards coming back. There's chicken wire in the shed that'll do the job. Without as much as a *howareyegettinon* or a glance at the roof, he disappeared back inside.

I was wary of getting a mouthful of crow feathers, so I held the edge of the chimney and peeped over the cowl. Stupid really, I knew there'd be no birds in there at that time of year, but my brain was ready for a fright, like when you flinch at something you know can't hit you. After tearing out the nest, I got the chicken wire and made a cap for the chimney.

Straddled across the ridge, I could see most of the village around me. The fields and forest looked like they were sprinkled with caster sugar. An old Ford came across the bridge and rounded the corner to Main Street. It was barely moving, in no hurry at all. I wondered how little the village had changed in fifty years, and if it would still be the same in another fifty.

A voice then from the street below. Bit late for Santy, a woman says. I look down, but can't see who's there. Cathy steps back into the middle of the road, shading her eyes with one hand like a child peering into the clouds. Does this place ever change? I ask her. Gets dark sometimes, she says. You'd want to mind that roof doesn't buck you off. It'll fall apart first, I tell her—thing's rotten. I threw my leg over side-saddle and straightened my arms against the ridge. I nodded out across the fields and the forestry beyond towards the old estate house. You ever remember anyone living in Rathmore? I ask her. Since I'd been in Kiltuam, I'd wanted to walk around it. Derelict as long as I've been alive, she says. I ask her if she's ever been out there and she cocks her lip. Not for years, she says. I edged across the ridge towards the ladder and made my way down. She was standing at the back gate when I opened it. Suppose you're going for a pint now, she said. I might, might not. You? Maybe a coffee, she said.

The pub was empty of customers. Christmas and New Year were over, and the January slump had hit. Joss was leaning on the bar reading the local paper. He looked at the two of us as we walked in. His eyes narrowed, and he must have got a fierce taste for gossip right then, because his tongue snailed across his lower lip. We talked about the roof again, and he said it'd do well enough till summer. The first drinks were on the house. Black? I said, nodding at Cathy's coffee. Milk makes me sick, she said with a smirk.

I sat with Cathy at one end of the bar for the rest of the evening. Her face was flushed from the drop of whiskey she'd been getting Joss to throw in the coffee. Now and then I caught our soft reflections in the mirror behind the bottles of spirits. When she said something surprising, she leaned towards me, and her breath warmed my face as she talked. She covered her mouth and laughed at her own jokes. Haven't been out since the funeral, she said. Drinking, socialising or anything like that. This is the first laugh I've had in weeks. She talked a bit about Christmas and how it had been the worst time, but with the new year here she was going to make a fresh start.

I told her about my Christmas with Quinn and his new friend, Rose—a widow who worked in the village shop. We were never big on Christmas after Ma and Maureen died and it was strange to see another person's hand about Quinn's house—flowers in a vase, papers tidied on the sideboard, a window open for airing. He tells me they go for walks and drinks together, I said. And the rest, she said, nudging me with her elbow.

More people came into the pub as the evening fell. They nodded when they saw us, some said hello and asked Cathy how she had been coping since the passing. It must have been too much because she changed with the darkening evening. She looked around the room as if trying to find a face. Is there somebody missing? I asked. No, she said. I'd better go. I must have looked disappointed. It's nothing, she said—not you, I mean. She was off the stool then, putting on her coat and scarf. Being a bit brave with the drink, I say I'll walk with her but she won't hear of it. Her smile says she might like that another time though. Fine so, I say, pretending to return to my pint. She puts her hands on my shoulders and leans in to whisper in my ear. Nobody likes a sulk, she says.

I felt giddy and a bit stupid as she waved at the door and left. I remembered Duffy, and wondered about him and Cathy and how we had just spent the evening together as if he didn't exist.

A slap on the shoulder then and Sticks Foley stumbles down beside me. Happy New Year and all that shite, he says. Didn't think you'd come back from wherever you were. His eyes drifted around the bar. When he shouted to Joss for another drink, Joss told him that if he kept it up, he'd be barred. I asked him what had him so drunk. Haven't stopped, he said. Nothing else to do. You should get yourself a woman, I said, laughing. He turned and looked at me as if he didn't know me. His head rocked gently and his eyelids struggled to stay open. She's all yours, he said. Wouldn't have me anyway. But wait till Duffy gets his hands on you. He had one arm around me and was fishing for money in his pocket. I asked what he meant about Duffy, but Foley wasn't interested in conversation, just blather. You're a sly lad, he said. I saw the two of you here, very cosy.

Sticks Foley didn't see anything funny about being called Sticks and working at a saw mill. Stick would have been better, because that's what he was—a stick of a lad—branches for limbs, swollen knots for joints. One of the men at the mill called him a dying cunt once. He didn't like it and walked away cursing under his breath. When that same man lost two fingers in a saw at the mill, we wondered if Sticks was involved. It could have been any of us who got injured. I remember looking at my own arms, imagining what life would be like without fingers or hands. I clasped my hands and squeezed, just to make sure. The strength of them surprised me. All the things made possible by fingers. And how weak the wrists really are.

Foley went around behind me then and put his hands on my shoulders just as Cathy had done before she left. He whispered into my ear, mimicking a woman's voice, Goodbye, Mr Murt. I swung back my elbow. Joss scowled at us from across the bar. Sit down you gobshite, I said, pushing my own money across the counter to pay for Foley's drink.


I walked across the damaged bridge on my way to the mill. A few white flakes appeared in front of me, twirling through the morning air. They stuck to my face and on the sleeves of my coat. The day before there had been showers of hail and frozen rain. A white dust had settled on the ground, then disappeared. But these were proper flakes, the kind that could smother you in a blizzard once they got going. The clouds were battle-grey—low and full. A car crawled past and snow gathered in its tracks. The road ahead began to change and all sounds were absorbed by the snow. I'd never heard the countryside so quiet.

The gates to the mill were open when I arrived. Already a layer of white covered the yard, hiding the gravel and slop. The atmosphere had been tense around the mill since the accident, but work continued. Wallace was difficult to work for and there would be no more messing. The saws and machinery sounded louder, angrier. The trees around the yard were darker too, as if the shadows of winter had grown.

Foley and Smithy were in the portacabin when I walked in. Still no sign of Foley easing off the drink. He had the raw eyes and lips of a poisoned animal. What has it got to do with anyone? he barked, when Smithy asked him if he'd been out the night before. Maybe that would have been a fair reply if he wasn't operating a saw. The three of us sat in silence as the kettle boiled. Jesus, Smithy said, if they could make electricity from the smell of drink, we'd be a rich little country. Nuclear, I said.

The kettle clicked off.

Foley didn't look up as he filled the cups. There's not many countries with a natural resource like that, Smithy said. Foley growled as he whipped up the milk. It splashed on the table and across a newspaper and Smithy shouted at him to cop the fuck on to himself. With that, Foley swung his arm, knocked the three cups across the table and stormed out. We watched him cross the yard, huddled together in his torn coat. That lad's not safe, Smithy said. What's got into him? I don't know, but he'll want to sort himself out. Wallace is no fool.

The sky looked to be within reach. Snow fell all day and didn't ease up till evening. By then, it was three or four inches deep on the yard and had settled in mounds on every log, branch and machine. The forecast said it was going to freeze that night. Roads would be impassable the next day. Wallace said that he was going to close the mill for a few days, the rest of the week probably. Anyone with a car had left earlier in the day, afraid that they might not get home.

People expect snow every year. If it doesn't come, the winter is considered mild. When it does fall, nobody knows what to do and the country shuts down.

The road and ditches glowed navy-white in front of me as I walked home. Snow crunched under my boots. It tightened between the grips. Somewhere in the sky, moonlight was trying to push through. I could have kept walking that road for days. The countryside belonged to me and I belonged to it.

# cathy

I lost a few days sitting around Curran's. The windows looked as if they'd been covered with damp newspaper. Pulpy-grey snow was piled on the frames and stuck to the glass. Quinn had given me two books at Christmas, so I sat around reading those or else chatting with Joss. Conversation was hit and miss. Most of the time he just moped about grumbling to himself. When he did get a burst of chat though, he was all rant and gossip. His favourite topic: people from the village. He repeated himself a lot, said the same thing from different angles, all the time eyeing me for a reaction. What did I think? And had I heard anything myself? Most people filled Joss with nonsense. They got a kick out of hearing their own rumours and lies told back with a different slant.

Friday started with a rant about the priest—Joss hated religion. Auld Father Scab, as he called him, had been in the pub the other day asking if he could put a collection box on the bar counter. Trying to raise money for a sound system in the church, if you wouldn't mind—microphones and speakers so that the people could hear him better. We were at the bar counter slurping soup— the best food for when the snows come. Hear him better, Joss said to me. It's ear muffs the congregation wants for that lad. Steam was rising up between us. Joss never sat down. Leaning on the bar was enough rest. He stuffed a crust of butter-thick brown bread into his mouth. You never thought of selling up and getting out of here? I said with a grin. Crumbs of bread flew across the bar when he laughed. Not in the village a wet week and you're telling people what to do. Courting the dead boss's daughter and all. A nice little dig, but I couldn't let on to be annoyed. You wouldn't have to go abroad, I said. Galway maybe. I think you'd like Galway. Joss didn't take kindly to anything personal. He said, She's half-Protestant you know? I told him I didn't think people could be half anything and that anyway I wasn't courting her.

His chin hovered above the bowl as he scooped and slurped soup into his mouth. Word going round, he said, thinking that I was biting. And maybe I was. This place must be worth a few bob, I told him. You could travel the world. Might even pick up an auld-lady for yourself. He stared across the counter at me. How many counties have you been to? Mr Tour of Ireland—that's something to boast about all right. A tiny envelope of butter flew from his hands as he struggled with the wrapper. Bastardin' butter, he said through gritted teeth. Seeing as I had a go on him now, I pushed on. America, I said. The cowboy McNabb, you could call yourself. Less of it you, he said, straightening himself. He waved the butter knife in the air.. That Duffy is a tricky customer, he said. With a big stupid-looking Stetson hat on you, I said. He threw the squashed packet of butter across the bar, dunked the unbuttered heel of bread into the soup and took a merciless bite. The chewing seemed to calm him down. Dangerous too, he said when he'd finished. I hear them boys don't see eye to eye with the Síochána. I told him I didn't care about Duffy or his cronies. You can't have a friendly conversation with a woman now, I said, is that it? Jesus no, he said. That's one thing you can't do. He bared his teeth in a smile, and I could've counted the bits of bread stuck between them. Then he whipped up the empty bowls and made for the kitchen.

The street was covered in a thick layer of snow that rolled over everything. It made edges curl and surfaces soft. The doorway of the shop was piled with fresh snow and melting snow from people's boots. Inside, half the village were shuffling around with armfuls and baskets of supplies, wrapped up and stuffed into coats, scarves and hats. People were giddy with chat after having been stuck at home for days. Smithy was there with his wife and child. It's like a holiday, he said, Christmas all over. The little girl was waddling around, her arms barely moving she was layered that tight with clothes. We laughed as she tried to pick something off the shelf but couldn't grip it with her mittens. When it fell on the floor, she looked to her mother as if she'd done something wrong, then came running back with arms outstretched. They lived way out in the country and had borrowed a neighbour's tractor to come in and get supplies. A family adventure, the wife called it. I liked the sound of that.

I was at the freezer with a packet of meat in my hand when Cathy came up beside me. You have to cook that, she says. Really? Never have before. She whipped the mince from me and weighed it in her hand. There's a lot there for one, she says. Sure can't I freeze the rest? Next thing she's rooting through the things in my basket. I ask her if she goes through people's wardrobes as well and she says she does if she gets a chance. She makes a dive for my basket. Herbs and all, she says. Herbs and all, says I, trying to see into her basket, but she holds it behind her knees. Don't be nosey, she says.

I waited by the door until she had paid. A few flakes were falling again, but nothing much. Trying too hard—that's what Quinn would say about such weather. We walked up the street together, a bag in each hand. So, she said. You know about cooking? Enough to stay alive, I said. That's not much. It's not. A blue tractor grumbled past and its horn let out a blast. Smithy's daughter was sitting on his lap holding the steering wheel. The wife was squashed against the side window, cleaning the glass with a wave.

Outside Curran's, Cathy slipped on ice and fell in a heap. She sat there on the ground like a bold child, groceries scattered all around her. When she realised that her clothes were getting wet, she scrambled to get up. I could see Joss watching from the window as we cleaned snow off the packets and tins of food. He said nothing as we went through the bar.

Other than soup and toasted sandwiches, you wouldn't get much of a feed in Curran's. There was a small kitchen out the back and it did me well enough. Do you cook here? Cathy asked me. I have the run of this stove anyway, I said. I spread some packets of soup on the table and asked her to pick one. Jesus, she said, it's all soup this weather—vegetable if you have it. How do you put up with him? I took out a saucepan, filled it with water and put it on the cooker. Joss is all right, I said. I don't be down here that much. She took off her coat and hung it on the back of a chair. You like living with uncle types, she said. I stirred the soup. I told her I'd never really thought about it like that before. Living with Quinn had been grand. I'd settled in on the farm. Without him, I might have gone haywire after Ma died. I must have known what question was coming next because I started making a fuss with the bowls and cutlery. What about your father? she asked. I didn't reply. My father was a man I didn't know, had never even heard a mention of. When you're older, Ma had always said. The soup was spluttering and I went back to stirring it. Sorry, she said, none of my business. She shifted on her chair and I thought she might get up and leave. Bread, I said, louder than I needed to. It's in the bag there. I served the soup and we sat at the table to eat. This room of yours, she said. It's just a room, I said. I'd like to see it, she said.

After the soup, we went upstairs. The room was strange, she said. It had character, but felt like it had never been warm. She laughed at the size of the sink, reckoned she'd nearly fit into it. When she got to the wardrobe, she opened the doors and stuck her head inside. I told her she wouldn't find out too much about me in there. Well, she said, where will I look? Then she was down on the floor by the bed. Under here maybe? she says, pulling out a pair of old shoes and shaking her head. Back on her feet again, she lifts up the bed covers. In there, I'd say. Not so much, I tell her. She pulls at the curtains and they take a buck-lep as if a gust of wind has caught them. I walk towards her, but she ducks past me and makes for the dresser. What are we hiding in here? she says, picking up one of my books. She reads the title out loud. A history man—interesting. I'm standing in front of her now, and my head is all light like it might float off my shoulders. When she looks at me I don't know if she is waiting or screaming inside. Is it good? she asks. I say nothing. What is she talking about? The book, you eejit. She's talking about the book. Rathmore is mentioned in that one, I say, stepping back. I had come too close. Must be lovely out there in the snow, I said. We could get out and back before dark. You and that place, she says, putting down the book. Alright then.

Rathmore House was two miles outside the village, but you could cut half a mile off that through a few fields if you wanted. We stuck to the road. The clouds had broken in places and blue sky was appearing. We walked along the footpath until it ended outside the village. Then we walked in the middle of the road. She talked about times when she was younger, the first snow she could remember, her father leading her by the hand. She cut herself off quickly, then and we walked in silence.

When a jeep came along, we stood off the road onto the verge. The snow was piled up, and she slipped and grabbed my arm for balance. The jeep slowed as it came alongside us. Slowed right down to a crawl. Cathy cursed to herself, turned her head and waved at the jeep to go on. The engine roared as it swerved across the road and sent snow showering into the air from under the wheels. They don't like you, I joked. Not sure that's the issue, she said. Was it Duffy? I asked. She looked away as if she didn't want to talk about it or couldn't face me while she did talk about him. How long ago was it? I asked. Months, she said—nearly a year. Of all the questions I had for her, Duffy was top of the list. There was the picture in the newspaper, but I couldn't ask about that now. Then there was the funeral—Duffy coming over to us and Cathy squirming away from him. And now? I asked. See for yourself, she said. I get this shite all the time.

She linked my arm and we walked on. Duffy was bad news, she said. His father, the crowd he was in with. He'd done some things. The Guards were watching him. Sooner or later, he'll be locked up, she said.

The entrance to Rathmore House was in front of us. No signs or fancy gates, just high stone walls that curved back from round pillars. We stood in the middle of the road watching the wilderness and trying to decide whether to step in the perfect snow—was a derelict house really that important? I didn't tell you, she said, but this place gives me the willies. Me too, I think. Come on.

We walked slowly. The driveway was a snowy sea that rose and sank around us. Cathy had one hand to her mouth as if she might scream at any minute. It made no sense to me that she had lived so close to this place all her life and was scared to be here.

The house revealed itself in lumps as we approached—a crumbling corner, a black opening, the snow-covered parapet open to the sky. She held my arm tight. I can still remember the strength of her grip. It's just walls, I said. I know it's just walls but I don't trust them. See, I said pointing, stones and openings. It's like a relic though, she said. The bones of something big and strong and once beautiful but now dead. I told her that I liked it—the isolation. It says something. The ruins tell a story of a way of life that's gone. She curled her lip and frowned. I like life, she said, busy places, not sad lonely places. Why is it about trust? I asked and she frowned more. Trust? You just said earlier that you don't trust it. She shrugged. Feels like the walls know things, hold secrets from before. See, those windows and doors look like a mouth. It's gaping at us. I could see what she meant. We were looking at a square stone skull. I walked up what was left of the steps but Cathy didn't follow me. Standing in the doorway, I shivered but kept going. I stepped inside. The place was a jungle of wild shrubs and scrub. Trees broke out above parapet level. High up the walls there were holes in the stone which probably held timber joists at one time. In a corner, shaded from the snow, there was broken glass and the charred remains of a fire. The four walls of that place were both a prison yard and the most secret garden. Cathy called out. I asked her to come in, but she said we should be getting back before dark.

There she was waiting, arms crossed at the bottom of the steps when I went out. I have an idea, I said. Do you like the trees? Course I like trees, she says. They're alive. Not yearning for some past. So I take her hand and lead her over to a small clearing between a group of trees. The white day is turning navy. I ask her to close her eyes for a minute. She refuses. Trust me, I tell her. She agrees. I climb up into a tree and walk out on a branch above her. I tell her to lean her head right back. When she does, I jump and shake as many branches as I can. A waterfall of snow rains down on her. She gasps from the shock but then leans back once more, opening her eyes this time. Again, she says. Again.

# III

# Sticks

# 7

Murt liked the Moss Hotel. There were few places left that you could say had character, that had not been butchered and tarted up for the tourists. Not a hand had been laid on the Moss; it knew nothing of good times or bad.

People around Balroe took little notice of the Moss. You didn't go there unless you had reason. The sign at the entrance said Hotel, but it was converted from an old estate house—Georgian or one of those period types. Most of its guests were the kind who liked to pretend they had money. They wore riding gear, went trekking in the woods and drank brandy and hot ports in the tiny front room bar.

If you believed in ghosts, you might think twice about staying at the Moss—riddled with the fuckers, Donoghue reckoned. He often went up there for a quiet drink—a sneaky one, as he called it. And, of course, there was Eliza.

As Murt drove up the avenue to the Moss Hotel, he wondered about Donoghue and his sneaky ones. How many times had he met Christopher up here? What had they told each other?

Trees lined the avenue on both sides, the canopy converging to enclose the road like the vault of a cathedral. When Murt turned into the yard, Eliza appeared from one of the stables and directed him where to park. The first question she asked when he got out was how he got the coop up there on his own. The second, how he was going to get it down.

Murt said, 'Donoghue and yourself. In that order.'

Opening the latches, he let down the sides of the flatbed.

When he had arrived at the sale yard earlier that morning, the gates were open, but there was no one around. He had tried to lift the chicken coop himself but could not manage it. Donoghue was a last resort, but at least he was a resort. Murt called him, and he said he'd be delighted to be of assistance. As usual, Murt had a difficult job getting rid of him afterwards. Once Donoghue heard that Murt was going to the Moss Hotel, he was edging towards coming along.

'The Moss: my kind of place,' he said, as if it was another world, somewhere exotic that he had heard about in whispers. Murt told him that he had a busy day ahead and did not know when he might be back. This got Donoghue thinking that he might miss a few of the afternoon races. 'Well, I have a few things to do myself,' he said, 'but if you do need a hand now, Murtagh, just say. I'm your man—you know me.'

Eliza stood with folded arms as Murt untied the ropes and dragged the chicken coop to one side.

'You'll never manage,' she said.

'Many hands.'

'Oh right. Ok. I didn't think it was as big.'

'We'll manage. Just grab there.'

Murt counted to three and they lifted down the coop.

'Where to?'

'The paddock,' she said.

Walking as if their ankles were tied together, they carried the coop to the paddock and left it on the grass. Eliza rubbed her hands along her denimed thighs.

'I had to keep the chickens in the shed,' she said. 'Was beginning to think you had forgotten about me.'

'Let's get them out to pasture so.'

Two horses stood watching as they brought out the chickens.

'Look after your new friends,' Eliza said to the horses as she scratched their necks and rubbed their chins. The horses snorted and threw their heads in the air. Eliza turned with a start.

'Before I forget,' she said. 'The gutters are in an awful state, and that window needs a new pane of glass; and can you see the top of the roof up there? Rain comes gushing in through that.'

She almost lost balance as she strained, on her toes, to point out the damaged roof. Murt caught her by the arm and got a mouthful of her wiry hair as she fell into him.

'I'll come back another day,' he said. 'There's a lot of work in all that.'

'Yes, of course—another day. Are you hungry? Let's eat something,' she said and made off across the yard. He followed her through a porch to an annex off the main house—a low-ceilinged room that was kitchen, living room and dining area.

'Don't mind the mess,' she said. 'These are the work quarters.'

He sat at the table which was scalded and stained and looked as if it had been attacked by a hatchet at some stage. Magazines and envelopes were stacked at one end. Gathered together in the centre of the table were jars of jam, bottles of sauce, salt and pepper, a silver butter tray, mustard, sugar, vinegar, a glass jug half-full of milk. Along the back wall, stood a timber dresser stacked with plates. Cups hung from hooks along the high board, bits of paper were pinned and stuck to every surface. It was a room where everything was kept at hand. A rush of grey smoke hit the ceiling when Eliza opened the range cooker and threw in two sticks.

'See my rosettes over there,' she said.

A selection of coloured rosettes was arranged around photographs of Eliza with her horses. She told Murt the history behind each rosette as she prepared lunch: where she had won them, the horses' names, what the weather was like on each particular day—details seemed important to her.

'You like animals, Murt?'

'Of course.'

'When I was a little girl, my dog ran away. I cried for weeks. Eventually my mother told me that the dog had been hit by a car. I got all the lines from my mother then: She's ok now, She's safe in heaven, We'll get you another dog. Then I overheard her tell someone on the phone that father had killed my dog. And it just didn't make sense. Still doesn't.'

She shook her head and sighed.

'You didn't bring it up with him?'

'You didn't bring things up with my father.'

When they finished eating, she pulled out a bottle of whiskey.

'Too early for me,' Murt said.

'Who made the rules?'

She poured two glasses.

He sat in an armchair as Eliza talked. She asked him where he was from, said that it must be lonely, coming from somewhere else, not really knowing anyone in the town.

'Do you like living out here,' he asked, 'on the wild side of the valley?'

She seemed to read it as an answer to her question on loneliness, an implication, but that was not what he had meant.

A rosette ribbon slipped through her fingers as she talked.

'It's funny,' she said. 'Things don't add up. Do you ever feel that your past is a different life, somebody else's? You remember doing things, you were present when they happened, but the feelings are gone.'

Murt wondered if she was drunk already.

He said, 'Memories are like that, I guess.'

'What good are memories without feelings?'

'Depends on what you want to remember.'

'The future too—it will never be what we expect. You reach an age when you realise that the things you want will never happen. How do you lift yourself out after that?'

If it was answers she was looking for, Murt was the wrong man. Too preoccupied to notice that he had not touched his drink, she refilled her own glass.

'Because,' she said, 'you never find freedom from your own expectations.'

'Freedom—is there such a thing?'

When she smiled over at him, she looked, for a moment, like an old lady. What age was Eliza anyway? He had never thought of it before. Older than him? At one time she might have been beautiful. He wondered what she would be like in bed; he imagined her wiry hair catching in his fingers, her cheek cold against his.

'And Charlie?' he asked.

'Charlie?'

'Does he like animals?'

Would she thrash around the bed, screaming and grabbing like a woman without control?

'He doesn't get much time, but yes, I think for the most part.'

Murt had heard a story doing the rounds that Eliza's husband, Charlie, had left the country. Who knows what happens between two people after years together? What a glance says; the arguments they have had. Who can know either, the truths they tell each other, the intimacy they share, what familiarities hold them together. Lies too—what lies they know that the other has told. The anger a kiss can dissolve, or what it betrays.

She looked at Murt and said, 'I've no real idea who you are. But you're easy to talk to.'

The revelation seemed to please her, as if this was what she needed now—a nobody. Was her stare an invitation for something more; had she made an assumption about his life—that he was lonely and open to her advance? He imagined what it would be like: something fundamental between their bodies—a primal weakness, one moment of fulfilment in their lives that would leave a deeper loneliness on the other side.

He stood and walked to the door.

'You're leaving?'

'Yes, I have someone to see. In the hotel.'

The daylight surprised him when he walked outside. Why had he expected it to be dark? He drove out of the yard, turned right and went around to the guests' car park in front of the Moss Hotel.

Parked facing a lawn that looked out across the valley below was the car that had followed him from the beach, the same car that had been parked at Seamus Cowman's gate. He pulled his truck to a stop beside the car, waited for a few minutes, then walked across the gravel courtyard.

Inside, the main room was scattered with attic-dusty furniture that could have been rescued from skips and brought there, like old folk, to rest. It was the kind of place where you could fall into a spring-dead chair and forget things like hours, and what you had to do the next day.

Foley sat cross-legged in an armchair beneath a pair of tall bay windows. He lifted a cup to his mouth and watched, brows raised, as Murt approached. When Murt stopped at the table in front of him, Foley replaced the cup in its saucer and stood up. They faced each other for the first time in nearly seventeen years.

'That was you at the beach,' Murt said. 'Spying on me.'

'Spying implies looking to discover secrets. I know yours.'

'What do you want?'

Foley tugged at the lapels of his dark grey suit and fastened a button.

'We have somewhat of a fractured history, you and I. The way things went wasn't very pleasant for either of us. I guess we all hoped this day wouldn't come, but we knew it would. Question is, what will we do now that it has arrived?'

'You came dressed for the occasion.'

'I'm a businessman now. Long time since I wore work boots. You know that. I believe you're fond of the odd day's spying yourself.' There was no gloating smile on Foley's face. He had not said this for his own satisfaction, or to show that he had the upper hand. This was no business negotiation. The statement was plain, levelling some imaginary field between them. Murt was disarmed. Yes, he had found out where they lived, but he had only gone there three times, to catch a glimpse of Gráinne. And he had kept such a distance—how could Foley know? So far away had he stayed, in fact, that Gráinne was never more than a distant figure in the background. They were separated, and always would be, by the world of foreground between them. Dealing with this realisation had been too much for Murt, and after the third time he went there no more.

Did it matter now that Foley knew?

'I remember Sticks Foley,' Murt said.

'Always hated that name. Sticks was a means, a stepping stone between waster and success. Did you even know my name was Chris? I had to be Sticks to become Mr Christopher Foley. Sticks served his purpose.'

He sat back down awkwardly and offered Murt the seat opposite, but Murt stayed standing.

'What do you want?' Murt said.

'We think it would be better if you don't try to contact Gráinne again.'

Still no smugness, nothing to indicate that he was trying to belittle Murt, or show off his superiority.

'She's my daughter.'

'No, she's *our* daughter.'

'You can't stop it happening if she wants it to.'

'Maybe she doesn't want to know.'

'She doesn't know, you mean. You stopped her getting my letter.'

Holding the teapot's lid in place with his finger, Foley poured himself another cup without spilling a drop.

'I was supposed to tell you at the beach,' he said. 'You must have watched that ship not moving for hours. Reminded me of one of those poles that were buried along lonely shorelines years ago to help rescue fishermen—the world just passing you by, until someone comes one night and chops you down: a heartless vandal. I couldn't find the heart to swing an axe at you like that. I just watched. And those people with the dog. Finally, you must have thought, after all these years. I tried to imagine what you were going to say.'

'If you've come to laugh at me—'

'You see me laughing? There's a difference between compassion and condescension. I was hoping we could settle this amicably and leave it at that.'

'I won't give up. I deserve to see my daughter.'

'No man deserves anything in this life. There is no such thing as deserving—you earn. That's not something you understood though. You never cared for much other than what was in front of you. A bit of ambition, and you could have gone far.'

A door slammed in the reception area, and Eliza hurried through. She stopped when she saw the two men talking.

'Oh,' she said. 'You know Mr Foley?'

'He does indeed, Eliza. Thank you.'

She threw a hand up in the air and shuffled out through another door.

Murt said, 'What do you know about my ambition? It was taken away from me. All that I have left, you seem to think you own.' He sank into an armchair. 'You could have told me at the beach,' he said. 'Why did you follow me here?'

'Curiosity maybe, I'm not sure. I wanted to see about you, where you live.'

'Wanted to find out what people around here say about me, you mean. Don't be talking to Donoghue. You want to ruin my life here so I'll have to move on?'

'I know about Duffy—what you did. You should think about that. The Guards will be interested. And your life here will be difficult if you persist with Gráinne.'

Through the bay window, Murt could see his Dyna and Foley's car parked outside. Foley was right, whatever made him want more out of life, Murt had never felt. The need was lacking in him.

'Why?'

'Are we so opposed? Helen's very protective of her family. She's, how shall I put it, like her mother—a bit neurotic. And of course she blames you for Cathy. Even the mention of your name gives her a migraine. It'd be better for all concerned.'

He glanced around the room as if distracted. He brushed lint or crumbs from his jacket.

'Gráinne should have the letter,' Murt said. 'Let her decide.'

'Helen won't allow it. For your own sake, leave it be.'

'This is wrong, what you are doing. Have you never wanted to make amends? No, you just walk over people and never look back.'

Foley sat up quickly.

'I don't have time to look back. It's dangerous, and it loses me money.'

'That's the only place I can look. All I see are shadows. And now, here's one sitting in front of me.'

'We've all got shadows.'

Murt watched him, not able to believe this image Foley was trying to project.

'Helen sent you, didn't she? You wouldn't have come otherwise.'

'I'd have come to tell you this is not the right time. Maybe if you wait a couple of years.'

Murt pulled himself forward onto the edge of the chair.

'I've waited long enough,' he said, standing and looking down at Foley. 'Is it enough, all your money and things? Do you feel like a big success?'

'I have everything I want. What do you think?'

'I think it'll never be enough. I think it's eating you up inside. You're trying hard, but I remember you. I remember the bitter fucker, the greedy, resentful Sticks Foley, and I bet he's still in there. Just because you've covered him with a fancy suit, and took a few evening courses means nothing. It's who you are.'

'I did whatever I needed to do to get ahead. You could have too.'

'I know all about how you got ahead, and who helped you out.'

Foley looked at him without expression, and Murt wished for something he could recognise, a flash of Sticks Foley, but there was none.

As he drove away from the Moss Hotel, Murt thought about Helen—Cathy's sister. Back in Kiltuam, Murt had had his run-ins with Helen. Although she was the younger of the two by five years, Helen held a spell over the family. They bent to her wishes and demands. As hard as they tried to please her, Helen was never happy. The more attention she was given, the more stubborn she appeared to be. Instead of the younger sister, she acted the cantankerous aunt. At first, Murt had been amused by how everyone bowed to Helen, how she got her own way. There was no reason why, in a family of two girls, one would be able to exert so much influence.

And yet, bow they did.

It might have made sense if she was a miracle child, conceived despite doctors saying more children would not be possible. Cathy had scoffed at this suggestion when Murt had said it, told him not to be ridiculous—when Cathy didn't want to talk about something, the subject was closed. Neither Cathy nor her mother could see—they refused to see—the dynamic that Helen controlled. Murt had often wondered if things had been different when Mr Shaw was alive. He could only speculate that maybe Cathy was daddy's girl, and Helen had felt aggrieved because of this. She bided her time and, when their father died, Helen stepped in to fill the vacuum that no one else seemed to notice.

After her husband's death, Kathleen Shaw began losing interest in life. While Cathy went to work at the school, and Wallace looked after the mill, Helen took charge of the house. If her mother would not get out of bed, Helen didn't mind because she then had the house to herself; the sitting room was her lair. After nights out, sometimes she would bring men back. Helen twisted and rebuffed Cathy's objections. One day Murt arrived at the house as a man twice Helen's age was leaving.

'Daddy would never have allowed this,' Cathy said in the kitchen.

'Oh, Sis, we all miss Daddy. I cried myself to sleep again the other night.'

Murt and Cathy were going steady by now. At the mention of her father, Cathy always went quiet. As a family, she thought they were managing the best they could without him. Helen, Cathy said, was dealing with things in her own way. Helen's hold over her mother and sister's emotions was powerful, and Murt didn't like to interfere. One day he caught her smile slyly to herself after another Daddy jibe at Cathy. She hadn't expected Murt to be standing in the doorway and she held his stare as she left the room. Her threat was clear and it had the desired effect. From that moment on, Murt and Helen would be guarded with each other. He tried to avoid conversations with Helen, or about her with Cathy.

It had always puzzled Murt how Helen and Foley had ended up together. They did not make sense to him as a couple. She certainly didn't marry Sticks Foley. No, it was Mr Christopher Foley whom she chose. And Christopher Foley was a man Murt knew nothing about.

# 8

When the phone started to ring, Murt wondered for a moment if it could be Gráinne. He was sitting in the front room of the guest house and the paper he was reading shook with the start; he let it collapse into his lap. He had been browsing through the ads, looking for spare parts for the carbide lamp, but he couldn't concentrate. Since meeting Foley at the Moss, Murt could think of little else.

The phone was the portable, cordless type—a handset with base station. As he considered answering it, the door was flung open and Ursula hurried in.

'Sorry,' she said. 'Expecting this.'

The ringing stopped.

'Shit.'

She grabbed the phone and left the room. A few moments after the front door slammed, Murt saw her pacing past the window outside. As she talked, her free hand changed from holding her hair off her forehead to waving with frustration. He couldn't hear what she was saying, but her voice was raised and agitated. When she saw Murt watching through the window, she turned away.

Murt woke sometime later when Donoghue came in to the front room and proceeded to shuffle and move things around. He mumbled and scratched his head as he searched. Murt wanted a word with Donoghue, but had never seen him this animated before. When he had given up rummaging, he sat down.

Murt said, 'Strange thing Seamus Cowman told me.'

Earlier that day, Murt had gone back to Seamus Cowman's to help him rebuild the wall. Cowman had been ratty and could not focus on the task. Eventually he had told Murt what was eating him. Safe to say that Donoghue wouldn't be on Seamus' Christmas card list.

'Many strange things in the world, Murtagh,' Donoghue said. 'What is Cowman's problem now?'

'Some man arrived into his yard and asked about shooting on the land.'

'Nothing strange about that surely.'

From the couch, Donoghue continued surveying the room, then lurched forward to riffle through a pile of old magazines and papers on the table.

Murt said, 'This man mentioned your name, said you told him Cowman's was good for a shot.'

He stopped rooting and looked at Murt.

'Me? I surely did not.'

'Auld Seamus reckoned the man was no hunter, whoever he was.'

It was rare to see Donoghue stuck for words. Sitting back in the chair, he bit his cheek as he racked his brain for answers or excuses.

'Seamus say what this man looked like?'

'Like he didn't belong around here. Between that and everything else, he's losing the plot up there. Keeps the shotgun very close at hand, you know.'

'And he's not happy with me?'

'The man used your name, like you still worked there. Maybe he wasn't really interested in shooting; maybe it was you he was looking for.'

There were shouts then from the kitchen—a panic—and the two men jumped up and ran to see what was happening. Mrs Kelleher was sitting on the tiles, slumped against the wall. Ursula was holding her mother's dazed head.

'Ambulance,' she said.

Donoghue fumbled with the phone and made the call. Murt got cushions and a blanket from the front room.

'She just collapsed,' Ursula said. 'Don't worry now, Mam—ambulance is on its way.'

'I just called it there, Martha,' Donoghue said. 'Won't be long.'

By the time the ambulance arrived, Mrs Kelleher was sitting up talking, saying she was fine, not to be worrying; a dizzy spell was all. Never been in hospital in her life, she said. Ursula reminded her that she'd been in hospital plenty of times. The ambulance men snapped their rubber gloves and joked about a wasted journey. Your carriage awaits, one said, pointing to the stretcher.

Blood trickled from a small cut on the side of Martha's head where she must have banged it against the countertop. Ursula held a cloth against the wound.

The ambulance men told her what was going to happen. 'Now, Martha, we're going to help you onto the stretcher. Easy does it. That's it, relax. Just putting a mask on your face to help you breathe.'

Mrs Kelleher smiled. She didn't look one bit worried or scared, but the same could not be said for Ursula.

# 9

There's a feeling of loss in the smallest villages, those back road places that are left behind: stony faces stare when a car from a different county passes through; a garage door swings in the wind; a clapped out car sits outside the shop, its door wide open, engine still running, as if it's been abandoned. In the next village, the same thing. And you start to wonder if these places will ever thrive or if they are dying. Until you see the young ones, the spitters and wall kickers sitting by the bridge, and you realise that things are just as they have always been.

Murt drove through the village of Ratheen, which shared boundaries with three counties, and on towards Quinn's farm. Although the village itself seemed deserted, he knew from the years he had spent there that it was not. The shop would be steady all day; when school finished, there would be a traffic jam outside; even the two or three alcoholics would be busy getting drunk. People are rarely idle.

He had noticed it over the years in backwaters around the country: except for your own place, the place where you grew up, every village and town is the same. Only when you get to know somewhere and have lived there for years does it feel like something recognisable.

The city was different. Murt knew little of cities, other than that he did not belong in them. When he worked on the keg lorry, coming in and out of Guinness', he would watch the city by night and day. It had felt strange to him, the hardness of everything, exposed like bones. He used to try to imagine some sort of shape that the city took. Then he thought about the shape of a forest, lines and lines of trees and all the space in between. Maybe a city was a bit like that. Except the buildings were not in lines; the city was more complex. His mind kept coming back to the gaps, the spaces in between buildings where the city could breathe. And he liked this idea, how the city, like the countryside, knows itself.

He used to watch people walking along the streets, standing at traffic lights, checking their watches and he had tried to imagine where they were going—to places he would never go to, never even know about. As the old lorry chugged along the quays, heading out of the city, it always make him smile that there were things in life that he would never know and just as many things that those people on the street could not know or even imagine.

Quinn was standing in the porch of the house towelling his hands as Murt got out of the truck.

'Just in time,' his uncle said.

Murt followed him into the kitchen where the kettle was boiling. Quinn shuffled around, took out another cup and put it on the table. He brought over sugar, the teapot, bread and jam.

'Been a while. Thought you had forgotten about me.'

'You're stiff,' Murt said and Quinn laughed.

'Hips, knees, back, hands, feet, the lot. Even the head is seizing.'

'I doubt that.'

Quinn told him about a recent trip to the doctor who said that he had never seen a fitter creature, and that he would most likely live to be the oldest man in the country.

'Rose is looking after you?'

'She's gone off to Kilkenny to meet her daughter.'

'What have you lined up for the day?'

'Thought we might go up to the fairy field with a few stakes.'

Like roads, every field and ditch has a name, called after a previous owner, or part of a townland maybe, and some are named for their features. The fairy field was so called because of a stumpy hawthorn tree on a mound in one corner of the field. When Murt was a boy, Quinn told him that it was bad luck to cut down or damage a fairy tree, that people used to tie ribbons around them and ask for favours from the fairies.

Quinn was keeping less stock now and there was not as much hurry on things around the farm. When they got to the fairy field, they took tools from the tractor and examined the fence before they started. The damage was minimal—would have done without being mended for another while—but this was Quinn's way of saying that little changes, that the work endures.

'I sent Gráinne a letter,' Murt said, when they stopped for a rest.

Quinn's eyes gleamed in the brisk day, the eyes of a man who still wanted to be young, but the skin beneath was crinkled and bunched on his cheekbones. He was wearing an old suit jacket over his jumper, but it sat crooked across his back. When he stood upright, there was a twist in his frame. His shoulders must have stopped heeding each other over the years and gone their separate ways. The left shoulder was higher than the right and edged forward as if it had always been dominant and only now, as he got older, was it winning out. The right shoulder shied away into the background. Stretching out an arm, he rested the hand on top of the fence. Murt had always been impressed by the length of his uncle's arms.

'And?' Quinn asked.

'Asked her to meet me.'

'She never showed up?'

Shaking his head, Quinn picked up the crowbar and jammed it into the ground between his feet. He jarred it left and right, backwards and forwards to widen the hole. 'Takes time, I suppose, that sort of thing.'

'Another eighteen years, maybe.'

'No, not another eighteen.'

Quinn lifted the stake into the hole and held it long-arm steady. Murt raised the sledge above his head and brought it down on top of the stake. The smack of pounded timber hung in the

November-crisp air. After four more belts, Quinn grabbed the stake with both hands to see if it was tight.

At the sound of a tractor from a few fields away, they stopped and listened.

'Woodcock,' Quinn said, checking the stake again.

'Do you ever see him at all, at the mart or anything?'

'He nods the odd time. Think he does anyway.'

'That should all be long forgotten about now anyway.'

'Nothing changes.'

'Did he ever get that bit of forest he was after?'

'He did.' Quinn gave the stake another chuck. 'That's good enough,' he said. 'We'll move along.'


After dinner, Murt went out to the van and brought back the carbide lamp to show Quinn. The vinegar solution had worked to free up the hardened lime; the drip mechanism was clean and, though the regulating lever was tight, Murt hoped that it would work all right. Quinn took the lamp in his hands to inspect it under the light.

'It's in good enough nick,' he said. Unscrewing the two chambers, he lifted the bottom chamber to his mouth and blew into it. 'Listen,' he said.

With his brow set in a frown, he blew again, carefully this time. A tiny hiss filled the air between the two men. Quinn moved his finger around the surface until he found the source. When he pressed down, the hissing dulled and stopped. He smiled across the table at Murt.

'Gas leak. You'll have to solder that up.'

'I have most of the parts,' Murt said. 'Just need a filter. And carbide for when I get her going.'

'That might be your problem—the carbide. Getting your hands on that stuff now is not easy.'

'Cavers and miners still use them.' Murt said.

'I wouldn't know anything about that. Hang on now till we see.'

When Quinn left the room, Murt took the lower chamber and

blew into it. He moved his finger around the surface as close to the metal as he could without touching it. At the tickle of air on his fingertip, he pressed down. The hissing stopped.

Quinn returned with a plastic bag. He rooted around inside and pulled out two balls of newspaper: the lamp they had restored when Murt was a boy.

'You still have it,' Murt said.

'Course.'

They unwrapped one-half each, examined them and screwed the two together. The brass gleamed here and there, but had mostly tarnished.

'It's in good order still,' Murt said. 'Not the same as this lamp though.'

'Different patent; same principle.'

From the bag, Quinn pulled out another ball of newspaper and unwrapped the calcium carbide.

'It'd be no good now anyway,' Quinn said. 'Damp, gone off.'

They sat tinkering with the lamps in silence. Quinn made more tea and when they drank that, he took out the whiskey. Murt said that he'd better not, with the drive back and all.

'You're not driving back tonight are you? Rose will want to say hello when she gets home. The bed is there, made and all.'

It had been a while since Murt had drunk whiskey. The taste had never been important before, but it was now. He tasted the bitterness, and he knew that it would grow on him again, like the beer he first drank in the hayshed, with Quinn and the other man, after a day cocking the hay.

'Those were summers all right,' Quinn agreed now, savouring his mouthful.

'Haycocks stacked across the fields like beehives.'

The things Murt remembered from the field: blinding white specks of houses scattered over distant hills; dried grass and dust in the men's hair and across their backs; shoulders glistening with sweat; the steady rhythm of work and the dog panting beside them.

At the shed afterwards, a few bottles waited in the water trough. The men had encouraged him to try the beer and he did; gulped down a mouthful first time and couldn't believe how bad it tasted, like stagnant water wrung out of dirty socks. It was so unreal to him that he needed to try again, in case he had missed something. Maybe his mouth was dusty raw, parched from the heat. The two men guzzled hard, as if the stuff was better than water. And you would never have thought by them that it could dehydrate you even more. They let it spill from the sides of their mouths and Murt tried this too, but it ran down his shirt and he spilled half of it. There was no laughing though. They all breathed hard between mouthfuls and he was one of them.

'That old dog,' Murt said to Quinn now, 'moving between spots of shade.'

'Bet by the heat, the poor auld divil.'

'She was on the way out for a long time,' Murt said.

Quinn had known it, of course, but he couldn't bring himself to have her put down. She went her own way, curled up one morning in a nest of hay that she had made for herself.

'When I found her,' Murt said, 'I didn't know she was dead and tried to wake her. Can still remember the bone of her lifeless skull, like a pine cone in my hand.'

The trickle of whiskey as Quinn poured another glass drowned out a whisper from the television's speakers.

'I see Balroe is in the news again,' Quinn said. 'Any go on another flat?'

'Not a word. I'd say I'm bottom of the list. Families first.'

'You don't have to stay there.'

Without getting up from his chair, he leaned forward and threw more coal on the fire.

'Do you think the parents had anything to do with Gráinne not meeting you?'

'The stepfather, Foley, came looking for me. He said they won't allow it.'

Murt told Quinn about meeting Foley and about the threats he had made. Quinn knew everything about Murt's past and always thought hard before giving advice. The fire crackled above the telly's murmur, and Quinn drained the contents of his glass.

'That's the thing about the past,' he said. 'It's always there behind you. Like an old dog, sooner or later it'll come and find you.'

After an early breakfast the next morning, Murt said his goodbyes to Quinn and Rose. He took the motorway east and later, when the mountains came into view, turned towards them. An expanse of forest and bog spread out around the foot of the mountains and stretched far up the mountainside. He remembered the days and nights spent somewhere in there, thinking he was training. He remembered the metal-cold air and Reilly, focused and giving everything he had.

The narrow mountain trek snaked upwards; the kind of road that keeps rising around the next corner, and just when you think the clouds are nearing, the road starts to fall away in front of you. A brown landscape of rushes, heather and sour grass, gorse bushes for miles in every direction. Sheep wandered the road, grazing along the verge where a fence had fallen away into the bog below. On the other side, huge mounds of mining deposits threw shadows across the road.

The top of the climb was a sparse landscape of stone and dust, bare mountain slopes, strewn with boulders that looked as if they had been shaken from the heights by an earthquake. This was wilderness. In every direction he saw curved summits, crests and troughs that held dark in the morning gloom. The mountains were alive, their backs arched as if in anticipation.

# 10

Ursula told Murt that she was trying really hard. At night, it was more difficult, but she was definitely drinking less. She said that it helped having another person in the house who wasn't drinking. No longer did they disturb each other in the front room. They chatted, mostly about Donoghue, and shared a laugh at his expense. She talked about the children and sometimes mentioned Ray, her husband. He was a Garda sergeant in the next town. Murt had heard his name—not a man you wanted to be on the wrong side of by all accounts. If Donoghue had known that Ursula was married to Garda Ray Quirke, he might have tempered his advances.

Ursula and Murt were in the front room talking about Donoghue.

Ursula said, 'It's kind of sad, Murtagh, don't you think?'

She called him Murtagh now. He let it go.

'How can people go through life that way?' she said. 'He's completely different from the man he thinks he is.'

This observation surprised her, as if she had, in a moment of inspiration, got to the core of Donoghue. She was pleased with herself, which, as far as Murt could see, did not happen often. He wondered if this was how she thought of him too. Maybe he had a deluded idea of himself?

'A lot of people think they're something they're not,' he said.

'What happens when they realise, when it's too late?'

'Most don't, or they do and they keep pretending.'

'Everyone has to keep going somehow, I suppose. We find a way.'

She was nibbling at a nail, making clicking sounds as she bit.

'He's kind of a social misfit really,' she said. 'Has he no family? What sort of a life is—'

She stopped, clasped a hand over her mouth and turned to Murt.

'I'm sorry, I don't mean. I wasn't implying you. Oh God.'

She hadn't meant to insult him, but it was true and they both knew it. The strange thing was that he felt more at ease than he had in a long time.

'There's a wife,' Murt said. 'And a son, I think, but I don't know if they want anything to do with him. Damaged bridges.'

Ursula scoffed, 'I'm hardly one to talk. Falling out with my own mother the way I did.'

Murt guessed what she was going to ask next, so he went ahead and said it.

'I have a daughter myself.'

The words appeared before him and hung in the air like a frosty breath. He heard himself speak them again. Ursula was surprised, and excited in the way women get—questions would follow such a revelation. He said that he had not seen his daughter in years, that he was no father to her. She nodded and asked if he knew where she was, if he had tried to contact her.

'Down south. About an hour from Kiltuam, maybe two from here. When I lived in Kiltuam, I went down there a few times and saw her from a distance.'

'Jesus, that must have been terrible. What's her name?'

'Gráinne.'

She repeated it as if she had never heard the name before.

'From the legend?' she said.

'Cathy liked that one.'

Now he had said more than he had intended. Ursula repeated Cathy's name in a way that made it another question.

'Gráinne's mother,' Murt said. 'She's—'

He didn't know which words to use—had he said them since her death?—or what order to put them in. They were in his mind somewhere, colliding with things like loss and regret, and in his throat now, making him choke.

'I see,' she said rescuing him..

They chatted about other things then—Ursula's mother, the Moss Hotel.

'I was there once for a wedding,' Ursula said. 'That woman, Eileen.'

'Eliza.'

'A bit odd. I hear she's—how should I say?—approachable.'

As Murt tried to decipher this, the front door opened and banged shut. Donoghue's heavy steps echoed along the hall and up the stairs.

'Must be time for the savages to feast,' Ursula said, as she got up and left the room.

Mrs Kelleher was in hospital still. Complications, the doctors said, something more serious than a dizzy spell. They were doing tests and more tests. Having to drive to the hospital kept Ursula off the drink for a while each day. Mrs Kelleher had entrusted her with the house: look after the lads, keep the cheques coming in. Maybe there was more to it in Mrs Kelleher's head—if Ursula is busy, maybe she'll drink less.

When Murt opened the kitchen door a few minutes later, Ursula scrambled to hide the wine glass. Her guilt stood uncorked on the counter beside her. Had she been sipping away all day? She looked at Murt, the silence begging him to pretend that he had not seen. Why had he come into the kitchen? Something to tell her: that he'd appreciate it if she kept their conversation to herself. It would be their secret.

'Sorry,' he said, and retreated back to the front room, knowing that everything between them now would stay that way.

Donoghue was quiet as he ate dinner—one of his thinking days, Murt guessed. They were sitting at their respective tables in the dining room, and had not spoken. This would usually suit Murt fine, but tonight Donoghue seemed to be down. Those things Ursula had said earlier, about feeling sorry for Donoghue, had got Murt thinking.

'You wouldn't know,' Murt said, 'where I might get a piece of scouring pad?'

Donoghue looked up from his plate, chewing slowly as he stared over.

'Scouring pad,' Murt said again. 'This much only.' He made a circle with his thumb and index finger and held it in the air.

'Supermarket, I'd say. What for?'

'The carbide lamp. I need to make a filter. Years ago they used felt, but it clogs up. Gauze is better.'

Unimpressed, Donoghue returned to his dinner as the door opened, and Ursula came in with another plate. She sat at a table in the centre of the room and started to eat. The two men looked around her and at each other with raised eyebrows.

'Well, this is a first,' Donoghue said.

'I have to eat.'

She told them that she had always hated the room—the wallpaper and clutter, the layout of the tables, like a classroom or a doll's house.

'You two,' she said. 'Always the same seats?'

'Neither of us has a better view this way,' Donoghue said, picking up his newspaper.

Murt laughed at this wryness that he hadn't heard from Donoghue before.

'Where did your adventures take you today, Oscar?' Ursula asked.

He rustled the newspaper and muttered an answer.

'How was the form?' Murt asked. 'Many winners?'

'Not so many today.'

With that, he folded the paper quickly, stood up, thanked Ursula for the meal—gorgeous, just gorgeous—and made for the door.

Perhaps his thinking days were losing streaks.

# 11

At the entrance to Knocklea forest, Murt opened the barrier, drove though, and closed it again as the man from the Forestry Service had instructed. Back when he worked at the mill, forests didn't have barriers and timber theft was rife. Mills and contractors always took more than they were contracted to take. Others used to come to the forests at night and help themselves to the stacked logs.

Sprawled across hills and glens, Knocklea forest covered hundreds of acres. Murt drove along the gravel roadway that wound up through the trees until he came to a flat straight where the road widened. The forest rose steeply on the left. To his right, where the land fell away, was an open expanse of yellow clearfell.

After clearfelling, the forest floor always looked like a wasteland. Harvesting was mostly done by machine now. Serious contractors came in with their eight-wheeled beasts worth hundreds of thousands of euro and flattened the forest in a few days. Huge jibs, nimble as a man's arm and fitted with all manner of blades, could grab whole trees and throw them around as if they were pencils; hydraulic rams hissing and spitting as trunks raced through metal teeth, stripping the branches. De-limbed trunks were then cut into shorter sections and either stacked or loaded. Murt often watched the machines in action, but had never got to use one.

Across the clearfell below him, branches and scrub had been bulldozed into piles that ran from one edge to the other like lines of bonfires waiting to be lit. In between, the scarred forest was a no man's land—abandoned stumps and deep furrows in every direction. A few splintered trunks stood as casualties of the harvest. No need of a tidy forest floor. The machines could go anywhere, and workmen didn't have to leave their cabs. In a few months, the surface would be disguised by a meadow of wild grass and briars.

Past the clearfell, Murt turned another corner and could see electrical wires strung between the trees ahead. The power line that cut through one corner of the forest had recently been upgraded, and Murt had asked about getting some of the old poles. He could cut them into shorter lengths and sell them as strainer posts for fences and gates. The old poles were lying in scrub along the side of the roadway. He got out of the truck and breathed in the forest air. On calm days, Murt's breath floated from his lungs and stayed right there in front of him. On other days, it bellowed, swirling in a race of wind.

Murt looked after his chainsaw—a bad saw wasn't worth the hardship it caused. The previous evening he had spent an hour in the workshop drawing a round file along each tooth of the blade. He filled the tanks now—one with two-stroke petrol, the other with burnt engine oil to keep the blade lubricated.

The morning's clouds were gathered in sandy grey bundles that tainted the landscape below. He flicked the choke switch on the chainsaw and yanked the pull chord three times in quick succession. The engine fired for a moment and died. He flicked off the choke. On the next pull, the saw started with a burst of white exhaust smoke, a flurry of fumes that were sweet in the cold air.

After stepping out a rough distance of eight or nine feet along the poles, he began cutting them into lengths. He dragged each post over to the truck. Standing it upright, he leaned the top against the side of the truck, lifted from the bottom and hoisted it onto the flatbed. When the truck was half-loaded, he stopped to take a break. He poured a cup of hot tea from his flask and sat down. The forest held a silence, something he would never tire of.

His peace was broken by the sight of a man rounding the corner below and struggling with laboured strides up the steep roadway. It was Foley.

Foley stopped by the van and leaned on the side, trying to hide the fact that he was out of breath.

Murt said, 'Knocklea'd be bigger than you think.'

'Didn't have a key.'

'Neither did I. No suit today?'

Ignoring this, Foley walked to the verge and stood with his hands in his coat pockets, looking out across the clearfell and the valley beyond.

'Some view,' Foley said. 'All the way to the sea.'

'You fancied a walk in the forest?'

'I did. Been a while. Oscar Donoghue told me you were up here.'

Murt lifted the chainsaw into the air as you might raise a stick to warn a person off. Foley stepped back.

'I have my own life here,' Murt said. 'Donoghue's got a big mouth.'

'He's a character—has a lot of time for you.'

Murt revved the saw to life and started into cutting another pole. Sawdust sprayed out behind him and Foley backed away from the stream. The engine roared and dipped as Murt worked the blade through. He wished that Foley would be gone when he turned around, but another part of him didn't want that. Right now, Foley was his best chance, his only chance—a connection to Gráinne that he'd never had before. Without him, Murt would be back to square one. Why was Foley still in Balroe anyway? His piece had been said, his terms laid out—Helen's terms. And yet he was hanging around, sniffing for more information.

Murt dragged a post over to the truck, reared it up and leaned it against the tailboard.

'Why did you say another year or two?'

'What's that?' Foley asked.

'The other day at the Moss, you said if I could wait another year or two. I didn't understand that—the difference like?'

Foley frowned, his eyes roaming for something to fix on as he thought—had he said that? His jaws clenched. Murt waited.

'There's no difference,' he said. 'Are we not clear on the arrangement?'

'I didn't know there was an arrangement.'

He stared at Murt before turning towards the valley again.

'It's an odd existence you have here,' he said, 'but you seem to like it.'

His voice was quiet. He was thinking out loud, trying to understand.

'Why are you still here?' Murt asked. 'You've said what you came here to say. Go back to your life with my daughter. Whatever you think you have on me—'

Foley took a step towards Murt and held his stare.

'His dog, Murt. You took Duffy's dog, kept it as your own. That's how I know.'

Duffy's dog—it might have starved to death if Murt had not taken it with him that day. Now he understood the guise of Foley's approach. Above, a crow squawked, and Murt watched it circle around, then land in a tree. People do the strangest things in a panic. He took a dog.

'You're wrong, you know,' Murt said, 'what you're thinking.'

Took it with him as his own—how did Foley know?

'I'm not the person you'll have to explain it to,' Foley said.

Left Duffy lying by the river and took his dog.

'Do what you have to,' Murt said. 'I'm going to see her.'

'This won't be good for any of us, dragging everything back up.'

'You didn't think I'd want to meet her some day?'

Murt crouched down, grabbed the bottom of the pole and lifted it onto the flatbed, growling with the effort. He'd had enough of Foley now; he needed time to think.

'Whatever about me,' Foley said, 'Helen will do everything to stop you.'

Murt shook his head. 'What are you not telling me?'

Foley turned to walk away and Murt shouted after him.

'Does Gráinne even know? Did she get my letter?'

As he watched Foley disappear down the gravel road, Murt listened to the whoosh and fizz of wind through the branches.

Nothing holds calm like a forest. The peaceful zone between ground and canopy, that's what Murt wished life would be like—shades of greens, browns and rust that are different in every light and yet always the same; the breeze that connects every branch like a net. He thought about trees being the real witnesses to the world. The secrets they would have, all the things they would not tell.

The guest house was quiet when he got back. Ursula had been spending most of her days at the hospital. The bottle of wine appeared only at night now—she couldn't sleep without it—or when she got upset about her mother. She was calmer, Murt thought, more relaxed. Keeping the mind busy helps, she said, and the doctor's tablets.

Lying in bed, Murt thought about the places where he had lived. A house is like a coat that you wear every day. Its shape is fixed, but it takes on your form after a while. You become used to the fit, you know its smell. The rooms are pockets that you can navigate in the dark. The sounds become familiar: opening, closing, scratching. You can sense if someone is near, and if something is different, not quite right, you know that too.

What if he had to leave Balroe? He needed to think about that now. Depending on what Foley and Helen did, he might not be able to stay. The Guards would have questions for him. Then all the talk around the town would be about him. People would look at him differently, ignore him, just when he was beginning to feel like one of them. Moving from place to place was fine when he was younger, but people are suspicious by nature. A man in his forties arriving out of nowhere would get the question and rumour mill going. If he left Balroe, he'd have to start from scratch again.

The following morning, he woke to the sound of uproar as if a car had crashed through the gable wall. Children's footsteps rumbled across the floorboards as they ran from room to room. Murt listened from the top of the stairs before coming down—voices, cries, shouting, a tantrum, pretend tears, and Ursula telling them to keep it down.

The noise stopped when he walked into the front room. Surprised at seeing a stranger, the two children took a few steps back to stare from a safe distance. The girl was taller, older by a year or two—around eight, Murt reckoned. She pulled a handful of hair across her eyes and the boy clutched her arm. Ursula told them to say hello, but they turned and disappeared through the door.

'Ray left them over for the day,' she said. 'To visit their granny. I'm taking them along.'

'And to see their mother, I'm sure.'

'They think I'm just staying here because she's not well, looking after the house and that.'

'You're happy to see them?'

'Course.'

The silence was an opportunity to talk about Ray, but it was none of Murt's business. He wasn't going to ask.

'He wants to know if I've sobered myself up yet,' she said. 'Never crossed his mind that maybe he's part of the problem.'

'She's very like you,' Murt said, when the little girl appeared again.

'They're good children. There's times when I can't remember one good reason why I married him. Do you think it should be like that?'

She checked herself and apologised.

Murt said, 'Maybe you're looking in the wrong places.'

'The bottle. I know.'

She shrugged and smiled, hoping he knew that she was really trying, but also that she couldn't fight it. Murt knew. She wanted someone to tell her that there was a secret, a knack to it, or a tablet she could take to cure the thirst. She wanted him to tell her how he had stopped, how he could live without it—he hoped she wouldn't ask him that. What could he tell her? About the years he had lost, or the damage he had caused; about losing his mind. No, none of that was for Ursula to hear. It would make no difference; everyone had their own story. She stood and left the room.

He could not tell her either the hardest part—that time doesn't heal. It stays with you every day, the desire is a starving animal following you around, and you have to try and be strong. That's all you can do, your only defence, even when you cannot think of one good reason—which is just about all the time.

He knew too, that people said things when they were upset, things that they might later want to take back.

Through the kitchen window, he watched the three of them playing in the garden. Ursula tried to grab the girl but slipped and landed on her back in the wet grass; giggles and gasps then as the children climbed over her, all hands and legs. When Ursula got up, her blue jumper was soaked to patches of darker navy. Did she see Murt watching through the window? She rubbed a hand slowly down along the curve of her back to her hip and started the chase again, using her wet hands as a playful weapon. Giddy with panic, the children shrieked.

Murt turned away.

# kathleen shaw

Before I'd ever met her, people around Kiltuam were telling me Kathleen Shaw was odd—*asoddasbefucked* they said. And she was too, but once I got a handle on her, she seemed to put up with me.

The first time I went around to the house, she didn't let me in. Cathy had warned me that she might be narky, so when the door opened, I hoped it wouldn't be her. It was her. You're from the mill, she said, pointing a sharp finger at me. I saw *ye* at the funeral. I introduced myself and asked if Cathy was home. Doran, she said. From where? The West originally, I said. You're the one lives above Curran's. Not much of a life. Are you a vagrant, Mr Doran? I'll not have my daughter—. Cathy was beside her then. She kissed her mother on the cheek and told her to go back inside. Later, Cathy explained more to me. That was something she did a lot—made excuses for her mother. About how she was sick with worry or was having a bad day and not to mind her too much.

Even after a few months, when I'd met Mrs Shaw a good few times, she had her little digs at me. At first it was hard to take, thinking I would never be enough for Cathy in her eyes. To Cathy though, it was hilarious that her mother was needling me like that. And me biting every time, taking it to heart. The woman's mad, she told me. Not mental-home mad, but cynical and crazy with the world. She stirs things up, gets a kick out of it. Just play along.

Turned out that indulging Mrs Shaw was one way to get around her. She smiled the odd time and cracked a joke—at my expense—when she let down her guard. There was banter in the woman. My husband was fond of you, she says to me one time. Of course, that doesn't mean I am. I was sitting at the kitchen table waiting for Cathy to get ready. I said to her, You make a mean cup of tea, Mrs Shaw. She was at the sink and threw her head up to the ceiling. A good worker, he said you were. Never mentioned anything about taking his daughter out to dances though. Hard work doesn't necessarily make good marriage material. Especially if you're fond of the soup. And no doubt you are—she spun around to face me—fond of the soup, I mean. All you lads are the same. Good for heating you up all right, Mrs Shaw. It's the only man for the bones in the depths of winter. She wrung the hands off herself in her apron. The other soup, she says. You know right well—the sauce. Black stuff and whiskey. I told her I might take a drop over the Christmas, and on Paddy's Day too. She wasn't having a bar of that lie. She said, He rarely touched the stuff himself, you know. Always compos mentis was my Daniel. I sniggered to myself. Mr Shaw often came to the pub on a Friday with us for a few scotches. He never had more than three, said that was his limit, that herself would start asking questions. Still, that's a long way from rarely touching the stuff. I want nothing but the best for my girls, she said. And that's what they'll get. The best. You're right there, Mrs Shaw. What mother wouldn't? She must have flinched then because her guard slipped. For God's sake, she said, would you stop with the *Mrs Shaw* nonsense. You know right well it's Kathleen. Now eat up that brack there. I told her thanks, but I was stuffed. Three slices is more than enough, I said. Sure I'm barely able to dance as it is. Cathy was standing in the kitchen then. I can vouch for that, she says. Now, are you going to sit here talking and eating cake all night or are you taking me out? Kathleen cut her off. He's going nowhere till he's finished his tea.

After the accident at the mill, Kathleen left the house less and less. Cathy was worried about her. She'd often tell me about hearing her mother's slippers shuffling across the floorboards, the kettle and the telly going on at all hours. She was fading away, Cathy reckoned, turning in on herself. Mr Shaw's death was the final straw in her scuffle with life. She didn't want to know too much about anything after that. Until her granddaughter came along, that is. She was made up, the world became bearable again for a while. There was a dusty glow in her face, as if caught in a shaft of sunlight.

Sometimes I met Helen at the house. She would have been sixteen or seventeen then. I remember her prowling around the place in her dressing gown. She was always looking for something, that one—her cardigan, a hair band, a book she'd been reading. No point in asking you, she snapped at me one day. I didn't know where to look. This was in the early days, before I understood her. Did you know that Cathy was fat at school? she said to me. Sure what does that matter, I said. Pudgy more so than fat, she said. That's what she was called—Pudge. I said Cathy would be delighted she'd told me that. Just saying, she said and off she went out the door, only to reappear a few minutes later looking for something else.

Other than smart comments, Helen said very little to me. Cathy ignored her sister's nonsense. She's just being difficult for the sake of it, Cathy said, making things up and looking for attention. We can't trust a word she says. Dad dying hit her hard—the age she was. Cathy could switch mid-sentence like that to see another side of someone. A more vulnerable side, I suppose you'd call it. She told me that Helen used to have some childish idea about life being fair and things working out. And when that happened to Daddy, she said, it blew all our lives apart. She's good with Mam though—you mightn't see it, but she is. Sounds like they both need you, I said. We need each other for different reasons. Without one, the other two might fall apart. It was too early to talk about marriage with Cathy, but I wondered what future we could have or where I might fit into this trinity.

It was wintertime during that first year when I was doing a line with Cathy, and Kathleen decided she wasn't going to her whist night any more. On Monday nights in the school hall, a group of them would meet to play. It was one of the few times during the week when Kathleen left the house those days. We were going to drop her off at the school on our way to the cinema. Don't think I'll go out in that weather tonight, Kathleen said. Listen to the wind. I told her I'd seen worse, that it was only a strong breeze. No, thanks though. Come on, Mam, Cathy said, you haven't missed it in years. Helen was standing in the doorway with a scowl on her face. She leaned into the room. It's whist, she said as if she was talking to a child. What's wrong with you? Kathleen snapped back at her. Why does there have to be something wrong with me? I just don't think I'm bothered with the whist any more. With that, she cleared out of the room leaving us gawking at each other.

After Whist, the supermarket became a no-go. Kathleen would do up a list for Cathy and leave money on the table with a note saying that she didn't feel up to it. Not up to what? I asked Cathy. People, faces, talking, she said. And cars and noise and nosey auld ones. She comes back fierce upset. They still ask her about Daddy and the mill and how she's coping. Suppose most of them are genuine but they can't keep quiet. What is it with people that they have to be talking all the time, that they feel they need to speak every thought they have? I asked her if Kathleen was just going to stay at home and never leave the house. It's better for her, she said. She's happier at home. Why should she put herself in upsetting situations? It's just life though, I said. But I was badgering her now. Mam doesn't want to deal with it any longer, she said. I know it's not right and that she should get help, but she won't listen. You've seen her at home—she's fine. Outside is different. The world frightens her. It took away her husband.

I'm not one of those people who has to say everything I think, so I decided to let Cathy and Helen look after their mother in their own way.

Wallace was only supposed to be running the mill for a few months after Mr Shaw's accident, until the family decided what they were going to do. He managed the place well enough and reported back to Cathy and her mother regularly. The mill was steady, the men were paid and work continued. Wallace got a decent pay rise and the manager's office. The men were always speculating though. Everyone had a theory or had heard a rumour about what would happen to the place in the long run. When it became common knowledge around the mill that I was seeing Cathy, there was no let-up in the abuse. Here comes the boss-to-be, they'd say. I was called Cuckoo and Artful Dodger. Most of the banter was harmless, but sometimes they made comments about Cathy. Sticks Foley was nastier than the rest. There was venom in that lad, and he pushed everything too far. At the back of it I reckoned he was jealous. We had been friends, but he turned sour with me.

It was only a matter of time before Kathleen heard the rumours. She was sitting in the garden one day, and I was waiting for Cathy. She said to me, I suppose you're after the mill. The old deckchair was blotched grey with damp and mould. A wide-brimmed foreign-type hat covered most of her face. I told her that Cathy was the only thing of hers that I wanted. Be a nice little dowry all the same, she said, considering you have nothing—never had. She didn't stir. There was no movement, only the sound of her voice. Her hands were holding tight to the armrests of the chair, as if to keep her steady, as if the thing was going to take off. All I ever wanted was a home and a family, I said. If I have that, I'll have enough. You've some cheek, she said. We don't know a thing about you and here you are, trying to sleeveen your way into our pockets. Still no movement. She could have been talking in her sleep if it wasn't for the cutting words. I told her that I had always earned my own money, never begged or stole from anybody.

Whatever I had to say made no difference to Kathleen. She had it in her mind that I was after their money. I couldn't blame her, I suppose. There's plenty of sleeveen whores like that out there. They pretend to be nice to you, but all the while they want something. Why should I be any different? My stomach was in a knot at all this fierce talk. I knew she wasn't winding me up. Then her hand moved off the armrest and raised the brim of her hat. She stared at me narrowed-eyed, looking for my reaction. Why now? Did she really dislike me that much? I wouldn't mind some water, she said.

When I came back out with a glass, she started talking about the garden. The roses were in full bloom, the rhododendron was taking over. For some reason, she hated rhododendrons. My father grew his own beetroot, she said. We'd boil them and cut big slices for sandwiches. At some point, as she rambled on, it hit me. This problem she had with me wasn't about money or the mill. It was Cathy. I was taking her daughter from her. None of them could see how the family would hold together without Cathy. If you don't want us to be together, I told her, then you should have said so before now. She's already agreed to marry me, Kathleen. I don't want to come between you three. But just as you think you can't live without her, I can't either. Scallions too, she said. I love the smell of fresh scallions. Reminds me of picnics and sandwiches when I was a child. It's a pity they boil up my throat. The deckchair creaked as she sat up. Above, a long cloud masked the sun. She took off her hat, shook it out and fixed her hair with a shuffle of her hand.

He saved me, you know, she said. There were eight children in my family. Eight hungry mouths, sixteen grabbing little hands at the table, seven voices louder than mine. And only two sets of eyes to watch us all. They did their best, my parents. We got by. They just couldn't see me among the constant racket. Whoever shouted loudest was heard. I was a frail thing, pushed and pinched to the back by my brothers. I longed for the day when they would leave and I'd get the attention. My father was a butcher and two of the boys worked for him. Another got a job as a farm hand. I had a sister who made clothes and things from home. And another sister who did nothing at all, just stayed around the house waiting for a man to knock on the door and ask for her hand. Only two of the boys left home in the end—America and England. A job was found for me as a milkmaid. I hated it but what could I do? There was only one princess in the house and it wasn't me.

The sun came back out and Kathleen finished the water and put the glass down on the stone patio slab. She fixed the hat on her head but didn't recline the deckchair. When I stopped going to the farm, she said, they threatened to kick me out of the house. Daddy said the farmer had done him a favour by giving me that job. And how was he going to face him now? There was no let-up in the abuse for days. Then they all just stopped talking to me and one night I packed a bag and left. Got a train to Dublin. She laughed and shook her head. I found this place run by the nuns. They took me in, I helped out around the kitchen. A few weeks later, the priest from home arrived and told me I had to go home, that Mammy wasn't well.

We both watched the sky. Islands of cloud floated across like countries lost at sea. You went back? I asked her. I missed home anyway, she said. Nineteen or twenty I must have been—imagine. When I got back, it was clear that I was expected to look after the house, make the meals, do the washing. And Mammy sick in bed needed constant watching. The others all had jobs except the princess but you couldn't ask her to do anything. She was a sickly child and would be treated as such for the rest of her life. Spoiled rotten. The boys wanted their dinner ready when they came in. I was running the house and yet I didn't exist. They hardly spoke to me. I was nothing but their skivvy—was even starting to believe it myself. That was my lot in life. I'd never been encouraged to expect something more.

Around the front of the house, I heard a car on the driveway.

And then Daniel and his father showed up. They'd heard that Daddy was looking to fall the five acres of trees he had. A deal was done there and then for the timber.

The front door of the house banged shut. Cathy called our names, but Kathleen continued as if there was something very important about her life that she wanted me to know. During the work, she said, Daniel would come over to our house every day, pretending to look for Daddy. He always had something with him from the forest—a leaf or flower, a tiny insect. By the time the work was finished, I was so in love that I couldn't hear Daddy cursing every Shaw in the country, for taking his timber and not giving him a fair price, he said, but really it was his skivvy that had been stolen.

Cathy caught the last few sentences. I thought you'd be keeping the Cinderella story for the wedding, Mam. I hadn't finished, she said. Laugh all you want. I told her it was a grand story. That's the problem with love, she said. If it's enough to make you happy, then you'll have nothing when it's gone.

The subject of where we would live after the wedding was a touchy one. Kathleen and Helen had their own solution. A room was cleared for us and given the name *yourroom* whenever it was mentioned. They painted the walls, got new carpet laid, invested in a queen-sized bed. After a few heated discussions with Cathy, the whole situation had become a big issue. It won't be for long, Cathy told me. And anyway, we don't have a place of our own yet. Isn't it good to have somewhere until we sort ourselves out? I told her that I was flat-out looking for a place and that we'd find somewhere soon. Of course, she said, but it'll have to be close. At this point the argument would kick off. How were we going to find a house in the village close to her mother's?

And so we moved into *ourroom*, which was more like a wardrobe. I'd have given anything to be back above Curran's. We were children sneaking behind the school shelter for a kiss. Kathleen's night-time habits kept Cathy awake, which meant I was awake or never fully asleep.

The three women nattered away non-stop. And argued. There was no end of snide remarks, rolling eyes, storming around the house and door-slamming, all soon forgotten about and they were ready to start again. Sure I couldn't keep up with them and had to find something to busy myself. The roads and woods became more familiar to me, as did the garden, the car and Curran's bar counter.

After a few months, it was Helen who finally cracked.

The arrangement wasn't working. Everyone knew. I was the only one saying it. Cathy was starting to come around to my way of thinking, but would she ever come around enough? Could she live with the guilt of leaving her mother and sister on their own? A cottage came on the market a few miles away. It needed work, but we could live in it. Cathy liked it—she saw what I saw. Pity it's too expensive, she said. I said we could use that money her father had left her and I'd get a small loan.

We were standing in the neglected front garden. It was as wild as a ditch but thick with all the smells and sounds of a country laneway in mid-July. It really is great, she said. I knew she was looking for faults. But I can't leave them, she said—not yet. Not yet or not ever? I said. She glared at me and told me to stop. We're killing each other in that house, I said. It's only a matter of time before—. Before what, Murt? Before you walk away? That's always been so easy for you, hasn't it? True to form, I turned and went back to the car.

Helen, who was becoming a crafty young woman, did her best to ignore me around the house. If Cathy or their mother told her something that she didn't want to hear, or if she was in a bad mood, she could throw tantrums that shook the walls. She didn't like that I was there listening to their arguments and saying nothing.

Finally, she rounded full-faced on me one day. Kathleen wouldn't allow her go off somewhere with her boyfriend—some lad she hadn't long met. Cathy agreed with her mother, and I just happened to be standing in Helen's way as the tantrum took hold. You're like a bad smell, she shouted. Who are you anyway? Get out of my way. I could feel my jaw tighten and my throat closing. I had a store of home truths ready for her, months of things bursting to be let loose. Don't speak to him like that, Cathy said before I could get going. I walked out and stood in the hallway. *Dontspeaktohimlikethat*, Helen mimicked her sister in a child's voice. I'm surprised at you, she said, Little Miss Perfect, marrying him, Mr Fucking Nobody. That's it, Cathy roared. We're leaving. Kathleen begged them to stop. She said we should all sit down for a few minutes. Let them leave, Helen said. You know he tried to touch me the other day, the creep.

Silence. The house held a huge breath.

That was enough for me. I walked back in to the Kitchen. Helen, I said, you'll get the man you deserve. What does that mean? she screamed. What the fuck do you mean by that? Itinerant. Coming here and stealing my sister. My only sister.

Tears fell on the lino floor. Kathleen reached across the table and held her younger daughter's hand as I took Cathy's in mine and left.

# 12

The evening sky above Kiltuam was a ball of rolling grey. A shadow of rain passed over hills to the south as Murt drove across the stone bridge and rounded the sharp corner onto the main street for the first time in many years.

He passed the old petrol station and saw metal fencing across the forecourt, signs saying: 'No Entry – Construction Site'. There were no houses or apartments built, no work even underway. A graveyard site, it seemed to have been abandoned for years—half-built walls, stained from the weather, plastic flapping in the wind like torn flags, heaps of gravel and broken blocks, a dumper truck rotten with rust. It was as if the workers had dropped their tools and fled from something terrible.

He was relieved to see the name Curran still above the pub. At the far end of the street, the church looked more isolated than he remembered, sinking into long grass and unkempt shrubs. He drove on for a few miles more and turned around at a widening in the road, the entrance to Rathmore house barely recognisable. Maybe he would take a walk up to the house. A car slowed as it passed, and they stared at each other, the driver and Murt, as if they were both looking at a ghost.

Halfway up the driveway, he stopped and looked around at the bare trees, the ground covered with dead leaves. Farther on, through the trees, he could make out one corner of the old house, and the memory of the day he had come there with Cathy rooted him to the spot. There seemed to be a stillness that he should not disturb.

He looked down by his side and saw his own arm reaching out for something: her hand that was not there. A few leaves swirled past on a breeze that came from nowhere. He turned back.

He had wanted to make the memory more real, somehow bring it back to life or keep what was left of it alive. But memories don't work like that; they aren't for reliving.

The light was beginning to fade as he made his way back towards Kiltuam village. At Curran's, he turned right and drove out Station Road towards the cottage that was once his home, his family's home. He needed to look again, on the off chance that none of it had been real. He remembered dreams within dreams when he woke up imagining it had never happened. Those were rare dreams, where everything ebbed peacefully around him. But the tides changed quickly when he woke.

The cottage lay in ruins, just as he had left it—the skeleton of a house that had appeared so often in his other dreams, the nightmares. The roof of his caravan had collapsed, a coat of green moss creeping up the sides from its belly beneath. How had he lived in it for so long? He remembered the dread he felt back then, when the thoughts of rebuilding the house began to fade, when he realised that he would never do it. The dread, every day, of knowing that those walls were there—the haunted shell of what remained of his life. By the end, he could not even look at them. The place made him sick, but he must have been half-mad by then.

There had been offers; letters and visits from auctioneers telling him that he could get a great price, a little cottage like that out in the countryside. They'd give arms and legs. But it was still his place, and even if he never had anything else in life, he would not part with this ghost. Those black walls were all he had left of her, of their life together. He looked at it now, the only place that was ever really his, and he wondered what could be done. Maybe he should have let them have it, taken their money and walked away for good, but then he would have nothing, only money, which is nothing at all. Someone else would have rebuilt it, made it their home, and Murt's life with Cathy would fade away, disappear as if it had never even been. Irrelevant, just as strangers' lives are to each other.

As he drove back towards the village, he thought of Gráinne and how, if things had been different, if he had been a proper father, if he had been fair to her and had not just thought about himself, the two of them could be living in the cottage now.

Curran's pub was in front of him then and those thoughts hid themselves away. Inside, he hadn't missed a day. Joss gave him little more than a nod when he walked in and asked what he was having.

Murt shook his keys. 'Something soft.'

The place was empty except for two old men down at the far end of the bar.

'I don't know if this is a good or a bad thing,' Joss said.

'Seeing me walk in?'

The years had given Joss the silvery tone of an old oak stake.

'I suppose it's bad news,' he said.

'It's always bad news, Joss.'

'You driving out here. Maybe you're selling the place below. I don't know how the Knackers haven't moved in there in all the years.'

'Don't suppose they'd even live there.' Murt pushed money across the counter and Joss waved a hand.

'Be even worse luck to charge you.'

He kept himself busy wiping the counter as they talked. Joss told a few stories about people whom he thought Murt would know. This lad, that lad, yer one who used to grow the turnips. Murt smiled as he listened to the stiff hinge of Joss' voice, in no hurry at all with a story. Nothing like a bit of banter to escape from the world for a while.

'No sign of you retiring?' Murt asked.

'Barely scraping by these days. The Lodge gets whatever crowd there is, others head off into the town. Get a few in the evenings, but that's it. Been downhill since the mill closed. You remember the Friday nights?'

'Course. Any of that crowd ever around?'

'Not really. Where is it that you're stationed these days?'

When Murt told him about the guest house, Joss laughed hard, said he knew a man in the town beyond who lived in a guest house. 'Similar set-up. Gone fat as fuck from all the good food. Reckons he's never leaving.'

Murt wanted to tell him some stories of his own. About the gombeen Donoghue and the landlady's daughter, about the lamp he was restoring—he had it out in the truck, could bring it in and show him. They could be there all night.

But that would lead to many more questions.

'Thing is, Joss, I came down here for a reason. I need a bit of help.'

'Don't go trying to get me involved in anything illegal. I have enough lip from that cunt of a sergeant as it is.'

He waved a damp rag in the air to reinforce his point and Murt had to jerk his head back from the stale smell.

'It's only a small thing,' he said. 'Information.'

'The most dangerous of all.'

At the far side of the bar, one of the old men stood up, shouted 'I'm off' and walked out. Joss cleared the empty glasses, pulled another pint for the last remaining old codger.

'The mill,' Murt said. 'Anything been happening there?'

Joss glanced sideways at him, cautious of where this was going.

'No,' he said. 'It's still closed. There was a lot of talk that they were going to develop the place.'

'That right?'

'But the way things went, not looking like such a good idea now.'

'Sticks ever be around?'

Joss added a frown to the glance.

'Look, Murt, I don't know what to tell you. What happened was a mess. I only know what I hear—gossip. There hasn't been a word about the mill since Foley hit the wall.'

Murt did not look up. If he let on to be surprised by what he had just heard, Joss might not say any more. He turned a square beer mat on edge, walked it lazily along the countertop and waited for Joss to continue. That's the thing with people, once they start telling you something, they can't help but spit it all out.

'If he sold the mill now, it'd hardly cover his losses, I reckon. Rumour has it they don't even own the place, whoever the auld lady left it to.'

'Foley's friends didn't help him out?'

'There's not many of that crowd involved now, not around here anyway. The Cause didn't mean a whole lot to those lads when they started looking around at their friends and neighbours and saw bigger houses, cars, investments, all that shite. So they said fuck this fighting bollox, I'm joining this cash circus instead. Weren't we the right little modern country? And what happened to our history? Prosperity happened to it. The past didn't matter and, as for the future, it'd be grand as long as we were getting rich today—every man for himself in a race to the grave.'

'You missed out.'

'I surely fucking did.'

Somewhere beneath the counter, a tap gushed as Joss leaned down to rinse his rag.

'No,' he said, 'Foley doesn't be around here anymore. Goes by Christopher now if you wouldn't be minding.'

'So I believe.'

'I don't know what you're looking for exactly, but that's about all I can tell you. Is it the girl maybe?'

'You know yourself, Joss.'

He threw back his head and it bobbed along with the motion of his cloth on the countertop.

'Pity about the cottage all the same,' Joss said, with a smirk.

'It is.' Murt smiled across the bar at his old friend, always sniffing for an angle.

When he had finished his drink, Murt got off the stool and put on his coat. The two men nodded to each other as if that was all grand. 'Look after yourself,' Joss said. 'Drive easy.'

# 13

When the letter arrived, he knew it was from her. He looked at the envelope for a long time, turned it over, felt the weight—a lot of pages inside, more than a short note, more than a postcard. His address in her handwriting. Whatever the contents, this pleased him—it was enough to know that she had written his name. She knew that he existed. But what was inside? What words did she have for him? He left the envelope on the table, afraid now to open it, afraid to take the good—or the bad—out of it.

Outside, the wind was throwing rain against the windows in handfuls. Every so often it chanced a surge down the chimney, then retreated. The house was quiet otherwise. Ursula had left the boy and girl to school and had probably gone on to the hospital. The children were staying at the guest house now and had their own room. There had been a scene over the beds, but it was just for show in front of Donoghue and Murt. He hadn't expected the racket they would cause, doors opening and closing all over the house. And they could appear anywhere at any time. Ursula said that it was only for a few days, that Ray was away at some undercover training conference in Drogheda. There had been no progress on talks between the two of them, and she joked that she might even keep the children at the guest house with her.

Murt picked up the envelope again and tried to open along the seal without ripping the paper, as if keeping the thing intact, being able to reseal it, was important.

He took out some sort of stapled document, put it to one side, and read the letter first. She had found his letter buried in a stack of old post, ready for the bin. She was not supposed to find it. The photograph had made her cry: so many things she didn't understand. Her *parents* had told her that her father was not a good man. She had nothing else to go on. Why had it taken him so long to contact her? And why now?

The photograph he had sent was a small Polaroid in hazy beige-grey of the three of them together—Murt with his arm around Cathy, Gráinne in her arms, the half-open door of their cottage in the background. The postman had fancied himself as a photographer and always had his camera with him. They were outside in the garden when he arrived on his rounds and he insisted that they pose for a photograph. How could any of them have known that it would become so important? After the fire, Murt had found it undamaged among the scorched remains of the cottage.

He wanted her to have questions that only he could answer. That was why he had sent the photograph with the letter. So that she could see them all together. Maybe he had hoped that it would upset her. Did that make him a cheat, to have set her up and manipulated her like that? She could have cut him out and pretended he was never in the picture. But that would leave a jagged line beside Cathy—the photograph would be less real without him. He wanted her to see that. It was a selfish act.

The things she had written in the letter made it difficult for him to read. She was right: he was a coward. No one wants to admit that to themselves, and he knew it all along. But there was something in the letter that gave him hope. Maybe he had expected real anger and there was none, only confusion and disappointment. He could sense her youth in the sentences and between the lines. At eighteen she was too young yet to be scarred. Maybe there was a chance that she could forgive him.

He picked up the pages he had left down. What he had thought was a document of some sort turned out to be a story that she had started for school but just kept writing to finish for herself. It was not supposed to be about any family in particular, she said, but it turned out to be about her own.

*An Ordinary Family Drama*
by Gráinne Foley

When Gayle's mother and father told her that they weren't her real parents, she realised the distance between them. Gayle was thirteen and couldn't understand why they had not told her sooner.

It started with a chance meeting. While off shopping, a woman came up to Gayle and her mother and started talking. The two women remembered each other from years before. Gayle's mother was uncomfortable but could do little. The other woman kept glancing at Gayle.

She asked, 'Is this—'

'This is Gayle,' her mother snapped. 'The eldest.'

The woman whispered, 'Cathy's—' but was quickly cut off. 'And there's a boy. He's nearly eleven.'

Goodbyes were said hastily and they made for the car like a runaway trolley. Gayle said nothing but that didn't mean she hadn't heard. Cathy? The woman's meaning was clear and the gossipy way in which she'd said it only increased suspicions.

The father, by then, was a successful businessman. He poured his whole self into his business, as if compensating for a lack of interest in the family. The more successful he became, the more success he wanted. They moved into a bigger house. The children went to private schools. Mother had free rein on the credit card. The family had everything.

The father's frame was narrow and rigid like a metal gate. The boy, Gayle's brother, had the prominent cheekbones of his father, the high forehead and small ears. Luckily, he was more handsome than his father; however, at least there was no doubt or question about who his father was. Gayle could find nothing of the father's features in herself.

More than the physical traits, Gayle had no bond with the man. Their personalities clashed. His controlled aggression made her uncomfortable and anything she did seemed to grate on him. It was difficult to catch his eye and, when she did, he averted his gaze quickly. When they talked, he busied himself with small tasks. Gayle took his guilty behaviour as a disregard and dislike for her.

In her mother, there was something—a similar tone in their voice; the same wispy thin hair, the kind that's mousy brown and soft as fresh cut grass. Sometimes they had a laugh together, and Gayle liked to tease her mother.

She asked one day, 'Where was I born?'

They were driving to the equestrian centre, which was a good five miles away, and her mother could not escape.

'Born?' she said, glancing over. 'In hospital, of course.'

'What weight was I?'

'Seven and a half pounds,' she said, after a pause.

'Do you think we're an odd family?'

Gayle knew that this would cut right to the bone with her mother.

'How dare you say that, after all your father has done for us.'

'He doesn't even like me, acts like he doesn't know me. How did you two meet anyway? Did he fool you into it, pretend he was Mr Charming?'

Her mother stabbed the brakes in anger, and they both lunged forward.

'Don't talk about something you know nothing about. Don't turn into one of those girls.'

'Touchy.'

'You've a lot to learn.'

'Is he really my father?'

'Don't say things like that. Doesn't he give you everything you need? We both do.'

'I know. But you can't buy everyone, not your own family. He buys people, doesn't he? Uses them.'

'He's a businessman; you do what you have to do.'

They drove in silence for a while then. Arguing made Gayle giddy, and she wanted to comment on her mother's bad driving, but she wasn't quite ready to drop the questioning.

'I'm not like him,' she continued. 'It's pretty obvious. Maybe you had a run-in with Mick the Milkman. He's about your age. I get on great with him.'

'Stop that, young lady.'

Gayle was laughing and expected her mother to find this hilarious. But her mother wasn't laughing.

'No way,' Gayle said. 'I'm right aren't I? You and Mick the Milkman. Who'd have thought it? Other than me of course.'

'I said stop. Now that's the end of it.'

'You'd have a soft spot for old Mick though.'

Realising the conversation had gone to full out joking, the mother smiled at last.

'And I beg your pardon, he's far older than me. He should be retired, for God's sake.'

'In his day though.'

'That's enough!'

There was relief on her face when they reached the equestrian centre. Gayle had hit a nerve.

And so, a few weeks later, the truth came out. A family meeting was called. Her mother was jittery, tissue in hand; she didn't know how to begin. Gayle guessed what was coming. And it didn't really bother her. What difference would it make?

As it turned out, it made a big difference.

Now it was real, more than just an idea in Gayle's head. Why had they kept it from her?

'We wanted to wait until you could understand.'

'Tell me what happened,' Gayle said, but details weren't given.

The thing about her stepfather was that he would do anything to get what he wanted. If there was somebody he didn't like or resented, he'd pursue them and delight in their decline. When the delight faded, he was deflated, tired, depressed, as if victory had sucked the energy out of him, leaving him hollow and weak.

Gayle watched everything closely, especially her parents. At school she was a geek, a study swat. Outside of books, she made people nervous by watching them intensely. She liked to know what made them tick and what made them think.

To her mother, family was the most important thing in the world. It was all she had, and she clung to it with fingers, toes and teeth. The more distant her husband was, the longer the hours he stayed away, the harder she worked to pull her family together.

The children were mollycoddled, protected. Being smothered was unbearable to them. And there was nothing worse, for Gayle, than Christmas. Her mother would be up to ninety trying to pretend she was relaxed and enjoying life.

'Christmas is family time,' she said one year to Gayle. 'The only time we all get to be together.'

This sort of pretend nonsense drove Gayle crazy.

'What are you talking about? We're always together. We live here together.'

'Yes, but you know what I mean.'

She looked at Gayle with a smile you might give a child who is crying, a smile for the sake of smiling. It was glassy and fake, hiding her gritted teeth.

'No, I don't know what you mean,' Gayle said.

'You do. It's a time we can all relax, enjoy each other's company.'

'Well, going by that logic, we should really get away from each other for the week.'

Her mother flung the knife into the sink—a stainless steel attack.

'For God's sake, Gayle, can you just do this much for me? It's been a hard year. Your father and I—we'll all enjoy it. If you and your brother could just be a bit less selfish for once. Now, could you hand me the tea towel please, love.'

Having put the matter to bed, the pretend smile returned to her mother's face.

Despite the mother's best efforts, the children were unpredictable. At the age of thirteen, the boy borrowed his mother's car one night and drove it into a tree. He was found hours later, curled up in a bed of briars. The boy never cried; he wasn't one to respond. When the questions started at home, a shrug of his shoulders was as much of a reaction as he gave. This infuriated his father, who didn't need much reason to fly off the handle. He was always tense, as if his anger was wrapped around him like a blanket and held tight. But he didn't have the physique for violence. There were times when he looked like he would have given up everything he had to strike out and deliver a blow that would shake the world.

And anyway, his wife wouldn't allow him to hit her son, would not stand for it. When he didn't get any more than a shrug from the boy, he kicked out at a wall and cursed it for hurting his toe. He faced the boy, hunched and scowling.

'You won't play your games with me, young man,' he said. 'This will not be forgotten. You wrote off your mother's car. Are you even sorry?'

The boy shrugged, a little less carefree this time. His father's eyes widened to that shake-the-world point. The blood was bubbling inside him, the whistle about to sound.

Here's the thing: the father saw himself in his son, imagined him as a clone. He expected the boy to be moulded in his image, but he was never willing to devote the time to achieve this. As a result, the boy grew up without real influence. The more he realised that his son wasn't conforming to his expectations, the harder his father became on him.

While the mother would love her boy for ever, she rarely went against her husband's opinions and reprimands. You could say that she was afraid of him, but actually she believed that she could use her allegiance to bring the family closer together—to keep the knot tight.

She knew how her husband worked, what made him tick. If she had something to ask him or needed a favour, she knew the right time to ask, that certain mood. Catch him in a rare vulnerable moment and appeal to his weakness. She was in the good position of being one of the few people in the world to know his weaknesses, things that not even he himself was fully aware of. If he had been, he'd have fixed them, turned them into strengths. No doubt some involved sexual bartering: there was the unpleasant incident where Gayle found some cheap leather garments which she innocently produced in the kitchen and questioned her mother and father about. In the frenzy that followed, they tried so hard to pass it off that Gayle felt more uncomfortable than she ever had in her life. A few short years later, having more understanding of the issue, she still turned puce with embarrassment and shame at the thought of it.

Her mother's biggest fear was that the family would disintegrate. She would do whatever was necessary to prevent this from happening. She was an expert at manipulation, although in her view it was always for the good of the family. The most trickery was reserved for her husband.

For example: he liked to trade. Trading was how he operated. He believed you got nothing from him if you didn't give him something in return. Building a sunroom was a big ask. Gayle's mother knew she would have to work on him for a few months. She began by mentioning it in passing: the Ryans just finished their sunroom, it's fabulous, you'll have to come over with me and see it. His silence was expected. It's not that they couldn't afford a sunroom; they could afford several sunrooms, another house even. Asking him to part with money was like asking him to donate a hand to scientific research.

He often lectured the children about where he came from. About how his family never had anything, no money, no comforts. About how he was a self-made man. About how he dragged himself up, rung by rung. And it didn't happen by throwing money away. The only way to have it is not to spend it, he said. What the children knew, but never dared to say, was that it had also helped a little that he had married into a few pound.

Having got nothing more than a passing response after mentioning the sunroom several times, it was time for her to move into phase two. One of his business partners was being a bit cagey about a proposed property deal, couldn't be convinced to invest. Gayle, who had been silently following developments, listened as mother and father were discussing it in the kitchen one day.

'Appeal to his weakness,' her mother said.

'I'm not sure he has one.'

'You don't know him well enough then.'

'Maybe that bitch of a wife of his.'

'What about her?'

'He might listen to her.'

A long silence followed, broken by the sound of a giddy knife dancing on the chopping board.

'You could talk to her,' he said.

'Me? You know I can't stand the woman. That false accent, as if we don't know where she came from.'

'Just meet her once for lunch. Mention the deal in passing, tell her how much they stand to make. Let her see herself on a yacht in the Caribbean, far from the cowshed she was born in. That's what she likes.'

The chopping stopped as she thought about this.

'I might be able to do that, I suppose.'

'Of course you will.' he said, opening his newspaper satisfactorily. 'What time will dinner be ready?'

From the next room, Gayle overheard this whole conversation. At fifteen, she had just had her eyes opened to something real from the adult world. Something subtle that would take time to sink in and many attempts for her to perfect herself. The following spring, work began on the infamous sunroom.

If the boy was his parents' pet, then Gayle's position in the household was less clear. When in the house, the father conducted himself reasonably. If in good humour, he was agreeable but detached. Good humour was relative. Was she his daughter in a family sense? Yes, she supposed she was. But not in the same way as his son. During a conversation about which secondary school they would send the boy to, Gayle's opinion, when offered, was met with an awkward silence which there was no reason for. When she won a show jumping rosette, the father's congratulations were forced. Impersonal, that would be the word for him. It was possible that he had been having a rough day, but it was a reaction Gayle had come to expect. When she asked for money—small amounts—he would quiz her about what she needed it for. There was a sense that he didn't want her to have it. Her brother never got this treatment.

Apart from all that, there was one thing that could not be overlooked. Perhaps a bit like her mother's refusal to see what her husband was really like, it took many years for Gayle to admit that there was a problem between herself and her step-father. Because it wasn't anything confrontational. There were no shouting matches or threats. It was all in his eyes—he never looked at her. She would go as far as saying that he could not look her in the eye.

As a member of her mother's precious family, Gayle was treated fairly. There was always a feeling there though. It wasn't that her mother smiled less at her, turned away more abruptly once she had said something. Rather, it was the opposite. Everything was exaggerated. She didn't even know that she was doing it. What was she doing? Compensating? For not being Gayle's real mother? For the coldness of the man of the house? For fear that her daughter would find out whatever truth she was hiding? Sympathy for the orphaned child? Mother loved both her children, it just happened that she loved one more naturally than the other. And children are observant little fuckers.

Once they had told her they were not her real parents, things changed. Her mother made even more of an effort and her father even less. Cracks appeared in the family mask. Every day was a different argument in the house. At first, Gayle thought that she was the cause. It was her brother who pointed out to her that their mother was half-crazy and their father impossible. It was as if the reality of their relationship was bound together and kept hidden with the truth about Gayle. And now neither could be controlled.

Gayle wanted to know more. She had so many questions. Her father refused to speak about the subject. He would tell her to ask her mother and then walk straight out of the room.

From her mother, Gayle got the same story every time—about the accident and how lucky she was to be alive, about the neglect she had suffered and how the family had taken her and loved her as their own. What more did she need to know?

'Just about everything,' Gayle said.

To which her mother flashed the fake smile. Conversation over.

Murt read through the story again and again, each time a little more heartened and despairing in equal measure.

Donoghue burst into the room and started rummaging through the newspapers and magazines. The dark stubble, which had appeared recently, was thickening to a beard and his face was locked-jawed with tension. Whatever he was looking for, he could not find it. He stopped, crouched over the table, and looked red-eyed at Murt. He whipped Gráinne's letter from the table and began furiously scanning the page. Murt jumped up and demanded it back. Now that he knew these pages were important to Murt, Donoghue began inspecting the contents. Murt made a swipe, but he retreated and read aloud, 'The picture is beautiful. I've cried a lot since I saw it.'

'Give it to me,' Murt shouted. 'Now!'

Donoghue looked at Murt's fist and held his stare for a second before handing over the letter, cagey, in case he might lose an arm in the process.

Donoghue said, 'Gráinne? I knew there was something you were hiding.'

'It's a personal letter. What business is it of yours?'

'Indeed, but Gráinne, crying over pictures. Interesting.'

The wind swirled outside and a small cloud of ash rose from the fireplace. Murt sat down again.

'Get what you're looking for and fuck off back to the bookies.'

'All right, Murtagh. Calm down, I'm sorry.'

He started around the room again, resuming his search, but the hurry had left him. After lifting a few ornaments, opening the cabinet doors, peering in and closing them again, he turned to Murt.

'You have a daughter, I believe. Is that her, Gráinne?'

Murt didn't answer. He held her letter and story in his fist, rolled into a batten, the paper softening in his sweaty grip. Donoghue sat down too, drawing his own conclusions.

He scoffed, 'Well, I hope you're having better luck than me.'

Murt saw something forlorn in his face—that same sadness Ursula had talked about.

'How's that lamp of yours coming along?'

'Not lighting yet.'

For a while then, the old Donoghue had returned. He told Murt a story about one of the men from Dwyer's who had stumbled drunk off the footpath into a ditch the previous night and had to call the Guards to help get him out. The banter would be savage the next time the man showed his face in Dwyer's. They had a good laugh at the story, and when they went quiet, the wind was howling still.

'How many winners do you need?' Murt asked.

'Many, many winners. I might have something lined up though—a big one.'

There was a sudden flash of madness in Donoghue's eye, a glint of spittle on the tip of his tongue.

'That old chestnut,' Murt said. 'It could be your undoing.'

'More than likely. You know what they say: Live by the slip, die by the slip.'

'Who says that?'

The front door of the house opened and a rumble of feet filled the hallway. Donoghue made a face like he wanted to get out of the room quickly, but it was too late. The children burst in, and the strangest thing happened: they ran straight over to Donoghue and grabbed his hands. They were shouting, calling him Oscar, telling him to do it again, show us the trick. Go on Oscar, please. Murt looked at Ursula, who seemed to know what was going on. She told them to leave Oscar alone and to go change out of their school uniforms. They weren't having any of it.

Donoghue stood up slowly between the two tittering children, opened his arms wide above their heads. They stared at his hands, like pups waiting on a crust. Murt had no idea what happened then, but cheers and claps erupted and the children were gone, shrieking, out of the room. Donoghue tried to suppress a grin as he fixed his cuffs.

'One of those, what you call them?' he said. 'Family heirlooms, that trick.'

'What were you looking for in here anyway?' Murt asked.

'My notes.'

He saluted the air with an empty hand and left the room.

For once Murt was glad of all the disturbance. What he had read was too much to take in, too much to be left thinking about in the silence. He would read it again later and try to get his head around it. For the first time he realised that maybe soon he and his daughter would meet. On the other hand, Donoghue now knew a lot more than Murt wanted him to.

# a beating

I'm far from proud of myself. A few times when I was off my head with the drink, I went over to Kathleen's house and demanded that they give her back to me. The sergeant always showed up and took me away. Kathleen and Helen watched from the doorway. I probably frightened them, shouting and roaring like a madman. The courts had spoken. They had given Kathleen legal guardianship. And the sergeant was losing patience. I'll have to put you in a cell, he said, if you keep this up. Do you hear me, Doran? It's harassment, what you're at. Judge Buachall takes a very dim view of that kind of thing. Those women are looking after her now. You're in no state— look at yourself. Look at myself. That was the last thing I could do.

I called them witches and all sorts for poisoning her against me. You're happy now, I shouted at Helen. Here I am, exactly what you said—an itinerant. You're not fit to be a father, she said. Look at yourself. Why was everyone so obsessed with my appearance?

I was never brave enough to go past the front gate, just stood there shouting. I knew there was no point in what I was doing. The sergeant was right. It was pure harassment. They were all right. I limped off, back to the village, where people turned their faces away when they saw me coming.

Months later—one of the last times—I went to the house and saw Foley. There was always going to be a last time, when I'd go too far. It was raining. Soaked after walking to the village for a bottle, I found myself heading for their house. I did my usual rant from the gate, and when no one showed at the door, I threw stones at the windows and put one in. This was already too far. The door flung open, and Helen surprised me with a smile on her face. Well at last, the smile said, you've done something that the sergeant can prosecute you for. Thank you, she said. That's the last we'll be seeing of you. Might as well hang around, he's on his way. Not as if he won't find you anyway.

Kathleen looked frail beside Helen—she hadn't long left then I think—and I could see someone else, another head behind them. I wiped the rain from my eyes. A figure stepped forward and a familiar face appeared between the two women. Foley, I said, what the fuck are you doing here? He was the same pale stick I remembered, but something was different about him. He stood smirking as I eyed him a while longer. The suit—he was wearing a suit. Not a funeral suit, but a business get-up. Helen put her hand on his shoulder then as if to hold him back, as if his new image gave him the confidence to do something about me. Fucking Foley, I said, you sleeveen.

There was nothing left to do but laugh. Maybe I remembered that laughing at Foley was something he didn't like—drove him crazy. It was all I had to try cut him down. I started laughing. Next thing, here he comes taking big strides towards the gate like he wants to hit me. I knew he wouldn't do it. On either side of the gate now, head to head, he takes a big snort through his nose and spits in my face. Warm lumpy saliva ran down my cheek. It wasn't difficult to pull him across the gate. Between the rain and the anger in my eyes, I lost control. His head got smaller, farther away, every time I hit it. As I realised what I was doing and my hands became my own again, he slipped from my grip. He slumped onto the wet ground, holding himself like a beaten dog. I stood over him until the sergeant grabbed my arms and wrestled me into the patrol car.

# 14

The wind got under the gutters, twisted and snaked its way past the wallplate and into the workshop. At the gable, a loose sheet of galvanised iron was getting a good going over. Between violent clatters, as if being beaten with a stick, it trembled. Rain pelted the tin roof, filling the shed with static noise.

Murt found the pinhole in the lamp again and cleaned around it. New metal showed brilliantly under the file. He rubbed away the fine shavings with his thumb. In the window above the bench, a cracked and loose glass pane rapped itself in a panic against the frame. He twisted a length of solder around his finger. The light bulb swayed above his head. Holding the solder steady over the tiny hole it hissed against the hot iron. Molten drops lumped onto the cleaned metal. He touched the hot tip against the edges, kept the solder molten until it bonded. When it had cooled, he took the chamber from the vice, rubbed it with a rag and blew into it. The hole was sealed. After screwing the lamp back together, he stood it on the bench. The solder stain on the brass looked good, he thought, like a scar that said it had lived.

He tidied up, locked the workshop and went back into the house. The first thing he saw was a pile of broken glass in the kitchen sink, a splash of red on the countertop. Carefully, he lifted out the pieces, wrapped them in newspaper and put them in the bin. He noticed the smell then, something cooking, burning—plastic melting. He checked the cooker: the knobs were all turned off. Hinges whined as he opened the oven door. Nothing. Then he saw it: the grill was switched on. He turned it off and pulled open the door. The tray handle had melted to a pile of tar-black sludge. Smoke, like a mix of solder and ammonia, gripped his throat. Covering his mouth with his sleeve, he ducked and ran to open the windows and back door. Almost in a panic now, he grabbed a towel and started to fan the poisoned air.

A dazed Ursula appeared in the doorway and the glass she was holding knocked against the doorjamb and fell from her hand. Too drunk and confused to be shocked, she tried to help. Murt told her to go to the living room, that he would clean up. He would not tell her what she wanted to hear because it was not true: not to worry, it was an accident, could have happened to anyone, everything would be fine. No, not that. The house could have burnt to the ground and killed the children.

She crouched by the broken glass and lost her balance. When she stood up, blood ran along her arm to the elbow and began to drip on the tiled floor. Holding her wrist, she staggered towards the sink, leaving a trail of unjoined red dots across the floor. Murt turned her hand under running water. Drops of blood exploded, diluting as they hit the stainless steel sink. He wrapped her hand in a towel.

'Do you think I need stitches?'

'Maybe not,' he said.

She bit her lip as she looked around. The kitchen resembled a fight scene. Her face grew longer, then contracted as the tears came. Murt told her to go into the front room, that he would sort it out.

'It's all right,' he said, forgetting his promise to himself; 'don't worry.'

When he had cleaned up the kitchen, he brought her in a cup of tea, but she had found another glass of wine from somewhere.

'Is it a rocket you're building?' she asked.

'A rocket?'

'Out in the shed. To take you away from here.'

A few ambers glowed in the fire grate. Murt threw on a stick and shook some coal over the top. He told her about the carbide lamp and she said yes, she remembered now—the girl who looked like his daughter, Gráinne. If she asked about Gráinne now, he might tell her everything, such was his mood. The stick crackled and a lump of coal slipped down behind. Ursula looked at him as she drank, feet tucked up beside her legs.

'I saw you got a letter.'

He watched the giddy flames dance.

'From Gráinne.'

This was big news to a drunken Ursula and she waved her free hand in excitement. He told her about the photograph and how he felt like he had played a trick.

'You do what you have to do,' she said.

Surprised to find her glass empty, she excused herself. Murt wondered if the conversation was over. He knew that it should be, but he didn't get up. Flames jostled in the grate like a nestful of eager chicks.

When she returned, she took a silver photo frame from the mantelpiece and stared at the picture, drowsy-eyed.

'There they are,' she said. 'Never a cross word between them.'

'When was it taken?'

'Their honeymoon. Sligo, I think.'

She told Murt that her father had died a few years before from Motor Neurone Disease.

'Shut him down piece by piece. To think you could live your whole life and then watch yourself fall apart like that. It's in the genes too.'

She replaced the picture and sat on the couch.

'What about your parents?' she asked.

'My mother died a long time ago. I lived with my uncle then.'

'You want to make things right with Gráinne. I can see that it's hurting you.'

Had he let this develop between them? Ursula's eyes were wide and sad with the drink. Was he pathetic to her? She felt sorry for the life he had. Well, it was his life, he had lived it, done the things he had done, made his choices. He did not want pity. Her hand touched his shoulder, and it was careful. Her finger brushed against his neck then through his hair. Everything about this was wrong, surely she knew that too. And yet, here she was, moving towards him, leaning forward, eyes fixed but lost.

The spell was broken by the wine, as if it needed to make amends for the mischief it had already caused. The glass in her hand was at such an angle that the wine dribbled onto the floor. Ursula stared at it for a moment then straightened the glass. Murt stayed still. Grasp a thought, say something. Quickly then, as if a window had been thrown open to the wind, Ursula sat up. She looked at the glass in her hand, she looked around the room and finally, she looked at Murt. Slowly, she stood.

'I have to go.'

Murt was rooted to the couch. He needed to get his thoughts straight about what had just happened, or didn't happen, or had nearly happened. He watched the fire fade to cinders and did not stir until the room was dark.

# 15

It was early evening when Murt pulled into Quinn's yard. Clouds cruised the sky like sharks, white-bellied and grey-backed. Crows skulked in the trees. Winter was stirring. He found Quinn in the shed and helped him to shake straw underneath the animals. They spoke little until the job was done.

'You have them all in now?' Murt asked.

'Just about. A few dry cows in the Slough Field yet.'

They filled up a sack of meal to feed the weanling calves. Quinn scratched the animals' backs with a stick as they ate.

'Did you get the lamp going?'

'Not yet. Nearly. I soldered up the hole.'

'Good.' He pointed across the yard to a new tractor. 'Pick up a bale of silage there with that.'

'Well, it's about time,' Murt said. He took the new tractor out to the field, and got a bale from behind the sheds. Quinn waited at the cattle feeder with his penknife to cut plastic and chords from the bale.

'Grand machine all right,' Murt said, climbing down out of the cab. 'Long overdue.'

'I don't know myself now.'

Murt followed him across the yard towards the office.

'Just have to feed this calf and we'll be done.'

Quinn always called the small shed beside the feed store his office. Here he kept things like tools, wet gear, medicines, sprays. As the kettle boiled, Quinn mixed a measure of powered milk in a bucket with some cold water.

'Anything strange up your way?'

'I got a letter from Gráinne.'

'Be the holy! That is news.'

'I think she might be interested in meeting.'

The kettle clicked off, and Quinn poured hot water into the bucket, tested the temperature with his finger and added another drop. Murt told him about the story Gráinne had sent him and about Helen, Foley and the mill.

'Sounds like a man on the edge,' Quinn said.

The calf threw its head at the bucket as he sucked, and milk splashed into the air.

'Go easy! Mad whore of a calf, this one.'

'Not sure what's going to happen,' Murt said. 'Helen's out to get me.'

'She might soften. Stay out of her way, I suppose, is the best thing. She doesn't have to know about any meeting, does she? You can take it from there after that.'

He put down the empty bucket and rubbed the calf's neck.

'Barney's me auld pet, aren't you, Barney? Loves an auld scratch too. Get him a handful of meal. There's Start-a-Calf in that bag.'

Quinn washed out the milk bucket and they headed across the yard to the house.

'Is Rose here?' Murt asked.

'In here filling out the forms. She's a great woman with the books. Only for her. Sure it's all paperwork now—from Europe. Big Brother, Rose calls them. They're watching us from the satellite, arguing with me about how many acres I have, as if I didn't know.'

Surprised to see Murt, Rose gathered up the papers into a file and left the lot on the dresser before giving him a hug.

'Would you ever ring ahead, let us know? Bloody trick or treat with you always.'

'You may stay for dinner anyway,' Quinn said.

They talked about the same things as usual, and Murt could never get tired of it—neighbours, the village, the price things had gone in the Co-op. Quinn said his last bill was crazy money. 'And, to make it worse, when I checked it over, hadn't they charged me twice for some of the stuff?'

After dinner, they got talking about Gráinne. The old dog, having been tossed a few scraps, finally settled at Quinn's feet. Murt had brought the letter with him and they were quiet while Quinn read the story. When he'd finished, he handed it to Rose and sat with a puzzled look until he spoke again.

'Of course,' he said, 'Daddy used to write a bit of poetry.' Rose shushed him, but he felt he was on to something. 'And wasn't Cathy a teacher? The knack would be in her all right, for the writing like.'

'Very interesting,' said Rose, folding the pages and handing them to Murt.

'I have his little notebook somewhere,' Quinn said.

'She sounds happy,' Rose said.

Quinn straightened himself in the chair, let out a gravelly cough and looked at Rose.

'Well,' he said, 'she's not so happy that she wouldn't be interested in meeting her real father. Two different things altogether.'

Rose suddenly agreed and added a stern look to her nod.

'So, Mr Foley is in Balroe,' she said. 'They can't stop you two meeting, if Gráinne wants to.'

'They took my letter, tried to keep it from her. And there was the other incident; they know about that.'

He looked to Quinn whose face was telling him to be quiet, not to say any more because Rose did not know.

'Something that happened a few years ago,' Murt said to Rose. 'They'll try to use it against me, if I keep trying to contact Gráinne.'

'Why?'

'Pride,' Quinn said. 'And money, of course. What else? They go hand in hand.'

They talked about the mill then, and Kiltuam. It was only a matter of time before the subject of his cottage was brought up, and Murt knew what they were going to say.

'You should have let the place go, got a few pound for it when you could.'

'No one would want it now,' Murt said.

His wry smile was not understood. They knew he wouldn't part with the cottage, and although they might not agree, they respected his standpoint. Somewhat defeated, or bored, Rose took out a pack of cards and laid out a game of Patience on the table—she was able to talk and play. When Quinn stood up, without lifting her head from counting, flipping, laying cards, she gave him a warning.

'Not too much now, remember.'

Quinn threw back his head and grumbled to himself before returning with the whiskey.

'The tablets he's on,' she said, glancing at Murt. 'They thin his blood.'

The dog stirred too, ambled over to Murt and stood looking at him until he reached out a hand.

# 16

The foyer of the Moss Hotel glowed with a vague orange light. A brandy glass appeared beyond the armrest, and was met in mid-air by another. Cheers. Sláinte. They laughed like old gentry men. A long mirror above the fireplace revealed to Murt what he could not see as he approached the high-backed armchairs—the dusty reflections of two men slouched askew in an armchair each. They had the place to themselves. Apart from the blazing fire, the light was dull from bulbs caked with dust.

They did not recognise his reflection when they looked up. Another guest perhaps? A lonely traveller looking for company and a stiff drink beside the fire?

'Care to join us, good sir?' Donoghue said, without stirring from his position.

'Grab yourself a glass,' Foley added.

Murt stood in front of them. They looked at each other unfazed. Foley attempted to square himself but gave up on it and took a sip from his glass.

'A drink?'

'He's off it,' Donoghue said.

'Good for you, Murt.'

'I'm sure you knew that already,' Murt said, sitting down.

Donoghue looked to be half-asleep. His face was fixed with an idiotic grin. Foley stared at the brandy swirling in his glass as he spoke.

'You know what it is, Murt? We're not that different at the end of the day. Your place, the place where you are, is very close to the place where I am. We're side by side, swimming in all this shite.'

'What have you told him, Oscar?' Murt asked, nodding to Donoghue, whose head jolted an acknowledgement.

'Balroe isn't a bad place,' Foley said. 'Lounging around this time warp of a hotel—I could get used to it.'

'And what has he told you?'

Donoghue spilt brandy on himself and lurched forward as Eliza appeared in the doorway. She was surprised to see Murt sitting at the fire when she walked through. She spoke without stopping.

'The pleasure is all mine, Murt,' she said. 'After dark and all. To what do I owe it?'

Donoghue's grinning eyes followed Eliza's strut.

'Another drink?' he said, as he stood up and put a hand on Foley's shoulder to steady himself. 'More brandy.'

When he was out of earshot, Foley said, 'Helen rings me for updates, while I'm here. Wants me to find out if you're into any, you know, illegal stuff. The more we have on you, the more we can throw at you to strengthen our cause. That's the theory—her theory.'

'What about your cause? Does she know about that? The friends who set you up in business.'

'No. Maybe. I don't know. What does it matter?'

From the other room, the tiny bar, they could hear Donoghue and the cackle and titter of a woman's voice.

'The thing is, Murt, there's nothing to find out about you.'

'And yet here you are still.'

'I'm trying to understand—you've got this life of very little that you're ok with. Only one thing would make you a happy man, and I'm doing my best to keep that one thing from you. Why do you think that is?'

'It would kill you to know that I might be all right in life. You always wanted what everyone else had, and you'd do whatever it took to get it. You're not happy with your lot; never will be.'

Foley sat forward, elbows on the armrests, shoulders bunched.

'There's a lust inside me, Murt. A lust for everything I don't yet have. It drives me. It drives me and drives me and eats away at me.'

Donoghue came back whistling, or trying to whistle. The effort of leaning over to place Foley's glass on the table caused him to wobble. He suppressed a belch and looked at Murt and Foley.

'Excuse me, gentlemen. I shall return.'

On releasing his trapped air, he swayed towards the bar again.

'I have nothing you could want,' Murt said. 'Tell me why you're here. There's something else.'

'I don't know what it's like, being content—what a shit word that is. I've always had this burning need to take what someone else has, to take it from them and be better than them, to cut them down. You think it's a poison.'

'You don't?'

'What am I without it?'

'I wonder would you be saying these things if you weren't broke. Don't tell me it's sympathy you want.'

Surprised for a moment, he looked at Murt, then returned his gaze to the fire, nodding slowly. 'No, not sympathy. I don't expect that. I'm after something else. What am I after? I don't know. Is there something else for my kind?'

He downed his drink, picked up the fresh glass and flopped back into the chair. Murt was not interested in his broken man story, but there was something of the old Sticks in him now—the way he threw the brandy into him and sat staring at the fire.

'Helen thinks the mill will save us. If she only knew. I don't have the balls to tell her.'

'It's Gráinne's isn't it? Kathleen left her the mill.'

He downed the full measure of brandy. After a fit of coughing, he stared into the glass.

'She left us the rest, and still it wasn't enough. We could have got a lot of money for that mill at one stage.'

From the bottom of his stomach, Murt laughed for a long time, and it was not pettiness at Foley's demise. He was not trying to get one over on him. It was relief at the final card being turned. Foley watched him, unsure whether to join in or to read the laughter as an insult.

'I tried to make something of my life,' he said. 'You just cowered and ran.'

'So that's the reason—you and Helen think I'll go after the mill, get my grubby hands on it?'

Foley's brow straightened back to indifference when he too now realised the cards were out.

'I suppose you wouldn't, but there's no talking to Helen. Why do you think I'm still here?'

'Because you're afraid to face her, to tell her the truth—that you're ruined.'

'The family, it's all she has. It'd kill her to lose Gráinne.'

'Lose her? All I want is to spend some time with her, get to know her. I've a lot of making up to do.'

Foley was too drunk now to care either way. Even when Murt broke the next news to him, his head just bobbed up and down, side to side.

'She found my letter, you know. She wrote back. I'm going to meet her.' He told Foley that he did not want the mill. All he wanted was to see his daughter. He was going to arrange a meeting and Foley was going to help. There was a long silence. Foley tipped both of the already empty glasses into his mouth again and looked around for more. Murt went to the bar but there was no sign of Donoghue or Eliza. He poured another brandy and left money by the till.

When he returned, Foley's head was slumped against his shoulder. Murt kicked his legs and showed him the glass.

'What about Donoghue?' Murt asked.

'Probably down the back with Eliza.'

'You know about the money he owes?'

Foley sat up and looked at Murt as he reached for the brandy.

Murt continued, 'What about your friends—the shower who set you up. Could they help him?'

'I've no sway, never did. Sure isn't it them he owes.'

From the moment it got dark, the November sky was black and empty. Murt could not remember the last moon. Miles away, the Protestant church's bell was sounding like you might see the flash of a lighthouse way off in the darkness. He stood outside the guest house and listened. A rare thing, bells tolling.

He remembered sitting in the porch of a Protestant church as a boy, cracking open hazelnuts on the flagstoned floor. He was ten or eleven. All those years were the same to him. Everything he remembered as a boy seemed to have happened in the same year—the year before his mother went to Dublin. It was as if he had only lived for one year, only known his mother for that one year, before she died.

They had gathered the hazelnuts in their bags, himself and another boy from school. There was a hazel tree beside the Protestant church, overhanging the headstones. Not wanting to get too close to the Protestant graves, they picked nuts from the long grass by the ditch. The church looked the same as their own except for the windows, which were plain glass in a diamond pattern, and a big square tower at the front which had a door that was locked.

Finding the nuts in the schoolbag was an ordeal. They sat in the porch of the Protestant church fishing around between books and pencils and what was left of their lunches. In the end, they emptied the whole lot out onto the flagstones. The nuts rolled like oblong marbles. They looked for the biggest nuts, picked them out and kept them until last. They were focused on their own stash and did not speak, or they spoke very little, as if words would spoil the music of cracking shells. Shoe in hand was the best method they discovered. The nuts were like dry sweets and they chewed several at a time as they smashed more shells. When all the nuts had been eaten, they scattered the shells across the flagstone floor like dice. They shook handfuls and flung them up in the air, all the time chewing nuts, spitting out bits of shell. Before Murt reached home, the cramps kicked in.

He laughed to himself now outside the guest house. He could still see the other boy—what was his name?—the oversized head and bulging eyes, like he was bursting with divilment. How he walloped those hazelnuts, tongue clasped between his teeth.

His mother found out that he had been at the Protestant church, and he was told to stay away, that the priest would not be happy if he knew about this cavorting. Nor the rector either. You keep to your own, she said. He couldn't understand how people from the same place could be divided by this invisible line, and yet they were. People categorised and divided by something, some idea or belief. And that group in turn could be divided and so on until the only thing left was an individual—everybody, ultimately, left on their own.

Keep to your own, whoever your own are supposed to be.

He imagined people trickling into the church now as the night bell called them, broken shells crackling beneath their shoes. And they might look down and wonder, look to each other in surprise, but they would not say a word while the bell tolled in the tower above them.

One Sunday, he hid in the ditch near the hazelnut tree. The Protestants walked slower and were better dressed, but other than that he could see little difference. It was only later, when Quinn talked to him about how the country was, that he began to understand what the words Catholic and Protestant meant. It was more to do with people than with God. They said the same prayers to the same God, but one crowd belonged here and the other did not. And he could always sense something: that the Protestants were not wanted, that they were allowed to stay because there were only a few of them, but a close eye had to be kept on them. Where had all that gone, Murt wondered now—the distrust? Or if it was gone. Things like that did not seem to matter to people any more, but back then it was ingrained in the thinking, vital to the very future of the country.

When he opened the guest house door, Donoghue surprised him in the porch. He was muttering to himself as he rushed past Murt: October, November, Christmas. A layer of sandy stubble covered his face in grains.

'Everything all right, Oscar?'

He batted a hand in the air and closed the door behind him. Through the side window, Murt saw the lights of a car approach and stop down at the gateway.

Ursula was in the front room. If she had been avoiding Murt, he did not mind. It was better to let what had happened between them fade or settle or whatever memories needed to do to stop slapping you in the face.

If she had not spilled her wine, would he have stopped it from happening? It had been a long time for him. Maybe it was the attention that had made him stay there on the sofa when he should have left, the attention that made him wait for her approach. How had the situation developed? Attraction had masked itself, dressed itself up in drink and loneliness and tried to fool them both. He hoped this was true. She loved the children. She missed her family and was trying hard to fix herself. It would have been wrong.

She busied herself not looking at him now. She talked fast, as if there was no time to lose on whatever she was not doing.

'Just in from the hospital,' she said. 'She's not well at all. Bloody doctors. And you'd think in this day and age, what with all they can do now–.'

'How's the finger?' Murt asked as he sat down.

They were only one look away from the conversation that neither of them wanted to have.

'Not too bad, thanks.'

'Good. I thought we were going to lose it.'

She laughed, relieved that her struggle for words, despite all the babble, was not necessary.

'I nearly burnt the place down,' she said, putting her hands to her face.

'You did.'

'Ray says I need the meetings.'

When she went out to the kitchen, he wondered if she would go for the stash again—that was how it worked. You want to give up so badly, but you're not sure if you can. Doubt has an awful thirst. Checking on her would do no good. It was her battle, not his. He heard the kettle boil, and she came back in with two cups of tea. She agreed that Donoghue had been acting strangely.

'He looks rough, rougher than usual,' she said.

A newspaper lay open on the table, pen scribbles in the margins—betting odds, amounts of money, totals. The figures were much bigger than a man like Donoghue should have been dealing with.

'Maybe he's in trouble,' she said.

'The gambler's life.'

'But this much?'

'As he says himself, good days and bad days.'

They sat then in silence as an easy fire flickered in front of them. The flame reached a wick of withered ivy that hung from a log. It flared for a few seconds and died away.

# IV

# Stones

# the cottage

Turn off the main street at Curran's and you're on Station Road. It used to be pure countryside out that way, only the odd house interrupting the landscape. Our cottage was about two miles outside Kiltuam on a plot of land cut from the corner of a field. Neighbours were more than a stone's throw in any direction.

I always thought the cottage was out of place on its own. It looked like it belonged with other houses, the sort you might pass coming in to a village—five or six identical cottages in a row, neighbours talking to each other across low walls and hedges, front doors left open for people to wander in, to talk and drink tea and look around, pick things up, put them down. Ours was that kind of a cottage but without the neighbours.

There were trees all around us and the greeny-damp shadows of forests touched everything. Some days were darker than others. Without Cathy, the shadows never lifted. When they took Gráinne away from me, it was black dark. Then there was the fire. It gutted the place, left bits of rafters like black ribs sticking into the air. I couldn't look at them and eventually cut them down. It took a long time to clean out the place. Everything was burnt and charred. There wasn't much worth keeping. What was left was a roofless shell, as if the top half of the house had been sliced off or never finished. The cottage was there, it existed, but there was no life or soul. Bones without skin.

I bought the caravan to tide me over till I fixed the house. A belt of vexed wind could tilt the thing on its side. Some nights, in a stupor, I woke up not knowing what angle I was at. I held on to whatever I could. Days were no better. There was nowhere to get away from myself except for the bottle. I adapted, isn't that what they say we're best at? Time passes—that's one thing I learned. The years don't be long going. I can't say I didn't think about what would become of me living like that, but there were no solutions or conclusions. Routine kept me alive. I numbed myself to not thinking by making every day the same.

Visitors were rare. After Cathy, neighbours dropped in with things. They offered help, the odd bottle. Once they realised what I was doing with their generosity, they weren't long getting offended. Soon they only slowed down to have a good gawk as they drove past.

Who was the last person I expected to see there? People always say that. One of those stupid sayings to make a situation more unbelievable. The last person I expected to see was Cathy, but Reilly would have been a close second.

I remember it was a slimy-damp morning, and from the caravan window I saw a car stop by the gate. Reilly got out. I didn't recognise him at first. He stood by the car for a long time, as if he was unsure about the address or of what he was doing there. The small gate squealed on its hinges. He walked steadily along the pathway, his open trench coat rippling at the bottom like a dress. He held it together as he passed the threshold of the cottage and stepped inside the charred shell. Who did he think he was? I leapt from the caravan and went after him.

It's not for sale, I said, thinking he would turn, but he just looked right and left as if trying to get something straight in his head before facing me. The kitchen, I said, is where it started. When he eventually looked at me and smiled, I was a bit overcome at the sight of him. We shook hands.

I said, This was the sitting room we're in now. Come on, in here. He followed me to the kitchen and walked around the perimeter of the room. He asked if it was the wiring. No, I said, my fault—the cooker. He touched the walls, smelled his fingers and rubbed them together as if sprinkling the soot. You own the place? he asked. I do. He nodded slowly, still looking around. I couldn't take my eyes off him. What kind of a man had he become? The last time I'd seen him he was nearly a man, but not quite. There was something about him, a self-control or a confidence that he might have worked very hard at. I remember thinking he was the kind of man that would look good at a funeral, in a long black gabardine. For a start, he was taller than most people so he would be seen. The hair was freshly combed into a neat parting. He wore a pair of silver-rimmed glasses that tinted in daylight, hiding his eyes. The moustache made him look official. And the way he stood there, his head titled back with a friendly *isthatso?* look on his face. You'd see him in a crowd all right and you'd wonder who he was and what he had to say.

That caravan, he said, breaking into a smile, it's comfortable? For a moment he was the Reilly I remembered. I wanted him to throw an arm around me and tell me things would be better from now on. His eyes were busy though, like he was a few steps ahead in a discussion he'd had many times before. Not really, I said, but I'm scarce on options.

We walked out the back, down through the weeds and wild grass and turned to look at the cottage from the rear. After much squinting and tilting of his head, he said to me, What about insurance? I shook my head. Pity, he said. You should have talked to me when you moved in. We could have sorted all that out. If you need a hand now, to get started like.

Without the smile, he wore a mask that I couldn't read. I laughed and asked him why he had really come to see me. You know as well as I do, Murt, this is a small country. A man in my position, not much gets past me. We were friends for a time, he said. We were only chaps, I said. Are we not still, he said, at heart? He flashed the smile again, and I wanted to believe we were the same boys from school, the two eejits who jumped into a van with no idea where we were going and slammed the door shut behind us. We haven't seen each other, Reilly said. That doesn't mean I forgot about you. You often cross my mind. Loyalty is important. I told him he hadn't come to rekindle friendships either. There's nothing to rekindle, he said. Was it ever lost?

We walked around to the front of the house, and he repeated the squinting routine as he visualised something that had left me a long time before—a future for the place. Could make a fine job of this spot, Murt. That was all very easy for him to say. To change the subject, I asked him how his sister was, and he paused for a second. Sarah's Sarah, he said. Will we go in for a swift one? He pointed to the caravan.

I didn't want him in the caravan. Maybe I was afraid of being confined in such a small space with him. Outside in the open was fine but inside there would be no distractions. It'd be him and me face to face across the plank-wide table. I didn't know what he really wanted to say. What had changed in the years since I left to get away from those people? He was right about one thing—the country was small. Only place a man could really get lost was inside of himself.

The caravan's low roof took something from the shape of him and he had to stoop forward inside. All I had left was a few dribbles of Jemmie. Grand, he said, looking around. He struggled out of his coat and sat down. Big changes on the horizon in the organisation, he said. A lot of opinions and loyalties divided. Maybe it's no harm. Getting more difficult to know who to trust, he said. I asked him if he'd ever thought of stepping back or getting out altogether. He smiled like he'd been expecting the question. I do often wonder, he said, where I'd be now if I'd left with you that time. Not in a caravan anyway, I said. Reilly offered his glass to the air, tilted it towards mine. He took a big gulp of the whiskey and savoured it for a long time.

Do you know that he's getting released soon, he said. I wished that I didn't know this, that I'd lost count of how long it had been. I'd hoped that when the day came, it would pass me by and I'd be none the wiser. But that was never going to happen. I had been keeping track. I knew the exact day. What happened to Cathy, Reilly said, was terrible. I wanted to come to the funeral but you know, with him involved, it wouldn't have looked good. I sent flowers. I told him I knew about the flowers, and thanked him. Anyway, he said, I'm sorry.

Did he think I might hold a grudge against him for not going to the funeral? Was it guilt that had brought him there to see me? I could have laughed. It didn't make one blind bit of a difference who had showed up at the funeral, nobody could have brought Cathy back. And yet there he was, for whatever reason. I knew it wasn't guilt. I can't explain why, but somehow it was important to him. He hadn't forgotten me.

I just thought I'd let you know, he said, in person, see if I could do anything for you. He looked up from his swirling glass then and his words spun too, open in the air around us. And our faces were close—the kind of distance that truth is spoken at. How long had it been since I'd held someone's stare or since they'd held mine?

You're a mess, Murt. Do you even have a mirror? You need to get out of here. After this, in a few weeks, leave here. Go somewhere else for a while. Somewhere where the memories aren't as strong. Give the memories time to drain. Surely you want to see your daughter eventually. Not like this—you know that.

I remembered then what it felt like to be grateful. For someone being fair and honest, nothing much. Sometimes it's the simplest thing, the fewest words—or no words at all—that can help. It was important that he left then and he understood this. He'd given me something and I needed him to leave me with that.

I walked with him to the gate. We shook hands as friends still. He said, She's doing well, Gráinne. Don't worry about Foley—his day will come.

After he had driven off, I stood by the gate for a long time listening to it squeal as I swung it open and closed. Then I went to get oil for the hinges.

# 17

Soaked in winter sun, the afternoon landscape crawled with deep colours, making it difficult to tell shadow from tree among the browns, greens and evergreens. Red-nosed tourists—teenagers, couples, families—snapped pictures; they pointed and spoke in different languages.

She walked beside Murt.

'You live in a guest house?'

It was the first question she had asked him.

'Supposed to be temporary, until the council gives me another place.'

He told her what had happened with the building collapsing and she laughed. It had never struck him as funny before.

They were walking along a gravel path among the maze of tracks and forest walkways above the lower lake.

'I can drive myself,' she said, 'but he insisted on bringing me. Helen will kill him if she finds out about this; and you too.'

She glanced over and smiled. Her gestures made no sense to him. If he could gather his thoughts, stop thinking that the situation was a set-up or a trap, then maybe he could relax. He felt as if he was being followed by shadows not cast by the sun—shadows of questions to come and memories resurrected. Any moment now he would be found out. When do you start saying sorry?

She was holding the photograph he had sent. She wanted the story behind it, where it was taken and by whom; what age he and her mother were then.

'And the house,' she said. 'What happened to it?'

He told her about the fire and she did not seem surprised, as if she knew already.

'You don't have much luck with houses.'

'Never thought about it like that.'

'You didn't sell it, the cottage?'

'No, it's a shell. I meant to rebuild it.'

'It looks nice—here in the picture, I mean.'

The pathway narrowed to single file where part of the track and fence had fallen away. There were warning signs, and tourists stood peering over the edge.

'When did it happen, the fire? Was it long after she died? My mother—Cathy.'

'Not long, no.'

A little farther on, the track forked, and they followed a sign for the upper lake.

'When did you leave Kiltuam?' she asked, drawing out the final letters—something which Kiltuam people would never do. 'We lived there too for a while, I think.'

'We all lived there,' he said. 'Still do in a way.'

'I want to go and have a look sometime. What's it like?'

'Same as most places—rural.'

'That's your thing?.'

'I suppose it is.'

If she was nervous or unsure, it did not show. He had expected a cool reception. Where was the hostility? Her tone was friendly, a bit detached. And yet this was her, the same person who had written the story.

'That's a grand bit of writing you sent me.'

'If it wasn't true maybe.'

The path fell away sharply and changed to steps as they descended towards the edge of the upper lake. A small beach-like shore of pebbles separated grass from the water's edge. Valley and sky reflected exactly in the black stillness.

'We learned about this place in school,' she said. 'Geography and History. How the valley was formed, and the monastery.'

'You've never been here before?'

'No, it's nice though—peaceful.'

The valley greens were sheer all around them. Pines and spruces scaled the sides. She pointed to the top of the valley's face where trees could not survive in the exposure and a few bare, grey trunks remained standing.

'Look at those,' she said. 'Like giant bones speared into the hillside.'

Close by, two boys kicked pebbles out of their hands. The pebbles arced high in the air and disappeared into the water with a plop, causing ripples that creased the reflections.

'Why did you wait so long?' she asked in a low voice.

A woman called out to the boys, beckoned them towards her. They flung their remaining stones in the air to rain down on the lake. He was caught off guard. Had she been luring him into an easy conversation, waiting to disarm him like this? He had expected this question, had imagined it would give him a chance to explain, but now the answer was far from clear to him. Where to start?

'I don't know,' he said, regretting it straight away.

She turned towards him—he had better start explaining.

'No, I do know. Guilt, self-pity.'

'You're a coward, you mean.'

They walked in silence as he thought about this. Through the woods, they came to a riverbank. Trees on both sides shared branches across the river's breadth where the water was clear, but dark to the bottom.

He said, 'When do reasons become excuses? I was drunk for years—a mess. It took me a long time to get my head around what had happened. By the time I copped myself on, I hadn't the guts, didn't want to intrude, make things worse for you.'

'So why now?'

'I think I've run out of excuses. Not before time, I suppose.'

Light broke through the canopy, and Murt could see stones deep in the river bed, showing as nuggets of rust and gold.

'I didn't think Helen would intercept the letter,' he said.

'You don't know Helen then.'

'I know her.'

'She's not that bad—just crazy. And she hates you. What happened?'

'Lots of small things. She didn't agree with your mother and me, and then blamed me for what happened.'

Farther on, where the banks widened, the waters swelled and were still. A fallen branch across the water held a crescent of foam. They sat on a bench by the gravel path.

'Tell me something about her,' she said.

He was quiet for a while. Somewhere beyond the stillness in front of them, water was racing, maybe spilling over a natural dam of leaves and sticks. What could he tell her about Cathy? His biggest fear: how memories change over time. He tried to think of the small things, of words, mannerisms and imperfections; the kind of things that are triggered or occur in the mind without explanation as life relentlessly continues.

'She used her hands when she spoke,' he said. 'Out in front of her, making something invisible. Must have been the teacher in her. She came up with these ideas and moulded them in her hands until you understood. Or maybe it was hypnotism. Whatever it was, it usually worked. She had that thing, like a lot of people, of speaking before she had thought something through—that's why she needed the hands. She would say something funny and laugh, but then have to go over it again with her hands.'

He kept his gaze fixed ahead, and the river's flow filled the silence between them.

'That day,' she said. 'Where were you? Helen has never talked about it.'

'I was late, forgot to pick her up. She wanted to go over to see Helen and Kathleen.'

Later, people had said to Murt: you weren't driving that car; there's nothing you could have done. They also said: it's not your

193

fault; don't blame yourself. But why was she on the road? He should have been there on time.

'What about the driver of the car?'

'We knew him. He used to go out with your mother.'

'Did he do it on purpose? It was an accident, wasn't it?'

'No, I suppose he didn't. He was drunk. He was a head case. You never know with people.'

'Did you ever see him after?'

'Yes, he's dead now.'

The river had lost its power over Murt. He stood up, nodded towards the path ahead and she walked beside him.

'What happened?'

'There was an accident. Just one of those things.'

They crossed a small hump-backed bridge. He wanted her to see the stone circles, the old church. As they walked back along the far side of the lower lake, he told her what he knew about the monks, some of the tales he had heard. She remembered from school that there was a cave in the valley where the saint had lived.

'I couldn't imagine living in those times,' she said. 'Weren't they so devout?'

'There was nothing else.'

They were on a wooden boardwalk that ran close to the road before it cut back in over the lake's marshy perimeter. Their steps rumbled along the timber platform.

'Did she believe in God?' she asked.

'In her way.'

'And you?'

'No, I don't suppose I ever did.'

'I want to believe. Everything would be easier then, but it's so far-fetched—might as well believe in Santy.'

The boardwalk curved out from a copse of trees and became a gravel track again. She pointed out the round tower as it came into view.

'It's like Rapunzel's tower,' she said.

'Who?'

'The girl with the long hair. It's a famous fable. The prince and the evil witch.'

'Always a prince and a witch.'

'He saved the girl and then fell from the tower and was blinded by thorns at the bottom.'

Tilting her head right back, she looked straight up the tower's face as they walked around it.

'Can't believe it's still here after all this time.'

She touched the stone wall as if it might be hot, then placed her palms against it.

'The monks who made this place were some of the best stone masons in Europe, he said.'

She crouched down and touched the grass, ruffled her hands through it.

'It's so soft, like moss or something.'

She tried not to walk on the graves as she squinted at faded names on headstones.

'Scary,' she said.

'What is?'

'Even headstones will eventually forget who we are.'

They walked around the stone church, and it seemed like an ornament to Murt, as if the whole site had been built as an attraction for these tourists who had no connection with the place, no understanding of its history. It was difficult to relate to the depth of the past.

'Where is she buried? I'd like to visit her grave sometime.'

'In Kiltuam—a quiet place.'

'That whole place sounds quiet.'

'Most of the time it is.'

She peered through the church doorway into the cool, dark interior. The shadows of what they had spoken about hovered between them.

The evening was closing in as they headed back towards the main car park. Tourists were fewer now.

She said, 'I was lucky wasn't I?'

'You were all right.'

The day had changed to grey tones, and a cold mountain wind breathed down the valley.

'We could get coffee,' she said.

They walked down the steps under an old arch that was the original entrance to the settlement. She held up the photograph again and wanted to know more about the house. What about her grandparents—could they not have looked after her?

'You don't remember Kathleen?'

'Sort of. I know about Kathleen, but what about your parents?'

'My mother was killed in Dublin, by a bomb.'

She looked at him in horror.

'Jesus! How old were you?'

'Twelve. I lived with my uncle after that.'

'That's awful.'

'It was.'

'And your father?'

They were at the coffee shop then and Murt rooted through his pocket for change. He gave her a handful of money and said he would have tea. She told him to get a table outside, so he sat and waited for her in the cold.

'It's my choice,' she said when she sat down.

'You're too young, for a start,' he said.

'To smoke?'

'To know better.'

She scoffed.

The aluminium table between them rattled and scratched across the concrete like a smoker's cough. Elbows, knees and lifting cups all had the same effect on the uneven legs. The wind gave it an occasional kick as well. It was a small circular thing. Murt had counted eleven tables while he waited for her, all exactly the same, the chairs too. When his arm glanced against the table edge, coffee and tea slopped from their cups.

'You've never been to a café before?' she asked, laughing.

'I drink my tea in mugs, usually indoors, where there's no wind or rain.'

'This must be an experience for you.'

He tried to wipe the spillage with a paper napkin, but it soaked to a mushy brown. A trickle of coffee moved across the table like a nosey fly. It mixed with the tea, creating another shade of brown.

Murt asked, 'Are you going to go to college?'

'I want to be a scientist.'

'A scientist.'

'I'm fascinated by how things work and the insignificance of it all.'

Murt laughed out loud but stopped when she did not join in.

'We think we are so significant but we aren't. Think about the size of the Earth in the universe, all the stars out there and we only know a small bit about one. I mean, the distance of the sun from here is unreal, and that's the closest star to us. Get your head around that.'

There was an intensity in her as she talked, a passion that was Cathy all over.

'What do you hope to do or prove?'

'I just want to understand.'

'And that's science?'

'Part of it. There is this group of scientists who have built this tunnel under the Alps. They are trying to recreate the beginning of the universe.'

'You want to recreate the universe?'

'I don't know, but isn't that crazy? Sometimes I wonder if the universe is only a tiny speck, nothing but a cell in something infinitely bigger again.'

Her words were like tiny explosions. He looked at her, his daughter whom he did not know, and he saw something beautiful. He saw the possibility of youth. He saw wonder and freedom.

As they walked slowly towards the car park, he hoped that she was in no hurry to leave. She waved across the car park at Foley, who was waiting by the car, fiddling with his phone.

'I have to see this little truck thing of yours,' she said. 'Sounds really cool. Is that it?'

He nodded. Her eyes were wide, and she gasped.

'I love it,' she said.

She was talking in explosions again.

'Can I get in for a second?'

Murt unlocked the door. She got in and held the steering wheel. She looked around left, right, rear mirrors.

'It's great being this high up. My car is tiny, but I'm still only learning.'

She wanted to take it for a drive but Murt said no, that Foley would not be happy.

'What's this?'

She picked something from the seat beside her and held it up to inspect it.

'A carbide lamp. I'm doing it up. Just a little hobby.'

She frowned like she didn't know if this was impressive or strange. Murt told her about the lamp but she seemed indifferent.

'I thought you said you like to know how things work,' he said.

'I do, yes. This is really old?'

'Fairly old all right.'

'Old things make me sad.'

# 18

The elbow work on the lamp had been done out in the workshop with steel wool and a solution from the hardware shop. Polishing was the final stage.

Murt ripped a shirt into rags with cuffs and collars and buttons. When was the last time he had worn the shirt?—a heavy cotton thing with red and blue checks. If he had lots of shirts, he would have called this an old shirt, one for the bin.

He had not seen much of Ursula or Donoghue for a few days. In the front room, he spread an old newspaper on the table and laid out the separate parts of the lamp. He started with the bottom chamber, working the rag over the metal, rolling it in his hands like a piece of fruit. The metal began to reflect the light. He remembered his mother shining cutlery, turning a spoon around in the cloth, stopping to breathe against the bowl, laughing at her inverted reflection.

What would Gráinne think of the lamp when he was finished? She had given him her phone number, said that she would like to meet him again. As he worked the cloth now, bunched to a small bulb to get under a rim, he shook his head. How easy it had been talking to her; the years he had wasted making excuses, convincing himself to stay away. And for what? Guilt had tempered him to expect her not to trust him, to hate him. That was one excuse the guilt had given him. She was right to call him a coward. He had always blocked out this thought—another trick he had played on himself. All those years were like heavy stones of regret which he would now have to carry, stuffed into a sack and flung over his shoulder.

No matter how much he polished, he could not see his face in the metal. It had been through so much over the years that the shine of newness, of youth, had long gone. Things like that cannot be retrieved.

She wasn't angry; she just needed to understand what had happened. And she wanted to know about himself and Cathy, about her real parents—the story was important to her. This pleased Murt more than anything. Even though it was only a few days old, they now had a past; there was hope.

There was also Helen. What would she do when she found out? It was her idea, not Foley's, to try to use what she thought she knew against Murt. She would take it as far as she could, and his life in Balroe would be finished. The Guards would want to question him. Before that, though, Helen would probably come looking for him.

He worked through the lamp's components several times. For the intricate parts, he used the very corners of the cuffs, where the material was stitched tight.

Foley had helped to organise the meeting, facilitated it, as he put it himself. He had no real objection, in the end, to Murt meeting Gráinne. Helen was the instigator, the screw turner. It was easier for Foley to find Murt than to tell Helen the truth. He was hiding from Helen, but also, Murt felt, from something else. The way he was hanging around Balroe, as if he was waiting for an opportunity, the right time. Maybe he now saw Murt, despite all that had happened between them, as an ally in whom he could confide. Or did he need to talk to someone whom he thought was beneath him and who wouldn't judge him?

Impatient to see the finished lamp, Murt hurried the cloth around the reflector's face and started to reassemble it for the final time.

He was still confused about Foley—the parts weren't adding up. What was missing? He considered what he knew: Foley was broke, talking like a man who was chewing the frayed ends of his tether. The last thing he needed was to be judged. A man at the bottom, as Murt knew, did not care. He did not care about what he did next or about the consequences. There was little left to hide from. A man who reckoned he had nothing else to lose was in a pure state of mind—giddy, loose-tongued and likely to talk in truths. Foley still had his family. He was not at the bottom quite yet, but he was close. Murt held up the lamp, rotated it like a carousel in front of his eyes and read the inscriptions:

Made by
Joseph J. Lucas Ltd.
Birmingham
England

Underneath, an embossed line of metal ran around the lower chamber's circumference. Below this he read:

Do not fill carbide above this line

A crude mark which looked like an arrow pointing to the embossed fill level was nothing more than a scratch; one of many which no amount of polish could remove. Murt liked the thing all the more for the damage it had suffered. He pressed his thumb against a curved indentation in the metal—what might have caused that? Did it strike a door frame as its owner rushed from the house? It might have suffered a fall from a bicycle or a clumsy hand. Maybe it had survived with superficial injuries after being flung in anger against some stubborn obstacle?

There was a weight in the metal. You knew you were holding something durable and also something intricate. It needed care, but could handle the knocks. He imagined its beam projected against a plain wall, a dark pie shape nicked from the circle of light by the damage at the reflector's edge. To Murt, it was the imperfections that gave the thing its beauty, its worth. It had taken the knocks and bore the scars. Who could know the exploits such a thing had been through?

Behind him, the door to the front room opened quietly and Donoghue looked in as if checking to see if the room was empty. He seemed to enter reluctantly, closed the door and ambled across the room. A feigned limp accompanied his tuneless whistle. It surprised Murt that Donoghue, despite all the bravado, could not act when he needed to.

He stood shifty-eyed by the window, hands clasped behind his back as if getting heat from a fire.

'That's not a bad day,' he said.

'Not great either.'

It was Donoghue's arms that gave him away—he did not know what to do with them. When he moved towards the chair, Murt saw the bandage. It covered most of Donoghue's right hand. His fingers and thumb were free, the rest was wrapped in white material which disappeared under his sleeve, making it impossible for Murt to know how far up the arm it went. Hoping to disguise the fact, Donoghue held the cuff of his jacket farther down by clasping it against his palm with his fingers. This appeared to be causing him pain. He went for the trouser pocket, but jerked back his arm. Finally, he crossed his arms and used the left elbow as cover, which looked ridiculous when he was still standing. He sat down, licked his lips, bit his cheek, looked around, avoiding Murt's gaze.

When he saw the lamp, he focused on it, wide-eyed.

'Do you have it going?'

'Nearly.'

'Looking well now. And tell me this: would it be worth much?'

'Not really. It was just something to do, to keep me sane.'

'A little project like?'

'That's it.'

'Great. Fair play to you.'

Donoghue produced his newspaper, flicked through it one-handed and grunted when he came to a good story: Be the holy, listen about this lad, he said to Murt, before reading out a few lines. Isn't that a good one? When he shifted, Murt glanced over at the bandaged hand. The game, for Donoghue, was all but up.

'Much stirring today?' Murt asked.

'Some young fella threw a rock through Dwyer's window last night. Little bollox – the place was closed all day.'

'That must have put you out all right.'

'Ordinarily I wouldn't mind, just that I need to have a word, you know yourself, with Dwyer. Where's Ursula and the children?'

'At the hospital. I don't think Mrs Kelleher is too good.'

'Maybe we'll go in and see her again?'

Murt winced at the thought of this. They had visited her a few days after she was taken in. It was the first time Murt had been in a hospital. The stuffy-clean hospital air smelled like a mixture of soup and new plastic. He did not know whether he wanted to sleep or get sick. Hospitals, he decided, were to be avoided.

'By the looks of it,' Murt said, 'you were there earlier.'

Donoghue bought some time for his reply with a confused frown. Murt held his own hand in the air to make his meaning clearer.

'That yoke?' Donoghue scoffed, as he produced his bandaged paw, turning the palm towards himself. 'Nothing at all. Wouldn't mind that, just a scratch. I'll be good as new in a few days.'

'What happened?'

'Had a bit of a fall.'

There was more to it, as they both well knew. No amount of questions would make Donoghue talk if he did not want to. Murt was worried about him—the way he had been acting, the money he owed. He remembered that man who had been up at Cowman's asking about shooting.

Donoghue pulled himself forward in the armchair tug-of-war style. On seeing that Murt was going to help, he switched to bad acting mode, forgot about the pain and staggered forward.

'I'll see you later,' he said.

'Look after yourself.'

'Don't be worrying, Murtagh. I'll be grand.'

In the three or four steps it took Donoghue to get to the door, it was clear that the limp was not an act.

# 19

When the time came that they could afford a bigger house, the Foleys moved counties. Closing the mill meant that they did not need to be in Kiltuam any longer. They didn't sell the mill or whatever other properties they owned, just upped sticks.

The reasons they left Kiltuam were not secret. People around the village knew about Murt's habit of showing up at the Foley's door to torment them. After all that had happened, it was perfectly understandable that they might want a clean slate. Murt too, thought that it was a good idea. So much so that he showed up at their house on the day they were leaving to say good riddance. According to the sergeant, if it wasn't for the circumstances of this being the final act, as he put it, he would have arrested and charged Murt for sure. Murt did not care. He was glad to see the back of the Foleys, but they were taking his daughter with them. At least he would not feel the need to visit them any more, or if he did get the urge, there would be little he could do about it because he would not know where they lived.

He had learned over the years that, given the option, people would rather talk than keep quiet. After asking around, Murt soon found out where the Foleys had moved to. The first time he went to their new home out of curiosity, just to see the place. The second time he watched Helen leaving the house with Gráinne and the boy. They were holding hands, one at either side. What age was Gráinne then? He remembered a navy uniform.

Each time he went there, he kept a good distance—no shouting or harassing.

The third time, Gráinne was a few years older and he saw her out walking with two friends. He was too far away to hear her voice, but he could see her smile. Driving back to Kiltuam that day, he realised it was wrong of him to be watching. That was to be the last time he would go there, until now.

The gates were open, and he drove up the driveway. The house itself was a square two-storey block, an ugly mask of stone with brick corners and reveals. It was showing off, trying to be a farmhouse, but without a screed of character, same as most of the new houses he saw around the countryside.

Helen answered the door herself, and Murt could not tell if she was surprised. After a brief stand-off, she spoke.

'It's hardly trouble you want,' she said. 'Although that's all you've ever brought.'

'No.'

'I suppose you knew that I'd find out about your little meeting— that's why you're here. Come to try and talk some reason into me?'

'You don't think it's time we talked?'

'About what? Cathy? Or is it Gráinne? She's fine. You won't make shite of her life. Or maybe Christopher—we could talk about him. He's going off the rails. Do you know anything about that?'

'I noticed.'

'Started around the time he met you actually.'

'You should talk to him.'

She threw back her head and laughed as if she had opened the door to a clown.

'You're talking to me about my family?'

There was movement in the hallway and Murt tried to glance around Helen. Someone was leaning against a wall, listening to the conversation. She pulled the door towards herself, blocking the opening.

'Sorry, we only invite friends inside, people we trust.'

Murt shrugged. 'Words are the same out here as in there.'

'You might think we have things to say to each other, but we don't.'

'If it's about the mill, the reason you're so opposed—'

She frowned, surprised that Murt had mentioned the mill.

'The mill,' she said, 'no concern of yours.'

'I know, that's one of the things I came to say.'

'One of the things?'

'About Gráinne, I don't see any reason why you don't want me to talk to her. I'm her father. Maybe she wants to get to know me.'

'We raised her; she's our daughter. You weren't able to be a father, remember?'

The door she was holding slipped from her hand. Gráinne stood glaring at both of them.

'You shouldn't have come here,' she said to Murt.

'I had to talk to her.'

'Why is that?' Helen asked, her voice rising in pitch. 'Go on, tell Gráinne why you are here: to try and stop me from going to the Guards.'

'Guards?' Gráinne's eyes narrowed. 'For what?'

'This man here, your so-called father, took the law into his own hands and killed a man.'

Murt had hoped that Helen would not tell Gráinne this. It was a big risk he had taken by coming to the house.

'Killed who?' The confusion on Gráinne's face was changing to disgust.

'The man who was driving the car,' Helen said.

'Jesus.'

'Isn't he a right hero?'

As Gráinne backed into the hallway and disappeared from view, Helen pulled the door towards her again.

Murt said, 'Sometimes things aren't as black and white as you want to see them, Helen. You think you know everything.'

'I know what happened to Oisín Duffy.'

'No, you don't.'

'Your explanations are wasted on me. Save them for the judge.'

Maybe it was too late, and she had already talked to the Guards? Murt heard Foley's voice and then he, too, was standing in the doorway. Helen rounded on him; voices were raised, shouting became screaming. Murt backed away. He had made a mistake by coming.

As he reached his truck, the screaming stopped and a door slammed. 'Hang on.'

He turned to see Foley following him across the yard.

Foley said, 'Park your yoke by the church in the village. I'll pick you up.'

Foley's driving skills had improved little in the days since they had worked at the mill. He drove north for a while in the shadow of the mountain that gave their village its name—a lopsided bald peak that was known for its colour: blue in winter, dusty orange in summer. Murt watched the mountain through the windscreen. The clouded peak appeared and disappeared between forests, fields and ditches, the slope dark now, as if in its own shadow.

They spoke little until they were out of the mountain's view and heading east.

'Isn't there always a bigger man?' Foley said, breaking the silence. Murt looked at him, unsure of the subject. 'There were bigger men around Kiltuam, at the mill—taller, fitter, darker, hairier, stronger, meaner, more handsome, more intense men. All those things that get a young man noticed. Things that can bother lesser men like me, make us want more: poise and stature.'

Countryside reeled by and they hit a straight road that ribboned in crests ahead of them. A dry stone wall ran along the left-hand side, exposed beneath the recently cut-back ditch.

Foley continued, 'You didn't try to walk a certain way, with a swagger or strut. There was no showing of the chest, no tough male or hard man bullshit. There was no thought about how you did it, or what it could mean—you just walked.'

The ditches were neat. Murt wanted to talk about the ditches, how grand and tidy they were trimmed up, the habitats that the cutting process might have disturbed. He had no idea where this was going. His stomach rose and fell with the road.

'Arriving in the village the way you did, out of nowhere. Caused quite a stir around the place. People didn't just show up in kips like Kiltuam and decide to stay. If tourists appeared, we presumed they had gone wrong at the blind junction, and instead of being on the road to the waterfall, they found themselves freewheeling through rickety old Kiltuam. It lifted our hearts to see strangers: gaping, delighted, a little scared. And they'd stop, take a few snaps, ask if there was anywhere they could eat, as if they knew the chance was slim, but they thought they'd ask anyway.'

Murt knew the types. He had drank with them occasionally, had a laugh with some, took the piss out of others; once he sent a car-full of Americans the wrong way when they asked for directions.

'But a stranger arriving off the bus and sticking around was unheard of. Joss McNabb was delighted that you were staying with him. He told your stories in the pub, repeated things you had told him and added his own slant.'

The car rounded some bad bends and the ditches got wild again with *sceach*, briar and fern.

'Before you even got to the mill to ask for work, we knew you were coming; that's the kind of place you landed in. Of course, you knew that from wherever you'd been—one old bridge is as stony as the next in this country. I wondered if you weren't trying to play us, what your endgame was. If people had stopped to think about it, they would have been suspicious too. Not a chance though. Everyone wanted to meet you, get to know you. A bad word couldn't be said—isn't that always the way, at first?'

Murt recognised the road they were on. Back roads have a habit of lighting up in the memory when you travel them again. The junctions, the entrances, ditches, corners, signs: Yield, Stop, Dangerous Bend, Hump-back Bridge. Murt had never cared about other people's impressions. Why was Foley telling him this?

'It takes a certain kind of person,' Foley continued. 'They liked you. Mannerly, the women said in the shop; inoffensive was another; a grand chap for a pint. They liked someone who kept to himself—a quality sought after in others, especially a stranger, but not too much. And in reality, not at all.'

Unsure of what else to do, Murt nodded. If there had been stories going around Kiltuam about him, it hardly mattered now. People are interested only in themselves anyway; they can hear or tell a story and forget about it straight away. Foley had never understood this. He was obsessed with talk back then, jealous that it was never about himself.

Murt let down his window. Maybe some fresh air would bring Foley back to reality.

'Sure the fuss died down quickly. We're a fickle lot.'

Foley laughed through his nose—not a funny laugh of enjoyment, but something wry and indifferent that was leading somewhere else.

'You remember that first day we met at the mill? You were reading the paper in the cabin when I walked in. You're the new lad, I said. I did my practiced handshake and nod. Still, I didn't feel I had done it justice against your grip. Don't you find that? There's always a more dominant hand in a shake. Sometimes you get in there first and take them by surprise: you're more alert and ready. Other times, you get lifted by an electric jolt from someone more practiced or confident, more prepared and determined than yourself. I tried to never let that happen. You probably didn't notice. Small things matter though; everything matters.'

They came to a crossroads and Foley turned right. The air smelled of slurry and burnt hair.

'Rospak,' Foley said.

'What is this about?'

Foley closed the car window.

'When Mr Shaw asked me to show you the ropes around the mill, I was more than happy. It gave me a sort of status among the other men. I wasn't the best man in the yard—too scrawny for the heavy work, had a bit of a mouth on me too. I didn't see myself working at the mill for long though. I wanted more, fancied I had too much brain to be spitting damp sawdust for the rest of my days. Mr Shaw knew this and he liked me because of it. That's why I got the job of helping you start off.'

The factory was in front of them then: Rospak Food Processing Industries in huge letters across the face of a building that stretched way back into Ros village.

'You ever work in a slaughterhouse?' Foley asked.

'I went with my uncle once, to see cattle being killed.'

Murt did not feel like telling Foley about the slaughterhouse; about the pink killing hall, the white coats and walls, the wet concrete floors, everything tainted by fleshy shades. He remembered not being able to warm his hands, no matter how much he blew into them. Every sound was metal-cold. Gates clashed continuously; hooks ran on tracks, some empty, others with carcasses. Even the voices of men and roaring cattle sounded like hollow iron tubing being struck. There was a gaping hole in the floor, covered by a steel grid. One man's job was to hose blood all day. That was another sound that never stopped—the hiss of a spray nozzle, as if steel could spit. Blood and water ran continuously into the hole. Murt had nightmares afterwards, about a massive vat of red blood down there in the darkness and him falling through the hole and drowning in it.

They passed through Ros village and at the next junction Foley went straight through. Murt knew now for sure where they were going.

Foley said, 'I never fitted in with other workers at the mill; you could see that yourself. Always felt like they didn't trust me. As much as I wanted to be, I was never funny enough in the canteen. Good men, good workers, were popular men; they were respected. Not me though. So I decided I was better than that. I was going to do something more; I would show them. Wasn't a bother with you—everyone loves a fast learner. The way you took to things and applied yourself was impressive, and not just to me. The canteen responded. Whenever you had a question, you came to me, though, and the canteen responded to that too. They slagged me less, accepted me at the table so to speak. After that, my own suspicions about you evaporated. You treated me as a co-worker, sometimes even looked up to me as a source of information.'

The sky had darkened and rain spat on the windscreen.

'You know where we're going now?' Foley asked.

'I do.'

'I want to show you.'

He cut corners short, crossed solid white lines and didn't seem to notice or care. As they passed the entrance to Rathmore house, Foley started talking about Cathy. Murt didn't like that.

'I had seen her plenty of times,' Foley said. 'Any man would have wanted to be with her, but she was with Duffy. That was a no go area. Until she wasn't with him any more. I'm sure I wasn't the only one who was jealous when she showed interest in you. She would never have gone with me, but I didn't want you to have her.'

He looked over and laughed as if they were friends reuniting for a chat about old times, which was not how the situation felt to Murt.

'I remember intercepting a sandwich Cathy left in for you.' Foley said. 'She asked me to give it to you, knew who I was too. Sticks, she called me. When I thought about this afterwards, I wondered did you two have a little thing between you, a private joke that I was the butt of. Couples have those all the time—secrets to make each other laugh. I didn't trust anybody, didn't have the social skills to read people. I wasn't even a man back then. The real me—the person who resented, who thought people talked about him behind his back, the person who, in private, bit his fingers until they bled—I hid him by playing the fool.'

Foley slowed as he drove past the *Welcome to Kiltuam* sign and on down the shallow hill. At the junction with Station Road, they both glanced at Curran's pub on the corner. The street was deserted.

Murt wanted to get out of the car and start walking, anywhere, as long as he could put an end to this conversation.

They rounded the bad corner and crossed the bridge. Evening was filling the gaps between shadows before it made a wider sweep at the day. Murt's stomach cramped as Foley stopped at the gates to the mill yard. Drizzle smeared the windscreen. They sat still.

'That sandwich,' Foley said. 'I took it out in the canteen at lunchtime and ate it there in front of you. Thought it was pretty funny, as if Cathy and me had a little secret. Right under your nose. Part of me wanted you to know that I was eating your sandwich, how I had deceived you, how good it tasted. Of course, it didn't fill me, the sandwich. Everything always came back to you—what you had that I didn't, what Cathy saw in you. It's nonsense now, but at the time nothing was more important for me.'

He opened the door and got out. Murt followed. The air was heavy with damp and pine. Foley fiddled with the chain around the gates and opened a gap for them to squeeze through. They stood inside looking across at the sheds—piles of rotting timber and metal, the old crane twisted, leaning to one side.

'It looks the same,' Murt said, 'just more decayed.'

'I locked the gates one day, presumed that would be the end of it. We were offered over a million.'

'And now?'

'Fuck all. Out here in this kip, we couldn't give it away.'

They walked a familiar line across the yard to the portacabins, the doors of which had been left open years before. The roof of the office had collapsed. Standing in the doorway of the dilapidated canteen, they watched the yard.

'Mr Shaw always admired a good worker,' Foley said. 'And you could turn your hand to anything. Getting out into the forest the way you did—the rest of us would have loved that chance.'

Foley threw his hand out and struck Murt's arm with something.

'Hey,' he said. 'That girl I used to meet sometimes, from the village, you remember her?'

Murt nodded. It seemed important not to disrupt the story. What had Foley struck his arm with? He glanced down. A large flake of dead bark was gripped in Foley's fist like a batten.

'One night I asked that girl what she thought of you. We were all in Curran's, probably a Friday. She made me point you out, even though she knew right well who you were. So I pointed. She looked over at you and made a squinting face as she thought hard about it. You know what word she used?'

He was smiling. Murt shook his head.

'Rugged.'

Foley was laughing so much his shoulders shook.

'I asked her if that was attractive to her. She didn't need time to answer—yes, she thought you were handsome, but as well, you didn't say much. This seemed more attractive to her. I hadn't thought about that one. Soon after that, I stopped seeing her. The way she had looked at you drove me mad. If you had asked her out, she would have dropped me immediately. You wouldn't have asked her out, though; she wasn't good enough for you, with her chubby legs and smitten streak. That's why I went with her, because I knew she was safe. It's also why I had no real interest in her, why I dumped her. The calibre of girl that I could get would never satisfy me. I wanted yours. I wanted Cathy.'

Murt's jaw was set tight by all this talk about Cathy. He had hardly heard her name spoken since the accident except in his own head. Why was Foley talking about her in that way? His tone was calm, as if recounting tales from the past that no longer meant anything.

'Before it started with you two, I thought of you as my equal. You enjoyed my company, I could see that. But Cathy—the way she swooned for you—made me realise that you were better than me. That hurt. Better than me with the girl I wanted. She would never have been interested in me. Even Duffy—if she had stayed with Duffy—that I could have accepted. The life she would have had, the hardship, self-inflicted because of her own bad choices. That would have given me some solace. Not you though.'

214

Murt was getting more confused. Who was Foley trying to make a point about: himself, Cathy, Murt? Or all three?

'You two were good together. It was obvious to everyone except me. I couldn't see anything for what it was back then. Things were eating me up inside.'

'Was a long time ago,' Murt said. 'We're different people now. And Cathy's dead.' Murt glared at him hard, hoping Foley would see the anger in his eyes and stop talking about Cathy.

Foley kept his gaze fixed on the yard. His hands broke flakes of bark and crumbled them around his feet.

'How long has it been? Seventeen, eighteen years nearly. I'm a different person now, as you said. At some point I had to face the insecurities or I was going to end up in a river, or hanging from a steel truss. Everything that was happening to me back then was in my own head. That man, Willie, who lost his fingers—it was an accident, I was too slow to react, to warn him.'

The old crane was there in the middle of the yard. Murt had an urge to turn the handles to find out if it still worked. Maybe the grinding of gears and squealing metal could drown out Foley's talk.

'The men had less time for me after that.'

That was true. Murt remembered them having a meeting one evening when Foley had left.

'You were unpredictable,' Murt said. 'We didn't feel safe working with you.'

'Like a cousin who had just returned home from a spell in jail for setting fire to a shed. What line would I cross next? If someone had just come out and accused me, got drunk and hit me a slap, said what everyone was thinking. But no one had the guts.'

Murt said, 'If it's redemption you're looking for—'

'Willie should still have his fingers.'

'—I'm hardly the person.'

'That stuff's only for nuns and priests. In the real world, we have to live with ourselves.'

Foley flung the lump of bark and it spun and freefell through the air, landing like paper on a puddle of water in the yard.

'Come on,' he said.

They left the portacabin and walked past the drying shed where timber was still stacked in rows, long dried and greying. At the far boundary of the site, where a river ran through the old mill race, Foley told him about the plans he had had for the place. In the air with his hands, he shaped a new mill wheel which was to be a main feature of the development, a centrepiece.

'Even back when we worked here, I could see it. I didn't know how it would happen for me, but I was determined to make something of myself. I started with that bookkeeping course at night.'

'I remember. You had to cycle to the town and then get a lift to class.'

'Nearly killed me. I used to sleep in the toilet here at lunchtime. But I got through it. Fucking sure I did. That need filled the void of respect I had longed for, the attention that came so naturally to others. I felt hard done by. So I decided that there must be some way around it. Success, I resolved, would bring attention. People would stand up and take note then; they'd shake my hand with respect; they'd call me Mr Foley. No more fucking Sticks.'

It was raining more heavily now. As they stood in the main yard again, he talked more about his plans; about how Kiltuam was to become a town. Foley had made a deal to buy the adjoining land and the owner was now taking him to court for reneging. He stood proud and laughed with bitter regret.

'An awful hunger in me for success—a need to succeed, to win. I wanted to come out on top at everything. Whatever is inside a man, that thing that gnaws at him, causes him flushes of jealousy and rage, that's what makes us who we are. Do we have the courage to be led by the gnawing and to crush it, to become stronger in the hope that the gnawing will disappear, be defeated? Of course, it never will, but you can't know that unless you pursue it to the depths of yourself.

Whatever stands in the way must be ploughed over. You can't be shy about something like that. With Cathy, it was different. I never had a chance—I was too scrawny and had a bad attitude. I wasn't a handsome man, but that didn't stop other men before me. Cathy was gone, but I resolved not to lose again. A change was needed inside me. I watched and listened to see how other men talked to women. It came naturally to others. Not to me though. I had to learn.'

'Jesus,' Murt said. 'I knew you were a bit mad, Foley, but not a fucking nutcase.'

Foley kicked a sliding door that was full height across the front of the main shed, to see if it might go. Grabbing the handle, he motioned for Murt to help. They jerked and shoved against the rust-seized rollers and guides. Foley counted to three and they huffed one big shove. The thing cried in pain, ran for a moment but refused to budge any more. They squeezed through the gap.

Standing inside the main shed, they could see patches of cloud through the roof where sheets of galvanised metal had blown off or rotted away. Showers of water fell in columns around the shed. The machinery would be long seized. Foley continued with his design: the shed was to be removed, a planted courtyard created in its place like a park at the heart of the scheme. Murt liked the idea.

Foley said, 'Madness: yes, you're right. I'm like my father. You were the only person I told about his breakdown; I never expected you to repeat it. And yet Smithy told half of Curran's that very night. Everyone sitting around the table knew about it. All the women, laughing at me. You were laughing too. Imagine the fool I felt. How could I forgive you for that?'

'I didn't say anything. It was known about your father getting signed in. I knew before you told me; just didn't have the heart to say it to you. I'm sure that's not what we were laughing about that night.'

'Probably not, but I saw what I wanted to see. Either way, there was no point in trying to talk to me after that night in Curran's. I realised that you people didn't want me. You never had.'

They walked to the back of the shed where the bigger saws were kept, their huge blades patinaed with a barky rust. Foley pointed up towards the trusses, asked Murt if he remembered the dummy hanging from the roof. They laughed as they walked around, and it made Murt sad to think that it was so far in the past, and with everything that had happened since, was it even worth remembering?

Back out in the yard, they stood near the crane.

'After I left the mill,' Foley said, 'I started drinking with Duffy. I'd always been friends with him. I looked up to him too. The sheer danger associated with him, the scorn he had for the people he didn't like—you, the Shaws; and the potential in him to do something about it.'

Murt did not like hearing Duffy's name.

'He took me under his wing, introduced me to his father too— the Wrecker. The Wrecker was looking for a money man, and with me doing the accounting exams, he reckoned he could use me. The cash he offered was more than enticing: twice as much as I'd have got with a company. I was half-afraid to say no anyway—the Wrecker wasn't a man accustomed to being turned down, by all accounts. It was only small things for a year or so—doctoring books, tweaking figures, shifting funds around. I kept my head down, didn't ask questions.

'Duffy was a loose cannon, same as the Wrecker. He would be in a grand mood one minute and the next he'd be roaring abuse, lashing kicks at whatever or whoever was close by. He liked me, though, listened to what I said. When Duffy heard that you and Cathy were getting married, he flipped his lid, cursed the two of you from a height. It wasn't jealousy—Duffy had another girlfriend—but he was bitter. Any reason to lose the head. His ego was hurt after Cathy rejected him, and then she took up with you. Jesus, he hated the sight of you two, the mention of your names.'

'Why did you come to the wedding?'

'I have to tell you, I was surprised to get an invitation. I had no intention of going. Duffy convinced me, said I had to go and stir things up a bit, start a fight, wreck the place if I could. When I reported back, he was pleased that we had had words but disappointed there were no punches. He told me I was a useless fucking cunt and that he'd teach me how to break a nose, starting with my own. This was his banter.

'I didn't see much of you after you moved out to the cottage. I was busy making money, and Duffy was busy making trouble. The accident changed everything. I couldn't be around Kiltuam. I mentioned to the Wrecker that I was thinking of going away. He said I did right, that he'd be gone too if there wasn't so much shite to deal with. He told me to go to England; said he had a few contacts over there for me. A few days later, I left, swearing that I'd never come back. I was shook up something terrible; couldn't think straight after what had happened. Here's the thing, Murt, the thing you should know: I was with Duffy that day, in the car. It was me who was driving.'

In the moments that followed, Murt tried to comprehend what he had heard. His mind fuzzed, as if something warm had covered him, making him weak and slow and wanting to lie down.

How could Foley have been driving?

Murt imagined a forest clearing: lying on a mat of wild grass, soft like hair; watching clouds float across the opening above; and in a circle around him, straight pine trees speared towards the sky, looking infinite and dangerous.

How did Foley get away?

Looking beautiful and fragile, the trees swayed. Next, the hole above was closing in, the clouds darkening. He heard trunks crack and splinter as they began to fall.

The Guards arrested Duffy. He went to jail.

The trees moved in waves around him, making him dizzy. He closed his eyes. If he could only get to his feet. He felt a breeze, rain on his face.

Why did Duffy take the blame?

Opening his eyes, he saw the sky widening as trees fell away in every direction. Out, out, away from the centre where he was lying. A deafening assault of trunks hitting the ground.

Foley says the accident was his fault.

And the whole expanse of sky opened above Murt.

Foley was driving. Foley killed Cathy.

Murt looked around. Dusk was falling fast. He tried to focus, but the yard was a burning blur in shades of rust and decay: orange, yellow, ochre, surrounded by a ring of green. His eyes traced a line along the crane's boom to the pulley and handles, the snapped and frayed ends of wire ropes that would never be repaired.

'You're telling me this now?'

Murt's hands, heavy clumps of things, were cramped into fists from the cold.

Foley said, 'I thought it was about time.'

Cold air caught in Murt's throat and warm breath rose through the air in front of him.

'Nothing can be the same again,' Foley said. 'Everything I believed in before, the things that were driving me, none of it matters now. It never should have mattered—if I had known that then.'

'Why did Duffy take the blame?'

'He wouldn't have been the type to talk to the Guards about anything. They wanted him locked up. He'd got away with a couple of serious assaults, even a robbery. Wouldn't have mattered if he told them about me—maybe he did—they had him at the scene.'

'So you disappeared for a while.'

'I can't see a future for me now like I used to. It's been over with Helen for a long time. There's nothing left of who I am. The last few weeks I figured I would die as a person. But watching you, I started to see things differently. All you need or want is to get to know Gráinne. One simple, tangible thing. You have to live with the years you wasted but now you'll do everything

220

you can for a new start. And I thought, why die when you can start anew?'

Those wasted years were more real to Murt now than ever before. All the things he thought he had to live with: guilt, hatred, pity, the drink, the fire, the caravan, Duffy. Was any of it necessary?

Night was falling like a black sheet across the countryside. Murt tugged at the collar of his donkey jacket and lifted it against his neck. He stepped out across the mud-sloppy yard and squeezed through the gap between the gates.

His boots fell hard on the tarmac road and splashed through water where it lay or ran between puddles. He did not look down—dark now anyway. The rain eased to a spitting drizzle that would not make him any wetter than he already was. When had he last walked this road? After himself and Cathy had moved out to the cottage, it was rare that he walked to the mill. He would take the car or Cathy would give him a lift. He was not working at the mill on the day of her accident but had gone to survey a forest across the county. He needed the car to get there. Did it have to be that day? Wouldn't the next day have been as good? The small things life turns on. He shook his head as he walked. Water trickled down his forehead and filled his eyes.

Foley was driving. Not Duffy. Duffy didn't kill Cathy. Foley did. But Duffy took the blame. He went to jail for seven years. Why did he do that for Foley?

Murt stopped, as he used to do, at the bridge and leaned on the stone wall. Below, the swollen river raced. Foley did not want forgiveness, he knew it was not an option. But why had he brought Murt to the mill? Why the showy confession?

Maybe Foley would follow him and try to explain himself more. Murt listened for the murmur of an engine, the dance of headlights catching up, but nothing stirred in the dark behind. He walked on.

# 20

It was Ursula who told him, when he got back to the guest house, that the Guards were looking for him. Two of them had called to the door earlier.

'I thought something had happened to Ray,' she said.

She was breathing in gasps. She wiped her eyes. Donoghue appeared behind her as if he was equally concerned. She turned on him. 'And you, disappearing out the back.'

His mouth moved but no words came out.

'I don't know what the two of you are involved in, but you're not welcome in this house if you're putting my children in danger.'

'Did you talk to Ray?' Murt asked.

'Of course I talked to Ray. That man who killed your wife, he told me about it.'

Donoghue raised his head in the air as he eyed Murt's reaction.

'I'll go to the station,' Murt said. 'Sort it out.'

'Will you take your things with you? I'm sorry.'

She sat down and rubbed her forehead. He understood what this meant: when he left, when she was alone again, she would go to the cupboard for the only thing that could help. This was all she could think about.

'Now, Ursula,' Donoghue said. 'I'm not sure what's going on here, but is that really necessary? Where will Murt go?'

'I don't know, Oscar. Jail maybe.'

She stared at him till he left the room. She scoffed and shook her head.

'How do I know what's real any more? I thought you were genuine. And people wonder why I drink.'

'I'm sorry to have upset you,' Murt said. 'It's not—'

She waved a hand in the air for him to leave. There was no point in trying to explain—her mind was on only one thing.

Murt did not have many belongings. Donoghue offered to help carry out the bags but said he would not be much use with his injuries. He waited by the van, afraid to go back inside, wary of Ursula.

'I won't be able for this place on my own,' he said with a grunt.

'Don't think it's her you need to worry about,' Murt said, pointing to the bandaged arm.

'Suppose you're right.'

'If I can help you out—' Murt said.

He climbed onto the flatbed and threw a sheet of timber over his bags.

'Sounds like you're in more trouble than me,' Donoghue said.

When he was sure the wind would not take hold of anything, Murt climbed down and tied a strap across the timber. The two men stood facing each other.

'What do you need?' Murt asked.

'A few weeks is all.'

Despite himself, Murt would miss Donoghue—the tug-of-war for idle gossip, the dining room banter, even his lies and boasting. Donoghue was wrong: he was in more trouble than Murt.

'Was she talking out of her arse?' Donoghue asked, nodding towards the house. 'About the jail.'

'Let's hope so.'

He offered his bandaged paw and Murt patted him on the shoulder.

'I'll tell you all about it sometime, Oscar.'

He sat into the van and Donoghue held the door open.

'You know I had a brother?' Donoghue said. 'Lung cancer. Turned his chest to black marl. The most considerate, hospitable man you could meet. And braver than any too. Smoked till the end.'

Murt would have liked a brother. 'Was he older?'

'Three years. Spent my life looking up to him, trying to impress him. And if I ever did succeed in impressing him, he never let on, which just made me try harder.'

He looked down towards the garden and smiled like people do when they hear something fantastic.

'Such a way to be showing our love,' Donoghue said. 'We were a right pair of eejits.'

Closing the door, he took a step back to the gable wall and waved off Murt. Murt watched him in his mirror. What would become of Donoghue now? Could he get enough money together in a few weeks? Murt could not help him with money. There was one thing he could try: a phone call, one last favour from an old friend.

As he drove through Balroe towards the Garda Station, he was thinking about people. How easy it is to underestimate and pass others off as fools. We look for ways in which we are better than everyone else. That's how we all get by. Even if we are deluding ourselves, we have to keep going. People need to feel they are worth something, that there is a point to them being alive. Without that, you have nothing. And if you lose it somewhere along the line, you might never get it back. This is what Murt knew.

He would tell the truth about all that had happened. Without evidence, they would have to believe him. It didn't matter anyway—he had lived with it for so long now that he was ready to shake the guilt off like a damp old coat and to maybe feel, for a change, a lightness across his back.

# 21

He woke in the night and remembered something else: Foley could not look at him when he said Cathy's name. Murt had not noticed it at the time, when they had talked at the Moss Hotel—how Foley had distracted himself with brushing crumbs from his suit, looking out the window. That day in Knocklea too, wiping his shoes and looking away. And when Foley had said her name, it was as if he did not want to hear it or could not bear to hear himself speak it after what he had done.

After what he had done, Foley carried on, managed to live with himself. He tried to forget. He married Cathy's sister. Knocked Cathy down, killed her and married her sister. Lusted after Cathy, killed her, married her sister. And reared her daughter—Murt's daughter—as his own.

The year slipped into December with flurries of snow. Soon it would be Murt's birthday and not long after, the shortest day. He could hear Rose and Quinn in the kitchen, their voices humming through the walls, like an old fridge. There were long pauses—they must have been listening to the morning news. And all their talk would be about what they heard of the country going to the dogs and how it could have happened. Voices on the radio, but no answers. People were always on about the past, but no one wanted to think about where to go from here. They only wanted what they had before. But it was not coming back, and they did not know how they could go on.

Murt sat up in the bed.

When he left the Garda Station the day before, and headed west for Quinn's, the snow had already started. The country had not changed, but he felt less sure of himself. Every traffic light, flyover and turn-off he passed made him wonder if he was on the right road. Signs meant nothing, every direction looked the same. He had always imagined the country having a heart that beats deep under the ground, something that reassured him. But he was beginning to doubt that. Lost in the white landscape, he wondered about the country and about the things that had happened, the constant talk about the past. People think that nothing much will happen in the future, that the history books cannot take any more. But you can't stop the future. People never say: just wait and see.

He walked into the kitchen.

The air sizzled with rasher grease, sausage, black pudding and egg. Quinn threw an arm towards the radio and said to turn that auld thing off; he was sick listening to them.

'Though they're giving a bit of a thaw for today. I thought we were going to be snowed in till the new year.'

Rose told him not to be jinxing it; sure wasn't there more on the way for the weekend.

'Mightn't be much, please God.'

They still had not talked about what had happened with the Guards. Whereas Rose was mad for talk, Quinn let things take their own course. He would wait till Murt was ready. After breakfast they went outside to do the foddering. Quinn had gained a hobble but Murt could not tell which leg was the cause. Still, the man could master an icy yard with hands clasped behind his back. They worked steadily, feeding, throwing out straw. The water troughs were frozen and Quinn broke ice with the four-grain fork.

'Would have been a good morning for a shot,' he said with a smirk, 'if you'd been up in time.'

'There many around?'

'Nearly as many deer up in that forest as there are trees.'

'We'll go tomorrow.'

Murt was welcome to stay as long as he liked, he knew that, but they needed to know what had happened. Even the old could not lie easy around the house.

'They told me not to be leaving the country,' Murt said, that evening. 'Sure where would I be going?'

'They'll want to speak to you again.'

'Same questions no doubt. I've nothing more to say.'

Rose was leaning across the table, looking wide-eyed from one man to the other as Murt recounted the past few days.

'You didn't tell them,' Rose asked, 'about Foley?'

'No.'

'What about peace for yourself?' she asked.

'I didn't even think about Foley while I was there.'

His talk with the Guards had turned out to be an interview—questions repeated, rephrased, approached from different angles. He signed a statement. It didn't matter if they believed him; there was nothing else to go on. What he had told them would match their reports. He repeated it. They asked again. They broke it up, changed the sequence, jumped between different parts to try and catch him out. Maybe he wasn't sure?

He was sure.

As he answered their questions, he was thinking about the future—how long it had been since he had thought about the future. That landscape of mountaintops, sand, dusk without trees. The past had him surrounded.

The Guards went at him hard. A likely story, they said. He could see their point. Their job was to investigate, to get all the facts, and the facts would determine their conclusion. Murt had told them the facts as he remembered them—how could he forget? It was up to them.

He thought about Gráinne and the next time he would see her. And Ursula: she had done what she thought was right. He hoped they could talk again some day. It did not matter that he had no home now; he had contact with his daughter, and Quinn's door was never locked.

No, he hadn't thought about Foley at the Garda Station. Rose could not believe this.

Murt said, 'It's up to Foley if he wants to tell them. What difference would it make to me now?'

'What he did though.'

Quinn shook his head as you might do in half-sleep.

'A lot of damage done,' he said. 'Maybe it's enough now.'

His slippers dragged along the floor as he shuffled over to the window. Hands clasped behind his back, he watched the weather.

'At it again,' he said. 'Heavy too.'

He stoked up the fire and eased into his armchair with a groan.

'Any word since?' Rose asked after a long pause.

'No. He's her stepfather,' Murt said. 'Maybe he'll tell her.'

'So it's not over yet?'

Quinn said, 'It's certainly not over. Only starting for them.'

# 22

When the gates lifted, Murt drove across the tracks. The road swung around to the right and opened out to an expanse of promenade. A wide grass verge separated the road from a walkway, and the slate sea stretched out beyond. With the ramps along the road, he could go slowly, take the place in. Farther on, he passed a round, open-sided structure with steps up to a raised platform. This must be the bandstand she had told him about. Nobody waiting there yet. He was early, half an hour or more.

On the other side, a terrace of old houses, Georgian or Victorian, one of those British types. He would like to live there, facing the sea. Three storeys, bay windows, fancy stonework; long front gardens stretching down to the road. A top floor, that would be his—smallest windows, but the best view. Some of the buildings were pubs, with seating instead of a front garden, a canopy for the weather. Maybe she would be hungry; they could eat there.

He passed a red bricked hotel with pointed turrets, drove on and turned in front of the amusements, then drove back along the promenade. He kept an eye out—she could be early too.

Back at the far end of the street, he pulled into a small car park and sat for a while. He was less sure this time, of himself, of the place—too built up. It was difficult to get his bearings outside of valleys and trees; instead of lakes, the sea again. And he worried too about whether or not she would show up—those same fears. The first time, he had had nothing to lose. The slate was damaged but blank. This time was different. He wondered what else Helen had told her from her version?

He opened the van door and stepped out. He focused on a positive: she had agreed to meet him and had suggested this place. The air caught in his throat as he walked, and it reminded him of something chilled and tasty he used to savour from a glass. Nothing like a clear winter's day, brittle light that made the world jumpy. A sneaky easterly wind rasped against his cheeks as it readied the place up for the next flurry of snow.

He walked along the concrete path, a stony beach beyond the railing to his left. The promenade, straight and maybe a mile long, ran to a head of land that formed a hill and cliff at the end. If she did not turn up, he might climb to the top, have a look at the place from above.

He kept an eye on the bandstand as he walked. People passed him in both directions, walking, running, talking; wrapped up and not put off by the bite in the air, the kind of people who were probably not willing to admit that they liked this weather. More traipsed along the beach, struggling for steps in the stones. It was different to the countryside. He wondered what the promenade would be like at the height of a storm, waves crashing against the wall, gushing through the rails and flooding the road.

An air horn punched through the day, and he remembered the tracks he had crossed and the railway station behind the terrace of houses.

Murt climbed the few steps and stood on the bandstand, not circular but eight-sided, an octagon. There was no escape from the wind, and he imagined there would not be much from rain either. It was like a small version of the drying sheds at the mill. Being higher up, though, he felt a sense of importance, of being looked at and looking down. An illusion, like so many things.

Clouds moved on the eastern horizon, swollen white balloons making their way towards the land. He leaned on the bandstand railing and watched them, tried to estimate when the next fall would happen. Judging by the clouds, it would be bigger this time, a deluge of snow. And soon—tomorrow maybe.

When he turned around, they were standing on the platform. Another surprise: she had brought Helen with her. Or Helen had insisted. Maybe this was the only way she would allow them to meet. His eyes narrowed, jaw clenched at the thought of Helen trying to control Gráinne. She was eighteen years old—a young woman— and he was her father. He tensed a bit more when he wondered if it was him she was trying to control and this situation which he had created against her wishes.

Gráinne smiled, said hello, and gave a half-glance at Helen that was either apology or spite.

Helen said, 'You're not saying a word to her without me hearing it, and this will be the last time. I suppose there'll be a trial, a big scene.'

He nearly spoke up but in this weather, despite the short days, what was the hurry? There was time to let the icy breeze sting his lips, to watch people pass, time to be amused by the situation they were now in.

'Grand place for a final stand off,' he said.

Out at the road, a dog sniffed the concrete and a woman tugged its lead as she headed for the grass. Why should he tell Helen the truth? Truth was no good to Helen.

'Gráinne doesn't want anything to do with you,' Helen said.

Gráinne's gaze was fixed on the expanse of waves way ahead of her. Helen was a woman consumed by twisted ideas, manipulation and the fear of losing what little she had left. The family she had worked so hard to hold together had been destined to fall apart. It was all pretend.

'She hasn't heard my side,' Murt said.

By making him the focus of her wrath, Helen had blinded herself to the reality around her. Murt was merely a symptom of her fears. Still, he was getting annoyed by this charade.

'I don't owe you an explanation,' Murt said. 'Maybe your Garda friend will tell you.'

His mother would have called this a dirty dig.

Her face changed, as if a freezing gust had caught her square on.

Pressure always needs a release. So tense and uptight had Helen been in the last few years that she had eventually found solace in the friendship of a local Garda. Whether true or not, rumours float like smoke. They drift and spread, catch in the wind and get mentioned in passing: here's a good one; you'll never guess what; do you know her, you do?; friendly with Garda so-and-so I hear; there now, you didn't hear that from me. This kind of thing goes on all over the country, has done for years, which is how Murt happened to hear. Keeping company with such a man would do Helen no harm if Murt got too close to her family, if he came looking for Gráinne. It would do no harm at all. Would be very useful, in fact.

'What do you—fuck you,' she said, raising her voice.

A few heads turned on the promenade, looked up and quickened their step.

Murt said, 'People talk.'

Gráinne looked at him then, as if she had been betrayed by more secrets. He should not have said it, did not even know if it was true.

'Nice here,' he said. 'I like it. Good choice, Gráinne.'

'He didn't come back,' Gráinne said. 'That day you were at our house, he left and never came back.'

'If he's missing, tell the Guards. You can do that, Helen.'

Helen's rage was unblinking. Murt did not know or care what had happened to Foley after the mill. Maybe guilt had got the better of him.

He looked at the two women and saw now that they were facing him united. This never was a meeting with his daughter—it was an investigation. They thought that Murt knew where Foley was; maybe Murt had done something to Foley so that he could not return. Helen would think that. But Gráinne, was that how she saw him now?

Murt said, 'He took me to the mill.'

Helen laughed. 'You went there? For what?'

'Wanted to show me his plans.'

A seagull flew into the bandstand, arched its wings and landed on the platform. Keeping close to the edge, it stepped in a circle around them.

'She thinks we have food,' Gráinne said, rooting in her pocket.

The gull's head darted maniacally at the sound of a plastic wrapper.

After having been duped into going there, Murt wanted to leave. He was a fool for thinking it might be otherwise. Foley could rot. There was something about that day at the mill that Murt could not figure out. The real reason Foley had taken him there was only now becoming clear—he had expected, hoped for, the same fate as Duffy. He believed Murt would do it again. How easily Foley had confessed since everything was lost for him. Had he hoped that Murt would give him an easy way out?

Gráinne crouched to approach, hand out with an offering. The gull took a step forward and stood like a statue before losing its nerve and taking flight to the railing. Gráinne flung the crumbs and the bird dived to claim them.

Helen and Gráinne were there only to find out about Foley. They did not care about Murt. The pleasant air had turned stale in his mouth. He wanted to lash out at all of them. Turning to Gráinne, he said, 'I know why he couldn't look you in the eye.'

'Stop it,' Helen shouted. 'Stop right there, Murt. No more.' Spittle flew from her mouth and stuck on her chin

Did she know? Of all the twisted scenarios and possibilities that had gone through Murt's head, never once had he considered that Helen might know. How could she? How could she stay with him if she knew what he had done?

Murt said, 'You know?'

'Gráinne, give us a minute.'

Gráinne walked away and down onto the beach. They watched her go, both needing the silence to think.

'I only met him when he came back from England,' Helen said. 'Never knew him before. It was the suit. And he was nice to me. There was something missing, a sadness in him that I wanted to fix.'

'How long have you known?'

'The way he never really wanted to talk about Cathy, and always looked away. It's not until you really get to know someone that you understand what their gestures mean.'

'You stayed with him.'

'It was just a theory in my head. We had a good life. He provided it. He could be fierce, distant, cold, but I kept the family together. You don't ruin everything for a theory.'

'You must have wondered why he married you.'

'Second best, that's probably what you think. He could never have Cathy so he took her sister. If only it was that simple. It takes time to recognise guilt, to understand what someone is hiding. To everyone else he is something different. I've heard people call him a greedy, ruthless pig. He was hard to live with, but I saw another side. And it broke my heart. There are many ways to look at things. He married me because he loved me. Maybe it was the only way he could live with the guilt.'

'And what about Gráinne?'

'Don't you see? He dedicated his life in remorse to bringing up Cathy's daughter, giving her the best home he could.'

'You believe that?'

'It's all I have.'

'But then he would have to face that reminder every day.'

'He had to live with it anyway.'

'What about you? How do you feel knowing what he did?'

'It's hard to think about. By the time I realised the truth, we had been married for years. I had to decide if I wanted to throw that away. As I said, I could see the sadness in him. I believed his motives; I had to, or everything was gone. Of course it breaks my heart.'

Helen had not betrayed Murt. They had never been close enough for that. If not betrayal, then he didn't know what to call it. Is everyone so selfish in order to protect themselves?

'You might not see it,' she said, 'but I don't want to think the worst about people.'

234

'I didn't kill Duffy.'

'I hope not.'

He looked at her now, this woman who was so eager to keep him contained, to control his existence. If he had died or vanished for ever, it would have suited her. She had probably hoped for this. It was as if Gráinne did not come into the matter. But Gráinne was the link between them all and she didn't know the full truth. Quinn was right: it was only starting for them.

'You can't tell her.'

'She should know.'

'She's your daughter—there, isn't that what you want to hear? She seems strong, projects the impression. But she's vulnerable underneath, like Cathy that way. What good would it do to tell her now, at this stage?'

He wanted to clap his hands, to ask why it had taken Helen so long. Had it really been so hard for her to say that Gráinne was his daughter? But instead of a sense of triumph, he felt only sorrow and resignation. Such words as describe a life.

'I will see her when I want,' he said.

'Yes.'

# 23

Apart from the obvious lack of hiding places at a graveyard, there is no hiding from the pack that make it their business to know who showed up and, more importantly, who did not. A few heads nodded in Murt's direction, some waved. There were nudges, whispers. He wondered about the stories they were telling.

Standing some distance away, out of earshot of the prayers, he could see Donoghue up near the front, staying close to the family. The Balroe crowd were all there. He recognised some of them by the backs of their heads, or the way they were standing, the width of their shoulders. There's always a gang that go to every funeral in the county—the craw-thumpers, the ones squeezing to be up near the front, the ones with eager hands, the criers who didn't know the person well enough to be crying but are infected by upset, prone to it. Everyone with the same sayings that they take out like Christmas decorations when they hear someone has died. The only thing that changes at funerals is the number of people who show up, as if that is a reflection of how good or important the person was.

Murt was not there to pray, just to offer his condolences to Ursula. They had not spoken since the day she asked him to leave the guest house—a few months before. He did not know what terms they were on. At least she would have heard the truth from Ray.

Murt watched a train skirt along a far-off hill, heard the rattle of an uneven sleeper cackle through the air as they lowered the coffin. What would the funeral gathering look like from a distant carriage window? An ink stain on the landscape maybe; bleeding then in single file through the gate, finding their cars, forgetting already about the person they had just buried; some wondering if they would be next.

When most of the others had left, he talked to Ursula. She insisted that he go back to the house for a while. It was only family and close friends, so he would be safe from the town crowd and their questions.

He nearly used his key in the guest house door, but took it out of the lock and rang the bell instead. It was like that first day all over again, not knowing what to expect. Before the door opened, he looked around to see what had changed. Something was different around the place: more space or light now. The house still needed a coat of paint, so that was not it. Behind him, the front garden had received some attention, a first spring pruning. The hedge had been trimmed; a wheelbarrow, loaded with weeds and off-cuts, waited to be emptied. Mrs Kelleher had never given a thought to maintenance while Murt was living there, although he had offered several times.

When she opened the door, Ursula told him that he could have used his key. He looked at her for the signs, tried to smell her breath when she kissed his cheek. Nothing. She seemed fine, sober. He was annoyed with himself then for presuming otherwise.

He followed her into the front room. Some heads turned his way and then returned to their conversations. Inside, the house was different too. Toys were stacked in the corner of the front room and the old sofa was gone. To Murt, it no longer felt like the guest house. The people present were guests in somebody's home.

When the children ran past, Ursula made them stop and say hello. They did so without throwing Murt a second glance. In the kitchen, Ursula put a cup of tea in his hand. It was as if they were meeting again after years, having parted on bad terms.

'You've made some changes,' Murt said.

'Place needs a lot of work. It's a start.'

She watched the cup cradled in her hands, took quick sips, tasted and nodded.

'I'm on the dry,' she said a little too loudly. 'At last.'

'Good. That's good.'

The way she said it made him wonder. Battles had been raging inside her since the first time they had met. Battles for control or loss of herself, battles that are never fully won.

'They still talk about you around town,' she said. 'Where you disappeared to.'

'Plenty of theories I'm sure.'

'I wanted to say sorry for what I did.'

'No need.'

She put her cup down quickly and beckoned him to follow her. 'You have to see this.'

Murt followed her into the dining room. More children scurried past, their fists full with sandwiches. In the dining room, the small tables, including his and Donoghue's, were gone. In their place, one large table with rounded ends and six new chairs. The wallpaper had been removed and the walls painted.

'Almost a different room,' Murt said.

'Felt like visiting hours at a prison before.'

The table was laid out with sandwiches and salads.

'Take a few there,' Ursula said.

'The guest house is finished then?'

'This is our home now. We're renting out our own house.'

'What about the other lad. He's still here?'

'Oscar left a few weeks after you.'

By the look on her face, Murt wondered if there had been an argument between them. She was hinting at a story that he might like to know, a story that he would have to ask Donoghue himself about.

'I saw him at the graveyard,' Murt said. 'Did he come back here?'

'He was asked anyway.'

Ray Quirke came into the room.

'Mr Doran,' he said.

This was not their first meeting. Ray had been at the Garda Station when Murt was being interviewed. He had introduced himself and took an interest in how things were progressing, but he gave nothing away as to his involvement. Murt wanted to think that Ursula had asked him to be there, but that's not how the Guards work. They had not liked his story. His version did not suit them. What could they do without evidence? There had been things said outside the line of duty by some of the officers at the station: insults, abuse, personal slights. It was not right, but there was little Murt could do.

'That day at the station,' Murt said, but Ray Quirke cut him off with a slice of his hand through the air.

'We'll have no shop talk.'

He reached across Ursula towards the food, and Murt watched his other hand move from her shoulder to her waist. They talked about Mrs Kelleher for a while, and Ray said it was for the best, the way she had ended up.

'You're still out west at your uncle's,' he said to Murt. 'Ratheen isn't it?'

'Sometimes. Between there and Kiltuam.'

'Sure it's no distance now with the motorways—you'd swear the country wasn't small enough.'

Murt knew about the country. He knew about the shadows it could hide, the tales it could twist. He knew about the forests and ditches, the hills and mountains that flare up all over the place like brawls between villages. That's the size of the country.

Someone called Ray's name and he left the room. Ursula did not look at Murt as she talked, and he wondered what he might have seen in her face if she did. She tidied the table, said it was a difficult time, with her mother and all; how she regretted the falling out and how maybe it was her fault for not taking better care of her.

Murt was glad of the fresh air when they went outside. More changes to see, Ursula said. The rear of the house, the back garden, was an oblong plot of yellowing grass, maybe half an acre, dotted here and there with fruitless fruit trees.

He frowned and asked, 'Was the garden always this big?'

'The trees, we cut them down.'

'The leylandiis, yes.'

One side of the garden used to be lined with a wall of thick evergreens which had not been cut back for years, if ever.

'I always hated them,' Ursula said.

'A wild breed all right, never stop growing.'

'Can't believe the light now.'

They walked along a path worn in the grass and came to a patch of tilled soil.

'Veggie garden,' she said, sweeping a hand outwards, flinging imaginary seeds across the lumpy clay. 'If that goes ok, maybe a tunnel next year.'

'One step at a time, I suppose.'

'That's it.'

She smiled, but was not tempted to share the joke. As they walked back towards the house, Murt could see Donoghue through the window.

'Is that Eliza he's talking to? What's she doing here?'

'She came along with him,' Ursula said, not hiding her amusement.

Donoghue met Murt at the back door and ushered him across the yard before he could ask any questions. They went into the workshop, and Donoghue closed the door behind them.

'Now before you ask,' he said, 'and if you haven't already heard, don't say anything in front of Eliza about the other thing.'

'Is that where you are now—at the Moss?'

'It is.'

'You sorted out your problem?'

'They backed off, gave me more time. Said it was a favour for someone. I didn't ask. Anyway, I got a few quid off Eliza, but she doesn't know what for.'

'You didn't?'

'Will you keep your voice down.' He waved a frantic hand in the air.

'You're some fucking eejit,' Murt said. 'Lost it all?'

'Not all.' He leaned back against the workbench and crossed his arms. 'I'm a disaster.'

'That you are. But if she has taken you in up there, maybe she sees something in you that you don't see yourself.'

'I never saw anything in myself. She's just lonely.'

'You like trying to impress people, and finally someone is impressed with you, and you're still not happy.'

This snapped him out of his self-pity, and he laughed again.

'How is my old friend Foley keeping anyway? Haven't heard from him.'

Murt told some of the story, the details Donoghue might find interesting, things he could embellish and repeat. When he got to the part where the Guards called to the house, Donoghue stopped him, said that he knew the rest, no need to go over it. This suited Murt, although he was tempted to enquire as to the story Donoghue had pieced together from his sources.

'Come on,' Donoghue said, 'we'll go back inside.'

'Think I'll make tracks.'

'Not one for crowds at all, are you? Or people in general. Well, I'll not let you leave without saying goodbye to Ursula.'

As he drove across the country, it struck Murt how its features never looked the same, how his impressions constantly changed depending on the angle or time of day or year. A frosty hillside under a winter dawn looks very different as a storm approaches. Storms roll with the land. The landscape stitched together. It made him think of people and the way they seemed to him. He was never sure how to take people or what the things they said really meant, and maybe people are like the land they inhabit.

The road cut through a tract of forest and a hillside that was being clearfelled. On the other side, he could see a mat of fine green where a crop of young pines were rising from the scrub.

# fishing

He fished from a flat rock in the middle of the river pretending I wasn't watching him. A rollie hung from the side of his mouth. He scowled at the smoke rising towards his eyes. When he tugged the rod, his head jerked backwards and to the left. It was habit—a thing fishermen do to check that their line is still hooked and baited, or if there is anything biting. He picked the rollie from his lips, held it between his fingers and turned the reel. No bite.

His dog—soon to be my dog—was tied to a nearby tree with a length of rope. When it got bored of watching us, it foraged in the undergrowth.

The river cut through the middle of a wooded glen. It was the kind of scene you might see on a calendar, the water dancing and spewing, a mist of spray water hanging in the air from the energy of the thing.

He stood wide-legged, the rod butt resting against his stomach. This was a show. He had seen me approach, had stared hard for a long time before returning to the river. It must have crossed his mind when he was locked-up that we'd run into each other or that I might come and find him. Not here though.

Crouching down, he rooted in a plastic bag and wrestled a can of beer from its ring-holder. He opened it one-handed. The gas cracked above the river's roar like a branch snapping.

The riverbed was littered with rocks. In places, you could cross to the far bank. Water spilled over waterfalls and rocky ledges. It gushed through gaps and gathered in ponds, some deep enough to wade in.

I stood for a long while before sitting on a bolder by the riverbank. The dog's rope was at full stretch, and it skulked up beside me. It smelled my clothes, licked my hand. The fisherman stayed out in the rocks watching this, but still he said nothing.

Later, when he reeled in the hook, it looked like he was done. He sat down on the rock, took the lid off a plastic lunch box and placed it on his lap. He picked something and held it like thread in front of his eyes. I thought for a second he was going to eat it. As he threaded it onto the hook, I felt the urge to go over and see how it was done, maybe have a go myself.

Then he spoke.

You fish?

I could hear him above the forest as if he was right beside me. I wasn't ready for conversation, hadn't prepared for it. No, I said, choking as I swallowed. It's all about perception, he said. He was concentrating on his task and didn't look over at me. You fool the fish? I said. Trout are predators, he said. Hungry bastards. I use worms, hooked up fully. He tidied away the plastic box, raised the baited hook into the air like a medal and cast again.

I knew forests and rivers. This thing he was doing, finding a spot for the day, I could understand it. I watched him fish until evening and could probably have done it myself by the end. And then he caught one. I saw the rod bend and dive downwards. He leaned back against it. He pulled and wound the reel. My heart raced. There was no panic, no tearing the thing from the water as fast as possible. He eased in the fish. And when it broke the surface, I was relieved. Maybe I even felt what he was feeling. I watched to see how he would release the hook but he just cut the line with a penknife and left the hook in the fish's mouth or brain, wherever it was lodged. Holding the still wriggling body against the rock, he picked up a short bat and struck the fish one swift blow on the head.

Crouched over the dead fish, he lifted his head and stared at me. I had been lost in the process. Looking him in the eye was the last thing I had expected. He had caught me. Was it a threat?

We spoke no more until he was leaving. As he packed up his gear, I wished I had left earlier. I didn't want to be there, had lost any urge for a confrontation, but I couldn't leave now. It was dusk as he approached. I stood on the last rock between him and dry land. He stopped. He was thinner, had lost some of his menace, but the darkness beneath his brow was hollow and bitter still. He said, My time is done. I had a river of things to say but none came out. He sensed my confusion and stepped to the next rock, the one on which I was standing. His eyes were numb, drunk, his throat exposed for my hand to grab. A slap then, something smacked me across the face and head, slashed me like a blade. His fishing rod thrashed wildly in the air. I blocked it with my arms. He was flailing, off balance. I reached for his jacket or arm but grabbed only air.

He lay between the rocks, half-submerged in water. A scrawl of blood like a child's painting on the rock behind his head. I jumped back to land. The dog was barking, choking itself. I untangled the rope and took his dog with me.

# 24

Murt picked up odd jobs where he could, and when he had enough cash, he made the trip over to the builder's merchants. Never in any hurry to leave the place, if there was a queue, he let people go on ahead of him. Something about the smell of timber and new tools made him feel like a child, always a new fixing or blade to discover on the shelves.

The lads behind the counter and in the yard knew him by name. They kept an interest, asked him how things were progressing. He discussed the day's list of materials with one of the lads, what he required and if there was a better product on the market. They were good with the price too, and did him a deal where they could: 'Eighteen per metre. I'll do it for sixteen.' Sometimes the list price was the best they could do: 'We're cut to the bone on that one as it is, Murt. Can't go any better for you.' Out in the yard, he helped them load the truck, then tied everything down with rope.

He drove back to Kiltuam and turned out Station Road. When he got to the cottage, she had already arrived. Her little silver car was parked where the caravan used to be. She stood in the doorway of the house and tapped her watch when he got out.

'You're early,' he said.

'You said to come early.'

'Not this early. What time did you leave at?'

He loosened the straps and opened the side boards. She walked over to the truck and looked to see what he had bought.

'You can help so,' he said.

'Me?'

'Yes. Grab hold.'

They lifted off the lengths of timber first and carried them inside.

The cottage still held the burnt smell, but it seemed to be receding. Or maybe he was getting used to it. He liked to think that the wind took a small bit every day and dispersed it in the forests and fields around—his past settling with the shadows.

'You've done a good bit more,' she said. 'The roof's nearly finished..'

'Ready for the slates.'

It was starting to resemble a house again. There would never be peace in it for him but, fixed up, maybe there would be a little less chaos.

'Some days I do nothing, just walk around, sit on an upturned bucket in one of the rooms. Reminds me of a day when I was in school: my first taste of freedom. The school was deserted and I ran up and down corridors, in and out of classrooms, around desks and chairs. I skidded across the floor on my knees. I moved furniture around and scribbled all over the blackboard. But when I sat on a desk and faced the empty classroom, the excitement went. I looked down to where I might sit and yelled at myself to pay attention. What I had always imagined would be the most fun in the world, wasn't much fun at all. I thought about stuffing the toilets, flooding the floors, breaking windows, setting a fire. Instead, I just walked around. Everything was different. The building wasn't built for silence, but I liked it better like that. In the staff room, I opened cupboards. That place was like a secret control room. It smelled of smoke and stale upholstery. I sat in the teachers' chairs. There were biscuits on a saucer and I took one.'

When they had finished unloading the truck, Murt closed up and latched the sides. He opened the door and stood there for a moment.

'What is it?' she asked.

'Nothing, stupid really.'

'What?'

He reached between the seats.

'Thought you might like to read this sometime.'

He handed her his notebook and walked away, back towards the house.

'Any word from Foley?' he asked.

' Roscommon,' she said, turning the notebook over in her hands 'He's over there now. Keeps a few sheep and goats apparently.'

'What about Helen?'

'He's trying to convince her to join him.'

Murt started a small generator. When the kettle boiled he made tea, and they sat on upturned crates.

'Have you talked to him?'

'Last week. Small talk. Talk for the sake of talk. He couldn't wait to get off the phone.'

'Same as always then.'

Foley would never tell her. But people talk. Maybe sometime in the future she would find out, and he'd have to face her. Helen too.

Murt had never given the future enough thought. The past was always too important. But what if the past was a fraud? What if people knew this and were afraid to change?

Gráinne said, 'Tell me more about my granny, your mother.'

'She was good with a needle. People would come round to the house and ask her to mend a dress hem, or take up a pair of slacks, that sort of thing. Curtains, duvets, cushions, all that. In the evenings, she'd be crouched over her lap, as close to the side lamp as she could get. She took breaks to roll her shoulders and neck. I remember the way she cut thread with her teeth, bit it like a plastic wrapper. Her mouth would be twisted tight to one side, mad-looking. She'd wet the end, draw thread from her mouth, then fish it through the eye. From across the room, I couldn't see anything in her hands. It looked to me like she was pretending to sew. She laughed when I told her she should have been an actress.'

'Where did you live then?'

'De Paor, the councillor, owned our house. There was an arrangement: Ma paid rent to de Paor, although I never knew how much. When I went to live with Quinn, the house became de Paor's again. I remember de Paor coming to the house sometimes—to speak about work, Ma said. Once, while he was there, I stuck a needle through my finger.'

Murt reached out his hand and his daughter brought it close to her face. She found the scar and ran a finger gently across it.

'Ma had a sewing machine too, you see. It was like a small suitcase with two thick leathery straps to carry it around. Not that you would carry it very far, the weight of the thing. For a woman who always said how much she hated sewing, she had that machine out a lot. It ran steady, like an engine turning over when she pressed her foot on the switch. She could thread the spindle so fast, I never figured out how it made a stitch. I used to turn the wheel slowly by hand to try figure it out.

'She was sewing a big quilt the day I jabbed my finger. It was sprawled all across the table and floor. De Paor arrived, and she wasn't expecting him. She left the sewing machine, and they went to the living room. I was half-listening and fiddling with the machine at the same time. The switch was under my foot like an accelerator, and I pressed it. I knew what would happen, but I pressed it anyway. The needle tried to sew a stitch through my finger and then jammed. Ma came running in when I started screaming. De Paor stood in the hallway watching. Does he need to go to the hospital? he asked. When Ma didn't answer, he said he'd be off so. She was crying as she bandaged up my finger. I told her it wasn't that sore—there was no need to be crying—and she burst out laughing. She said to me, You'll always be honest won't you? I said I would. Promise me you'll be honest, she said. I promised.'

'I'd love to have known her.'

'Ma knew as well as anyone that being honest wasn't possible. And promises—they were for fairy tales. He was at Ma's funeral with his family, de Paor. I remember seeing him talking with Quinn for a long time. He shook my hand too. He bent low, crouched so his face was level with mine, and just looked at me. I couldn't understand it, a man like that, stuck for words.'

Gráinne was smiling but she wiped her eyes too. She stood up, said she'd be back in a minute, that she had to get something from her car. It was more than a minute but she came back and handed him a parcel.

'What's this now?'

'Open, open.'

He tried to be careful but ripped the paper in several places. From inside he took a bag of grey pebbles and held them in cupped hands as if they might spill off and soak into the ground. He smelled inside the bag, took out a few pebbles and scratched a fingernail along them. The carbide chalked and blew away like dust on the breeze.

'Where did you get this?'

'You can find anything on the internet. Now you can test your lamp.'

The internet meant nothing to him. His net had never stretched farther than the country, which had always been big enough for him. Past the beaches and cliffs there were things he would never know or understand: places, hills, names, rivers, languages that were not his. There was much more to the world, he knew that. This country was nothing major, a corner in a grand room, a niche off the main space, where anything could happen all the same.

When the rain started, they stood inside the cottage and watched the softening landscape through an opening in the wall where some day a window might be.

Thanks to ...ly my
parents, sis... r cre-
ating the ... ...nows
no bounds. ... win-
ners at the N... real
encouragemen... ...ious
workshops I a... ...n at
Listowel Writ... l the
staff at UCD... bell,
Paul Perry, Ja... ...ks to
people who re... ...avin
Gaffney and th... ...g for
his interes... who
incorrecte... ...terest
and supp... ...as Craven for opening the
half-door o... ...guages hut. Finally, a huge thanks to Eoin Purcell
at New Island, who has been behind the story from day one, and to
Jonathan Williams for his belief, dedication and meticulous editing.
Without those two people, you would not be holding this book.